A History of
Girls' Comics

A History of Girls' Comics

Susan Brewer

First published in Great Britain in 2010 by
Remember When
An imprint of
Pen & Sword Books Ltd
47 Church Street
Barnsley
South Yorkshire
S70 2AS

ISBN 978 1 84468 072 6

Typeset in 10pt Palatino by Mac Style, Beverley, East Yorkshire
Printed in China through Printworks Int. Ltd

Pen & Sword Books Ltd incorporates the Imprints of Pen & Sword Aviation, Pen & Sword
Maritime, Pen & Sword Military, Wharncliffe Local History, Pen & Sword Select, Pen &
Sword Military Classics, Leo Cooper, Seaforth Publishing and Frontline Publishing

For a complete list of Pen & Sword titles please contact
PEN & SWORD BOOKS LIMITED
47 Church Street, Barnsley, South Yorkshire, S70 2AS, England
E-mail: enquiries@pen-and-sword.co.uk
Website: www.pen-and-sword.co.uk

Contents

Model of a newsagent's shop, made by author, based on a kit by Streets Ahead.

Foreword by Mark Wynter

A s an 11-year-old newspaper delivery nipper in 1954, I wasn't given to reading girls' comics. But once promoted to chief paperboy at the grand old age of 13 years, it was my responsibility to mark the comics for the rounds of all the other paperboys before they arrived at 7am. Yes, I was out of my bed at 5.45am six days a week and at 6.15am on Sunday. Being a fan of the boys' comic *Eagle* (featuring 'Dan Dare: Space Explorer'), I occasionally flipped through its sister comic *Girl*,

The major influence on British girls' comic culture was the birth of *Bunty* in 1958, which emphasised stories in place of activities that were the mainstream of many girls' comics up until then. Amazingly *Bunty* survived the longest but, by 2001, the title had become a little tame for the new millennium. *Valentine*, as its name suggests, was ostensibly a romance comic, along with *Romeo*, which was slightly illicit. Inside its cover the exploits of 'Millie the Model' and 'Rose the Slave Girl' (frisson of sexual fantasy) were eagerly devoured. There were even nylons to be won: rather laughable now! There came a spate of girls' name titles: *Diana*, *Judy* and *Tammy*, which featured 'Common Cathy', 'Nell Nobody', 'Jumble Sale Jilly' and (biggest of all) 'Bella at the Bar'. Often depicted were miserable lives with nasty parents, relatives, guardians or employers, but there was always hope for a better life and kind treatment. In 1970 a grown-up version came along, selling over one million copies per month. This was *Jackie*, the comic strip being just one element amongst pop star posters, advice and quizzes.

The value of comics for girls really did bridge the gap between childhood and adolescence. That has been long erased and usurped by what is known as the march of progress. Without progress we stand still, wither and perish; but from the late 1960s the move from innocence and young girl/boy pre-teen adolescence, has surged to such a degree from comics to gossip/celebrity magazines that childhood is eroded long before puberty. No time to dally, to enjoy, or even to contemplate much of what is a part of growing up. The stages of mystery onto the next gradual leg of discovery have become almost non-existent. Why should this be? Well, of course America was always ahead of us in many areas of commercial enterprise.

I recall on my first visit to New York in 1961 being surprised at the teen and pre-teen magazines available; no comics, just a culture encouraging young children to be groomed as beauty queens or cheerleaders. Inevitably a semblance of that was bound to catch on in the United Kingdom. Throughout the 1960s we still had comics of a sort, and I speak with first hand authority as a pop singer of that period. With hit records such as *Image of Girl*, *Dream Girl*, *Go Away Little Girl*, *Venus in Blue Jeans*, etc. I featured in many girls comics, such as *Boyfriend*, *Cherie*, *Valentine* and well recall trotting along to the various publishers, suitcase of clothes in hand, to be photographed for 'speech bubble stories' of boy-meets-girl, boy-dates-girl. The stories often serialised, never even ending in a kiss!

These publications were important, leading up to and including teenage time. A young girl's dreams and hopes for the future, with regard to a partner. The dreams might have a

Mark Wynter, 1960s' Pop Star.

fairytale quality, but often they come true. Many of the girls' magazines of today scream gossip and headlines for articles offering not just sensible guidelines for sexual activity, but blatant tips on how to tantalise, tease and rush into some sort of relationship. Gone it seems are the days for young girls of "I wonder and I hope he notices me". Of course, Jane Austen had her own suggestions on how to attract a man; scheming, coquettish, learning to dance (at a distance) and, for the formally educated, letter writing, possibly the learning of an instrument and the all important art of conversation. Sadly, for many today, the latter is now being greatly reduced by that brilliant invention, email.

Lest you may feel I am a complaining, old-fashioned fellow, let's get back to the celebration of this collective on girls' comics. They served a purpose of fun, fantasy and, if ignorance truly is bliss, that too was represented. There was a moral stance, an unwritten borderline and a delight in simple imagination with girlie communication. Nothing was, as they say, 'full on', much better to let the nurturing process happen slowly.

In my current profession, many younger actors have referred to me as an 'old smoothy' for reasons I have never quite understood; perhaps it's down to my lack of Clint Eastwood

Mark Wynter, 2000s' Actor.

stubble! However, I have never been a 'Lothario' and, confronted today with teenage girls who say that their mothers and grandmothers remember me, I often take stock and think to myself, 'wow, these girls are so confident'. It has ever been thus with the opposite sex but often as I recall it was disguised – purposefully perhaps – with personality or quiet determination. Much of this behaviour is still in play, and the sweetness of young girls is total joy. Not sugary sweetness you understand; sugar and spice and all things nice has never been an apt description of any girl; far too simple a brief.

To delve into this book will, I'm sure, evoke a lantern slide of happy memories, situations and moments remembered, while younger readers will find not just another nostalgic look at history but a revelation that is both interesting and entertaining. I have known the author Susan Brewer since she was a young girl as a member of my fan club. Her numerous talents of prowess, originality, style and the freshness of her many articles and books continually astound me. I'm now in her fan club!

Mark Wynter

Introduction

As with many children of the immediate post-war era, comics played an important part in my life. From the earliest comics I can remember – *Chicks' Own* and *Tiny Tots* – through to the teen comics such as *Cherie* and *Boyfriend*, the visual joy of a comic paper brought me much pleasure. Along the way, I embraced other titles – *Bunty*, *Radio Fun*, *Girl*, *Jack and Jill*, *The Dandy*, *Robin*, *School Friend*, *Topper*, *Judy*, *The Beano*, *Girl's Crystal* – some a brief flirtation, but others, especially *Bunty* and *The Dandy*, proving steadfast companions for several years.

Comics were special, not just because of their colourful layouts, amusing cartoons, exciting stories and, occasionally, free gifts, but because they were a treasured weekly treat. It was exciting and made me feel grown up when a comic just for me came through the letterbox together with the daily paper.

If for any reason, the comic didn't arrive, I would hurry round to the newsagents, fearful it had been lost. It never was, of course. It was usually waiting in a pile on the counter, left behind because the comics were late coming in that morning and the paperboy hadn't had time to 'mark them up'.

Coming right up to date, recently there has been a craze for issuing compilations of pages from girls' comics in book form, helping us all to relieve our youth. This book is a kind of follow-on from these compilations, but it is so much more as it is a look at the history of the comics, and how the attitudes and aspirations of girls have changed over the years. I've spent months wallowing in armfuls of dusty, tattered comics, reading once more the adventures of 'The Four Marys', 'Belle of the Ballet' or 'Luv, Lisa', evaluating and enjoying the way styles in comics have changed over the years. The intense, wordy, moral stories of the early 1900s gradually gave way to the chummy 'all girls together' jolly hockey-sticks ideal of the 1930s and 40s. Things then progressed to the adventurous (with more freedom) fifties, sixties and seventies stories, and through to the modern, often flippant styles with less words, more pictures normally involving fashion/boys/music – or preferably a mix of all three. And we mustn't forget the scary late seventies' and eighties' comics, some of which have now reached cult status, with their tales of ghosts and the supernatural.

It's been intriguing, too, to note the themes of the stories from the mainstream comics; top of the list must certainly be school, with ballet, horse riding, ice-skating and gymnastics not far behind. Talented orphans, cruel guardians and girls solving mysteries, which have baffled their elders, are popular too. Problem pages proved enthralling – spotty skins worried 1800s' girls, just as they still worry girls today – while observing the ever-changing fashions in clothes, hair and music has been a joy, and an unexpected bonus. For humorous relief, Minnie the Minx, Lettice Leefe, Keyhole Kate and Beryl the Peril still have the power to raise a smile – some things never change.

Along the way, I have met some really friendly, helpful people; publishers, collectors, researchers and, of course, all those readers of comics – without them, the comic industry

Author enjoying a comic with her grandmother, 1950s.

would soon disappear. The worst thing about writing this book has been the angst caused by reading the stories right through to the cliffhanger – and then discovering I don't have the follow-up issue. So if anyone knows how 'Hannah in the House of Dolls' from *Bunty*, 'I Had To Know the Truth' from *Blue Jeans* or 'Strange Neighbours' from *Mandy & Judy* ends – please put me out of my misery by letting me know!

Susan Brewer

CHAPTER ONE

Early Comics

This first chapter is a look at the history and collectability of comic papers and other periodicals for girls, such as the *Girl's Own Paper*, which dates from 1880, as well as the girls' comics which appeared in the first half of the Twentieth Century, amongst them *School Girl* and *Schoolgirl's Own*. Later chapters will examine post-war comics for girls, coming right up to date with an investigation of what's out there now. Comics are becoming increasingly collectable, though for years it was the boys' comics collectors went for – the girls' comics were considered a very poor relation. Now though, the tables are being turned, with many issues of classics such as *Bunty*, *Girl*, *Girl's Crystal*, *School Friend* and others selling for comparatively large sums, especially early issues and those which had contained free gifts or were special commemorative comics. If the free gifts are still with the comics, then they are even more desirable.

I've tried to make this book an affectionate and nostalgic overview of the various comics intended for girls, or those which had girl appeal, and with an analysis of the contents of some chosen issues of comics. Hopefully, the accounts will trigger memories of happy, carefree childhood days, and will also act as a pointer for the type of comics you wish to collect, from toddlers' first papers through to the classics, not forgetting the romantic types and the part works. Sadly, it is impossible to discuss in detail all the comics beloved by girls, so I have selected my favourites, or those I felt were particularly influential in the history of British comic papers. I know there are many omissions; if your favourite isn't here, then I apologise – until I began, I had no idea that there were quite so many girl-orientated publications and it would have needed a far, far thicker book than this to accommodate every title.

Basically, though hopefully a help for collectors, this is intended as a nostalgia-inducing frolic through our childhood; a social history looking at a more leisurely way of life, a time when children had little money and made the most of what they spent it on. It's especially for those of us who rushed off to the newsagent each week with our pocket money, spending ages agonising over which comic to buy. Did you go for your favourite, did you choose the one bearing the enticing free gift, or did you take a chance on the newest title which had just come in, to give you a bit of street cred with your friends? Hopefully, the happy memories will come flooding back, and you may even be tempted to search flea markets and boot sales for titles from your own childhood. You'll find that as soon as you turn the pages and reacquaint yourself with half-forgotten characters, the nostalgia will come flooding back.

What is a comic?

A comic can mean various things to various people, but at its most simple, it is a few sheets of folded paper, usually A4-sized or larger, stapled together and containing a series of humorous stories recounted in brightly-coloured picture form. It employs the use of speech bubbles, frequently with a simple text underneath. Most comics have a banner at the top of the front page with the title printed in an eye-catching font, to make it easily recognisable to its regular readers amongst the other titles on display in a newsagent's shop. This device also helps to attract the casual or passing buyer, especially if printed in a bright red, such as on the front page of *Girl* or *Robin*, or in large colourful letters like those on the The *Beano* or *The Dandy* comics.

Often, too, the comic will have a logo, which may also be featured inside on a club page or on gift items. This logo is the magazine's identity, and becomes particularly important to those readers who send in a small subscription to join the club, rather like the school tie, regimental badge or team colours. It allows members to regard themselves as part of a special and select group. In return for their subscription, members will normally receive a badge, a free gift and a secret code. Club members are usually eligible for special prizes or offers in the comic, which might not be available to non-members. This gives the child a feeling of importance.

The Pocket Oxford Dictionary definition of a comic is 'comic paper, especially a periodical with narrative mainly in pictures', but for the purposes of this book, the term is used more loosely, encompassing children's magazines, educational periodicals, advertising story broadsheets and part works, as well as the basic comic paper. We think of comics as a modern development, yet, if you consider that, basically, comics are just stories told in a sequence of pictures, similar images were found in Ancient Egypt, and depicted on murals in Ancient Rome. Then there is the Bayeux Tapestry, embroidered with its intriguing knights and horses, which tells the story of the Battle of Hastings in a long strip of fabric presented almost in a cartoon format. The Bayeaux Tapestry is surely an early form of comic? You could even argue that sequential paintings such as William Hogarth's *A Harlot's Progress*, his later *A Rake's Progress* or the two paintings by Sir John Everett Millais, *Her First Sermon* and *Her Second Sermon* are a form of comic: because they tell a story. However, for most of us, a comic is a thin publication, stapled together, containing captioned pictures that tell a story, and, often – as the name suggests – humour.

How long have children had comics?

Queen Victoria was on the throne, Britain had taken a very moralistic tone and most children's books contained a solemn message – so, did children have comics then? Well, yes, in a way, though not as we know them today, and strictly speaking, they were magazines or picture papers. A girl's light reading matter in Victorian times looks extremely daunting nowadays, even to adult readers, with its many pages of tiny text, black and white line drawings and stories such as 'Forlorn, Yet Not Forsaken' or 'Only a Girl-Wife'. The text is very formal, with long words and convoluted sentences, and a modern child would be reaching for the dictionary before she finished the first paragraph. Even so, humorous episodes shine through, such as this gem from an 1885 copy of *The Girl's Own Paper*:

'A lady in a registry office observed, "I am afraid that little girl won't do for a nurse, she is too small; I would hesitate to trust her with the baby."

"Her size, Madam," said the clerk, "we look upon as her greatest recommendation."

"Indeed! But she is so very small."

"I know that she is diminutive, but you should remember that when she drops a baby, it doesn't have so far to fall!" '

Selection of girl's comics.

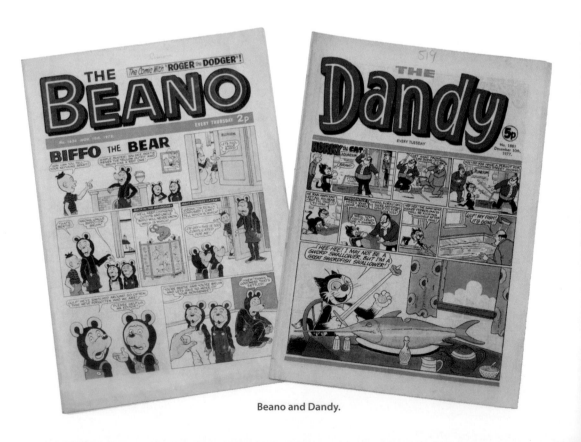

Beano and Dandy.

Girl's Own Paper.

The Girl's Own Paper was published by The Leisure Office in London's Paternoster Row, and first appeared in 1880. The Religious Tract Society was founded 1799, and was a British publisher of Christian literature. They particularly aimed their publications at the poorer people in society, and also the women and children. Another of their magazines was *The Boy's Own Paper*. These children's papers were produced with the idea of encouraging young children to read, and also of installing moral values into them at a tender age. Interestingly, issues of the newspapers were bound together at the end of each year and sold as an annual, and it was also possible to buy the covers separately to have your own copies bound together in book form – a forerunner of the modern magazine binder.

The earliest comics, or regularly produced publications which children might have read were the so-called penny-dreadfuls – sensational-type stories, often in dozens of parts, featuring adventures or blood-curdling stories, and aimed at the lower and semi-literate classes in Britain. Probably the first recognisable comic strip papers were *Funny Folks*, published by James Henderson in 1874 and which ran for twenty years, and *Ally Sloper's Half Holiday*, which first appeared in 1884 and continued until 1916. Both of these were intended to appeal to adults. *Funny Folks* was originally designed as a pull-out supplement to a magazine called *Weekly Budget*, but it proved so popular that the publisher decided to launch it as a weekly paper. It was the success of *Funny Folks* which inspired engraver and publisher, Gilbert Dalziel, to issue *Ally Sloper's Half Holiday*. Ally Sloper was a working-class scoundrel and the comic strips told of his exploits. Six years later, Amalgamated Press began publishing *Comic Cuts* and *Illustrated Chips*, and these proved so successful that the owner of the company was later able to launch the *Daily Mail* and the *Daily Mirror* on the proceeds.

Gradually, publishers realised that the juvenile market was an untapped source of revenue, and comics began to prosper, though comics for young children didn't come about till the early Twentieth Century, when *Puck* included a junior section. The first comic for youngsters was *Rainbow*, which was initially launched in 1914 and enjoyed a very long run, not closing till 1956. By the First World War, the majority of comic titles were aimed at children between the ages of eight up into the early teens. The 1930s saw the founding of the D. C. Thompson company, who went on to issue *The Beano* and *The Dandy*, two of the most popular and best-selling comics ever. This was the golden age of comics, with many classic titles appearing during this time. Unfortunately, a lot of comics also disappeared, due in many cases to the Second World War paper shortages, which came into effect on the 25th May 1940.

Wartime Troubles
Britain began to feel the paper squeeze in 1940, when German troops had overrun Scandinavia, effectively cutting off the main supply of wood pulp. British printing presses fell idle and paper was restricted; consequently the comic industry suffered badly. Suddenly, dozens of story papers and comics died, or were amalgamated with siblings. This closure of so many titles was a dreadful blow to all the artists and writers who had worked on the comics – when they returned after the war, they found themselves out of a job as so many of the titles they had been employed by had disappeared. It wasn't really until the early 1950s, even though the war had ceased in1945, that the British comic market prospered again.

After the Second World War
The 1950s gave us a second golden age (or maybe a silver age), a time when publications such as *Eagle*, *Girl*, *Bunty*, *Judy* and *Robin* were just a few of the dozens of titles to brighten the lives of post-war youngsters. Not long after the war, in February 1949, the Reverend Marcus Morris warned in the *Sunday Dispatch* that 'Morals of little girls in plaits and boys with marbles bulging in their pockets are being corrupted by a torrent of indecent coloured magazines that are flooding bookstalls and newsagents'. He envisioned a new, popular genre of comic that was innocent and wholesome, and 'where adventure is once more the clean and exciting business I remember in my school days'. Then he acted on his words by founding the *Eagle* comic, which he managed to sell to Hulton Press after traipsing around various publishers, determined to find someone to back him. Apparently, the model for the *Eagle* logo was the top of a brass inkwell bought at a vicarage garden party. *Eagle* proved a great success on its launch in 1950; it was different in both quality and content, and girls wanted a similar comic. It wasn't long before *Girl* appeared, another success. With these comics the high quality of the paper, as well as the artwork, design, printing and standard of writing, reached new heights. The colours were crisp and bright, brought to life by the photogravure printing method, the pictures were well drawn and featured plenty of detail, and the stories were exciting, not just run of the mill often 'soppy' tales as found in the pre-war girls' comics. (See Chapter 3.)

Before the 1950s many comics and story papers were still featuring tiny print, large blocks of text and just a few pictures, which often only used two or three colours – a long way from the full-colour glossies which began to appear during the next decade. To modern eyes, these so-called 'comics' are uninspiring and are not inviting to read. However, for a child of the era, they were unputdownable.

Loyalty
Comics have a major drawback, one not so much experienced by magazines and newspapers, and that is the question of loyalty. An adult will often take the same newspaper for years and years, or read the same magazine. It becomes a habit – if you expect to read the *Daily Express*

or *The Times* at breakfast, and you're given *The Daily Telegraph* or *The Sun* instead, it can unsettle you for the rest of the day. When young people finally flee the nest to set up home on their own, it is quite likely they will choose to take the newspaper their parents take, the one they grew up with. They will have become used to seeing it around the home, and it will have been the one they began to read, probably in their early teens – newspapers cater for adults. Comics, however, appeal to certain age groups, and children have a habit of growing up, so, with the best will in the world, no child will be buying her pre-school *Playhour* or kindergarten *Twinkle* when she is in her teens. The publishers therefore have an ongoing task to attract new readers, and can't afford to sit back on their heels. They must devise eye-catching covers, free gifts, character tie-ins or exciting stories to pull in – and then keep, in the short term – new readers. On the other hand, this transitional audience can be advantageous, because it allows publishers to rehash, or even re-use, previously published material, which goes a long way to explaining the themes which crop up time and again in comics.

Typically, comics enjoy an extra sales boost at Christmas when they publish an Annual, which is usually a large hardback book featuring picture strips and stories centred around favourite characters from the comics. However, as we have seen, in the past, some annuals such as those of *The Girl's Own Paper*, were just bound copies of the previous year's issues. In the summer, a Summer Special would often be issued, normally an extra-thick special edition of the comic, often bought by parents as a treat for the children to read whilst on their holidays. These Summer Specials were perfect entertainment for rainy days. Other publications issued by many comics were Library Specials – full-length slim paperbacks, either in strip format or in text with occasional illustrations, normally based on a character from the comic. Today, Summer Specials and Extras are still issued, though perhaps there isn't so much choice of titles as there once was.

How does a comic evolve?

The market for comics has varied over the years; from the heady years of the 1930s through to the 1970s, children would regularly buy a comic. Unfortunately, as television, computers, game consoles and iPods have become more popular, so the need for comics has tailed off – children have so much to do, that, sadly, in many cases reading is taking a back seat. Bill McLaughton, from D.C. Thomson, explained how a comic came into being in those earlier years.

'Back in the sixties there was a huge market for comics for both boys and girls in all age groups. We had freelance authors and artists who contributed to the existing publications so new story ideas were worked out, given to an author and scripted. They were then drawn. Once a stock, of, roughly, six weeks, was built up, a new comic was launched, traditionally early in the year. There wasn't market research as such, nor trials. The new comic was launched, usually, without advertising. It took approximately six months from conception to launch.

'Although we had a stable of girls' comics, they all catered for the differing tastes of the readers. *Bunty* and *Mandy* were similar, but nevertheless different. Others, such as *Spellbound* were totally different in content. We also had *Jackie*, preceded by *Romeo*, which were for the pop generation.

'The short answer is that a new comic could be launched in a remarkably short time, 4-6 weeks, but generally the planning took ages. I'd say nearly a year from the first discussion to launch. I was on the launch of the new *Adventure* in 1970. It came out on February 14th

McDonalds Beano characters.

1970, but we started putting it together in September 1969, around three months after the go ahead was given.'

As the decades progressed, comics, just like the world, evolved. By the 1970s, girls were no longer satisfied with the standard adventure stories centred around school, ballet, riding stables, theatres or days gone by. They wanted more thrills, excitement, mysticism – even horror. Naturally, the publishers soon cottoned on to this, and *Misty*, *Spellbound* and others of that ilk appeared, all eager to cater for these new tastes. Already, comics had seen a natural progression with boys, fashion, make-up, pop music, pin-ups, even, shock – sex – creeping in to the hallowed pages. Pre-war writers would have needed smelling salts when faced with some of the problem pages which graced the pages of *Jackie*, or the strip-stories which appeared in *Romeo* or *Valentine*. Yet, compared with some of the things which appear in today's girls' magazines, they were innocent.

Up to the early sixties, an ideal story for one of the girl's mainstream comics, such as *Bunty*, *Judy*, *Girl* or *School Friend*, would revolve around a talented girl ballet dancer who was teased at school, and, unknown to everyone, had a seriously ill twin sister. The girls probably lived with a strict aunt who refused to pay for the medical treatment for the sick twin. It would involve kidnapping, a kindly Swiss doctor, two bullies who finally saw the light, and maybe a friendly dog thrown in for good measure. Oh, and if the sick twin made a remarkable recovery which allowed her to become a champion horse rider, that would be a bonus. By the 1970s and 80s, though, the story would feature a strong, gutsy girl who, as she was very late for her judo class, made a slight error by rushing past a woman who asked for directions, and so was turned into a zombie. The girl would be made to walk the streets forever as a punishment – the woman was actually one of the living dead. It was probably around this time that writers realised that girls rather enjoyed being scared, or having a cry; some of the picture stories of the period could be quite distressing.

Incidentally, one of the most unpleasant and disturbing things which comes over when reading some of the older comics, especially those dating pre-1940s and immediate post-war, is the attitude to those characters which aren't British. Fun is made of the Japanese, German, Indian, French and, especially, black people: the characters are stereotyped, made to look inferior or as figures of fun. Black people are invariably shown as caricatures with large pouting lips, gold hoop earrings and woolly hair, an unsettling side of the traditional British comic. The differences of speech are presented in a patronising way, twisted and emphasised to appear funny, while the descriptive terms used for some of these people are completely unacceptable in today's society. It's a sad reflection of the way that many people in Britain were still hankering for the imperialistic days of the late 1800s and early 1900s, when Britain was still very much a major power.

It's easy to find fault and to mock the girls' comics, yet they served a positive purpose. The most important was – and is – to encourage girls to read. Many children are daunted by the sight of a page of closely worded text in a book. Pictures with simple captions or speech bubbles are much easier to assimilate. Of course, this doesn't apply so much to most of the pre-war girls' comics, which consisted in the main of stories printed in minute text, with just the occasional drawing to break them up. Nowadays, the sad fact is that thousands of children leave school barely able to read their own name: comics, much more so than books will help a child to recognise many words.

Critics of comics often condemn or mock the post-war issues featuring the endless adventures of ballerinas, gymnasts and crime-fighting schoolgirls. They seem to think that the publishers were churning out the same bland, lightweight matter without any attempt to introduce stronger or controversial themes. Yet the owners of the comic titles were not stupid, they knew that they needed to give girls what they wanted to read, and these were favourite themes at the time. Girls are not normally renowned for being particularly timid, most are quite vocal in their likes and dislikes, and all these comics would have received dozens if not hundreds of letters each week. The publishers would soon know if a story theme was disliked or unpopular.

The stories which appeared in the comics, though they may have been similar, invariably told of girls striving to achieve a goal, overcoming adversity, and managing to achieve their dreams even though numerous obstacles blocked her path. They inspired and encouraged their readers. These stories demonstrated that a girl from any background, not only a middle-class home, but from an orphanage or one-parent family where there was little money to spare, could still make good. They also showed how to stand up to school bullies, how to use initiative to solve problems and – importantly – how to communicate with both adults and other children. These skills would be absorbed painlessly as the girls read the comics. Publications such as *Girl*, *School Friend*, *Bunty*, *Mandy*, *Judy*, *Tammy* and all the rest served their purpose – they both educated and amused. Proof of that can be seen in the way they are so fondly remembered today by the women who read them as young girls. They not only recall the characters and the stories, but also the helpful hints, recipes and answers to questions, many of which were taken on board and used in later life. As the decades progressed, as we shall see, stories did become much stronger.

Modern Comics

According to Mel Gibson, a media studies lecturer at Sunderland University, barely one in twenty readers of comics now is female because of a growing divide between the sexes and an explosion in demand for sex-obsessed girls' magazines. When Mel investigated the cultural shift which has led to the downslide in the girls' comics market, she discovered that in just one generation girls have deserted the comics which, for so long, were the market's homely, if a little staid, foundation. Now girls prefer magazines with make-up, fashion and even sex tips, while an increasing number each year are shifting towards the Shojo Manga publications, such as *Fruits Basket* (See Chapter 12). Right up to the late 1970s, most of the girls' comic-based reading concerned adventures where heroines overcame problems and righted wrongs, but during the next decade magazines switched to becoming pop and fashion based, with scarcely any story content.

Although it could be argued that a similar cultural shift happened in the early 1960s, with the advent of *Boyfriend*, *Cherie*, *Valentine* and others, these comic papers still retained the story strips. Even though they might have included a few pages on fashion, pop, boyfriend problems and film stars, overall, they contained lots of fictional reading matter. Today's teen comics, which, strictly speaking, are mostly magazines, are blatant, up-front publications that treat ten-year-old girls as adults, and which are purely media based. There is no room for adventures, brave heroines, or even courageous canines.

On a recent investigatory visit to a major newsagent I counted around fifteen comics, of which at least a dozen were actively aimed at girls. With one exception, every comic had a free gift attached to the front cover; fun magnets, combs, stickers, dolls clothes or jewellery. Whereas twenty years ago a comic was a low-priced treat, costing no more than a daily newspaper, today these types of comics are luxuries, with prices averaging between £1.50 to £2.99. No wonder there is a slump in the comics' market. Why is a comic so expensive? Although paper costs have risen, a standard woman's magazine, which has more pages, costs a quarter or a half less than the price of a comic.

It's difficult to understand the justification for the price hike in a child's comic, but presumably the attachment of the gifts has to be paid for somehow. Make no mistake – the gifts given with modern comics are, in most cases, far superior to the cheap plastic novelties given with the comics of previous generations. It is very sad that manufacturers feel obliged to offer a free gift with every issue to entice buyers; at one time the longing to know the outcome of an adventure was the hook to catch the readers' attention and imagination. Now, it seems, it is the free toy that is the important part; the actual comic is secondary. Instead, readers' loyalty has disappeared and has been replaced by consumerist greed and the must-have mentality for the latest plastic gimmick. I have been given to understand that some supermarkets insist that comics contain free gifts, so that they can be marketed as toys, though whether this is correct I do not know.

Illustration and writing

With many comics, the stories are written in-house. Writers and general staff bandy ideas around, with regular staff meetings to talk over new trends and ideas. Sometimes the writers are well known, or become well known, through the strips, but often they remain

Typical picture strip.

anonymous and it can de difficult to determine who was responsible for which strip. Once the story is written, it is sent to an artist so that the idea can be depicted in a visual form.

Illustrator David Roach explains; 'As for drawing comics this is how it works. Usually the artist will sketch out very rough layouts of the strip, often on A4 paper based on the directions in the script. Then he will draw it up more accurately on a large piece of paper or board, traditionally at twice the size it will be printed, though different artists might choose a different size. The page will look pretty much as you see it in the comic, with all the panels drawn on the one page. I should say that these days some artists do draw individual panels and then construct the page on a computer, but this is still relatively rare. Once the strip is fully drawn in pencil the artist would go over the lines in ink, drawing with either a brush or a pen, using permanent India ink. Certainly back in the past, most comics employed very basic printing methods so they would need to shoot plates from a solid black line, rather than the more wishy-washy pencil line.

'The finished page would then be sent to the publishers either in person or by post, where word balloons would be stuck onto the art (usually these were written out onto a glue-backed paper and meticulously cut out). Any colour would usually be added in the editorial offices – to be precise, a colour guide would be worked out and then sent off to the printers who would add the colour themselves. There were exceptions to this – comics such as *Eagle, Girl, Diana, TV 21* etc used full colour photogravure printing which allowed artists the chance to create fully painted pages. A publisher would expect his artists to draw an episode a week – often 2 or 3 pages – but some artists were definitely faster and others much slower – I'm one of the slow ones!'

When studying lists of the comics that appeared over the Twentieth Century it is obvious that, certainly at first, the comic market was aimed at boys rather than girls. Although things changed after the Second World War, most comics, especially the funnies, were aimed fair and square at males. Of course, girls read them – no girl likes to be left out, and so she will read her brother's comics as well as his books – and many comics did, as a token gesture, include a girl character somewhere. Probably the most famous and most popular is Minnie the Minx, from *The Beano*, who is still going strong today, even though she is now getting on for sixty. Other girl cartoon characters from the various classic pure comics, such as *The Beano, Topper* and that ilk, include Beryl the Peril, Keyhole Kate and Pansy Potter. Dennis the Menace has a baby sister known as Bea, while Swanky Lanky Liz is one of the members of Lord Snooty's Gang. (See Chapter 5.)

Comics reflect the attitudes and the lifestyle of girls at the time, perhaps an obvious statement but one to bear in mind when we are bemoaning the loss of the older-type traditional comics and complaining about the media-obsessed modern titles. Titles such as *Schoolgirls' Own*, dating from the early decades of the Twentieth Century tend in the main to depict girls as middle-class boarding school inmates, who patronise the lower classes, help the poor, look after cripples and regard black people as something from another planet. It was, though, patently obvious that the sole ambition of the majority of the girls was to marry and have a family. After the Second World War, the introduction of comics such as *Girl* and, slightly later, *Bunty*, with their exciting adventure stories and stories set in hospitals and ballet schools reflected the comparative freedom of 1950s' and 1960s' girlhood. By the mid-1960s, pop music was becoming much more than just a teen craze – even pensioners could reel off the names of all The Beatles for instance – while fashion was playing an ever-important part in the modern lifestyle. Comic-type magazines such as *Jackie, Mates* and *Oh Boy!* replaced the more traditional teen romance comics of *Valentine, Cherie* and *Romeo,*

Free gifts with modern comics.

Media toys.

offering a colourful blend of stories, music, gossip and fashion. This trend snowballed throughout the 1980s and 1990s, and nowadays, media is everything. Most of the current crop of girls' magazines (it seems wrong to refer to them as comics now) reflect the current media-obsessed world we live in. Newspaper headlines scream the latest scandal about a soap 'star' or pop group, nonentities soar to stardom overnight after a brief few minutes on a reality show, and everyone seems obsessed with the latest fashions.

Saddest of all, most of the girl orientated publications seem to be pushing home the message that beauty is everything, that the only way to succeed in life is to be famous, and that the way to do it is to become a 'star'. Gone are the nursing and teaching ambitions, even the hairdressing ones seem to have faded. Today's girls want to be singers, dancers, actresses or models, a message which is being seconded by some of the modern magazines, even those aimed at the primary school age group.

In all fairness, though, today a girl doesn't really have the choice; if she doesn't want to read about fashion, pop or the media, but is after an old-fashioned in-depth longer read, she will have to buy a book. Comics are temporal, they will entertain for an hour, a lunch break or a treat after homework. Children are deemed to have a short attention span – which can't really be true given the thousands who happily read the latest Harry Potter blockbuster from cover to cover.

Why Did It Happen?

It's really a bit of a mystery. This shift in the appearance and content of the comics can't be blamed on the publishers – the world has moved on. Nowadays children are so overwhelmed by the thousands of new toy lines, new characters and new crazes which appear almost over night, that it's natural that they want to keep abreast of the times. Yet, when did this happen? D.C Thomson's Bill McLoughlin, talking about the demise of *Tracy* says; '*Tracy* was just stopped and didn't combine with anything else. Just another victim of the 1980s. *Debbie* went in 1983, *Etcetera* in 1986, *Looking Great* in 1988, *Patches* in 1989 and *Suzy* in 1987. The 1980s was the graveyard of comics, both boys' and girls', and comics have never really recovered. It is facile to blame the demise of all the titles on computers, which were not widespread then, but something happened in the late 1970s and 1980s that turned people away from comics. Whether kids became more adult earlier or comics became passé in the time of the New Romantics and such magazines such as *Jackie*, who knows. But I do think the greater access to TV and the kind of material it showed, perhaps changed people's attitudes and made comics seem old fashioned.'

Another cause could be the vast influx of media-based toys, which began to flood the market at the end of the 1970s with the introduction of the Star Wars series of films and consequent tie-ins. Before then, no one had attempted such enormous mass-marketing of film tie-ins, and once manufacturers noticed the huge success of toys which could be built up into a complex world, it wasn't long before the same idea was tried for girls. My Little Pony, Strawberry Shortcake, Care Bears, Flower Fairies, Wuzzels, Rainbow Brite and Moondreamers – suddenly children's toy boxes were changed beyond recognition. Gone were the traditional toys, especially baby dolls and domestic items; instead girls wanted the latest craze. Eventually, I believe, this filtered through to comics, and girls began to think that the titles they had loved for so long were out of date. The older titles seemed jaded and tired alongside the bright new media tie-in comics, and they didn't fit in with the new world of pink plastic and scented characters. So, the traditional comics died, or were brutally revamped in a desperate attempt to attract back the readers. Sadly, in most cases it didn't work.

CHAPTER TWO

Comics for Tots

Comics play an important part in the life of pre-school children: classics such as *Jack and Jill*, *Chicks' Own* and *Sunday Fairy* are now old fashioned, and instead we have a plethora of character-linked comics. So what are the differences between the older comics and the current comics for youngsters, and why did they change?

Were hyphens helpful?

I remember, as a small child in the early 1950s, seeing Mum's friend standing at our front door, clutching two comics. I knew they were a gift for me, and was so excited – I really looked forward to my weekly comics. I suppose I was lucky to be given comics, as we were not a well-off family, but both my parents encouraged reading and so each week I would be given popular titles of the day, such as *Chicks' Own*, *Tiny Tots* or *Rainbow*. I was always intrigued by the hyphenated words that appeared in many of the comics, it looked so odd – but comics helped me, I was reading fluently by the age of four. *Jack and Jill* was slightly too late for me, but I used to read my cousin's copy, marvelling at the shiny paper and bright illustrations.

Hyphens were used in some comics to split syllables of longer words, though I always thought it rather baffling. Thus, sentences such as these from a 1950s' *Tiny Tots*:

'When Tiny and Tot ask nursie if they may have another bathe, she shakes her head. "No, you cannot bathe again today, children," she says.' were rendered:

'When Ti-ny and Tot ask nur-sie if they may have an-oth-er bathe, she shakes her head. "No, you can-not bathe a-gain to-day, chil-dren," she says.'

All the two syllable and above words were split in this way, though the comic seemed to aim at mainly using one and two syllable words; even three syllables, such as 'aer-o-plane', 'round-a-bout' or 'an-oth-er' are quite hard to find. However, a closer examination shows that the splitting wasn't strictly just of the syllables, it was done at convenient breaks in a word. Hence, the two syllable word 'whispered' was split in three places to read 'whis-per-ed', which could give rise to some odd pronunciations – or pro-nun-ci-a-tions! The idea was good, and no doubt helped some children to read, but unfortunately, it could well have proved confusing (as in my case) as the majority of books given to a child did not contain split words. When a child started school, they were invariably exposed to 'Janet and John', not 'Ja-net and John'.

The tots' comic *Jack and Jill* didn't use hyphens. This publication was a bit more progressive – it looked different to my *Chicks' Own*. The shiny paper and bright colours photogravure format was similar to that used on *Girl*, *Robin*, *Eagle* and *Swift*, and was certainly very attractive. However, it didn't stop me from enjoying *The Beano*, *The Dandy*,

Chick's Own, Tiny Tots, Rainbow and Tiger Tim.

Topper and, later, *Bunty* and *Judy*, even though they continued to use the newsprint kind of paper. One of the earliest comics for children was *Rainbow*. *Rainbow* first appeared in 1914, and continued right through till 1956. An iconic *Rainbow* character was Tiger Tim, who, in early days had his own comic, *Tiger Tim*, before amalgamating with *Rainbow*. He later cropped up in *Jack and Jill*. Tiger Tim also appeared in his own annual tie-ins.

Comics versus books for tots

There is a plethora of books for young children, ranging from the indestructible first kind made from cloth or board, to the teaching kind, which pave the way for learning to read. So why on earth would a parent give a tot a comic? What possible benefit could there be? Well, surprisingly, comics have a lot going for them. For a start, inevitably they are colourful, with instant child appeal. Additionally, the large format is attractive, resembling a newspaper. If a child sees her parents regularly reading a newspaper or similar format magazine, she will think it grown-up to be given a comic newspaper for herself. Most comics feature regular characters, with, often, an ongoing story. Even though the child can't yet read, she will enjoy looking at the pictures as an adult reads the text to her, and she will invariably want to know what happens next. She will be looking forward to her next week's comic (although, as already noted, many modern comics nowadays use a regular free gift as the bait). At one time, comics featured serials ending on a dramatic note, thus providing an even greater hook, but nowadays, they are more likely to feature a complete tale. Even so, the urge to follow a favourite character's adventures remains. Often, the comic is bought at the supermarket, a sop to ensure the girl behaves, 'or you won't get your comic'! Nowadays, however, comics are fast falling from favour. As Bill McLoughlin of D.C Thomson points out; 'Japan uses comics to educate, so does Brazil and closer to home we have Spain, France and Germany who use the comic medium right through the age spectrum from kids to adults. Maybe one day we will realise that the comic medium is as effective as TV.'

The strip format of comics, with sets of pictures telling the story, enables even the youngest child to work out a storyline for herself. Sometimes, she may get it wrong, or go off on a tangent or misunderstand the meaning behind one of the illustrations. None of this matters, the main thing is that the child is using her imagination and her intelligence. Additionally, the simple, repetitive text underneath will soon have her recognising certain words, such as the characters' names. Most of the modern comics contain various puzzles involving colouring in, following a simple maze, discovering the odd one out or maybe learning a word. Comics nowadays tend to be television-based, featuring the adventures of characters popular with pre-schoolers: Teletubbies, Dora the Explorer, Cbeebies, Fifi and the Flowertots, In the Night Garden and others. These are an extension of the programmes the young girl might be watching regularly. The familiarisation of the screen adventures will help her to make sense of the pictures depicted in the comics, and because the characters and situations are already known to her, she will find it easier to link them with the text beneath the pictures.

This isn't a new phenomenon – back in the 1950s, comics such as *Robin* included television favourites, notably Andy Pandy, while amongst the comics for older children were *Radio Fun* and *Film Fun*. Other comics are character based, often on dolls such as Sindy or Barbie, or on toys such as Sylvanian Families or Glo Bugs, as opposed to media creations.

The following comics for toddlers and young children are really unisex; the switch to predominately small girl orientated comics came later, probably in the 1980s, with the arrival of such titles as *My Little Pony*, *Care Bears* and others, though even so, *Twinkle* and similar earlier titles were certainly girl-intended.

Bimbo

Launched in 1961 by D.C. Thomson, it survived for just over a decade before folding. *Bimbo* was a colour-cover gravure-printed weekly, which cost 5d. The first issue front page was enticingly colourful in blue and yellow, and free inside was a multicoloured balloon with 'a long long whistle'. It contained two text stories and several picture strips.

Apart from the front and back cover, which featured (in a 1962 issue) a story about Tom Thumb who was going on holiday in a caravan, and four inside pages, the rest was black and white. On the back cover was Bimbo's Alphabet, which had reached the letter O for owl, ostrich and otter. Stories such as 'Young Robinson Crusoe' featuring two children

TOM THUMB

1—Young Tom was going for a holiday in a lovely caravan his father had helped him to make. The caravan was tiny, for Tom was only a few inches tall.

2—When Tom had loaded all his furniture, he harnessed Monty Mouse to the caravan and set off. On the way he passed his pet baby mice.

3—The little mice, who lived in an old shoe, were very sad because Tom was going without them. "I DO wish I could take you," Tom said to them.

4—Then kind little Tom thought of a way to take the baby mice with him on holiday. First he borrowed a roller skate from Simon Jolly. *(Continued on back page.)*

living on an island in the Indian Ocean, 'Pip the Penguin', 'The Jingle-Bells School' and others, were all beautifully illustrated in a strip-story format, with clear brief text beneath. The two inside colour pages were devoted to a cartoon called 'Baby Crockett', a double page serial 'Little Snow White' (her dwarfs had different names to the Disney version, and included Thumpy, Chuckles, Mumpy and Bossy), and pictures sent in by readers, who were all awarded a paint box prize. The ages of entrants are worth noting; they range from an expected age five, up to a couple of unexpected eleven-year-olds – nowadays, eleven-year-olds would probably hate to be mentioned in such a babyish comic. Interestingly, this comic also contained a preview of what would be included in the following week's comic – tots could look forward to 'Robby Rabbit's Jack-in-the-box', 'Chirpy Chipmunk Goes Boating' and 'Pip the Penguin's Alarm Clock'. Most comics never bothered with this subtle hook, but it was a clever idea. *Bimbo* morphed into *Little Star* in 1971, no doubt partly because the word bimbo had changed its meaning somewhat since the more innocent early 1960s, and now was often used as a derogative term for a curvy female.

Buttons

Buttons was a comic published by Polystyle Publications and intended for playschool children. The company obviously did quite a bit of research, as the first issue I have is 'number 0' and dated 0 to 0 October 1981. It was given away at playschools, clinics and other places frequented by toddlers and their parents. Very much BBC based, it was filled with favourite characters from the time, and the first trial issue, 0, features Postman Pat on the cover. Inside is a mixture of colour, and black and white comic strips, as well as puzzles, ideas for things to do (make a grasshopper from a toilet roll, lump of play dough and pipe cleaners) and a feature on a one-man band. Cartoon strips include 'Morph', 'King Rollo', 'The Flumps', 'Pigeon Street' and 'Noah and Nelly'. *Buttons* was a well-thought out comic, and provided plenty of amusement for the youngest children. It was a follow-up to *Pippin in Playland*.

Candy

This short-lived comic was introduced at the beginning of 1967 by City Magazines, originally as photogravure, later switching to web offset, and, in the process, losing much of its attractiveness, as the colouring turned rather muddy. Inside the first issue, as well as a free *Candy*'s magic painting book, was an episode of the popular television boxer dog Bengo, drawn by Tim. Other television favourites inside that first issue included Topo Gigio and Thunderbirds.

Candy continued to hold on for three years, before finally becoming incorporated into *Jack and Jill* at the beginning of 1980. Looking into a November 1968 issue, we find 'Polly and Pussy-Cat in Nursery Rhyme Land', 'Monkey Tricks' – Monty Monkey has a mishap with a toy aeroplane – and 'A Story For Bedtime', which tells the traditional tale of Careful Hans. The centre-page colour spread is given over to a story about Tingha and Tucker who are koala bears, and their Australian friends Kiki Kangaroo and Willie Wombat. Tingha and Tucker were popular characters on children's television at the time. The rest of the magazine was devoted to puzzles and things to do, and there was also a reprint of the classic poem, *A Boy's Song*, in which I noticed that the word 'grey' had been rendered as 'gray' – it seemed an odd spelling for a British magazine. Finally, the back (colour) cover was a picture of a hot air balloon, 'b is for balloon', with a two-line rhyme.

Chicks' Own

One of the classics, this comic was first published in 1920 by Amalgamated Press, and was one of the experimental hyphenated comics. With cartoon text saying things such as, 'Well I nev-er. It is not rain-ing at all', 'Hur-ry in-doors ev-ery-one', 'Our boat has drift-ed a-way', and 'The trees I or-der-ed have not ar-rived', the idea was to make reading easier. Certainly, *Chicks' Own* was a popular comic, which ran for 37 years. It contained quite a lot of reading, with more text than found in most small children's comics of the post-war period, and, as well as the funny stories, had 'Sunshine Farm', which was illustrated in a more grown-up style with plenty of depth and shading.

Chicks' Own had an impressive, busy masthead which, as well as showing the title in large red letters, and the price – in 1953 it was 3d – in blue, also contained a delightful spring scene of six children, a house, tree, garden, flowers, a nest box, sheep and a puppy. All the illustrations have plenty to look at, ensuring that even the smallest child would gain enjoyment from looking at the pictures, even if she had no idea of the actual story line.

In 1941, *Chicks' Own* took over the ailing *Bubbles*, which had already amalgamated with *Sunday Fairy* and *Children's Fairy*. *Chicks' Own* had also taken over *Playtime, Bo-Peep and Little Boy Blue* and *Happy Days*. In 1957, *Chicks' Own* finally bowed out, after a wonderful run of 37 years, joining up with *Playhour*. Unfortunately it's just not possible to analyse all the comics here, but it's interesting to note that *Bubbles* printed the original Mickey Mouse in 1924, with a story by Roy Wilson called 'Micky The Mouse'. *Bubbles* also ran a less-than-politically-correct story called 'Nippi the Jap'.

Harold Hare's Own Paper

Harold Hare was a much-loved character who appeared in *Jack and Jill*, and also in *Knockout*. In 1959, on the 14th November, *Harold Hare's Own Paper* arrived in the newsagents. The first issue bore an attractive, eye-catching yellow cover with a picture of Harold flying a shiny red plane. He was clutching a blue balloon, and at the top of the comic it said, 'Free, 2 Wonderful Toys. Grand Harold Hare Balloon and Mask.' Also on the cover was a paw mark and a note which read, 'Sorry, this paw-mark is where I trod in the ink. Harold x.' The comic, or 'paper' cost 5d every Thursday, and that first issue contained such characters as Dagwood Duck, Wendy and her Toby Jug, Mr Toad, Peter Puffin and Flopsy Flufftail. It also contained the very popular Bengo, a picture strip featuring a boxer dog and his doggy friends, drawn by William Timyn alias Tim. (see also *Candy*.)

An issue dated 8th September 1962 features a full-colour picture-strip featuring Harold on both front and back covers. Inside the comic is black and white apart from the centre pages, and these contain an imaginative story, 'The Wonderful Island of Yum', where Peter and Pam are staying with Professor Yum and a baby whale called Splosh. They could breathe under the sea because Yum was 'a special dream island' and could ride on flying fish. Additional picture-strips include 'Snuggles' (a story about a koala bear), 'The Little Horses' (wild horses who try to help when forest creatures are in trouble), 'Katie Country Mouse' (knitting a scarf as a present for Mrs Mole) and 'Moony From the Moon' (adventures of a little alien). 'Wendy and her Toby Jug', 'Peter Puffin', 'Flopsy Flufftail' and 'Mr Toad' are still in evidence from the first issue. There is also a puzzle page and a short text story 'Billy the Beetle' labelled as 'An All By Yourself Story'.

The comic went on to run for four and a half years, embracing *Walt Disney's Weekly* along the way. *Harold Hare's Own Paper* also underwent a title change, to the less long-winded *Harold Hare*. In 1964, *Harold Hare* became amalgamated with *Playhour*.

✳ AN EXCITING NEW Mr TOAD STORY INSIDE

© Fleetway Publications Ltd., 1962

EVERY WEDNESDAY
8th SEPTEMBER, 1962
6D

Harold Hare's
OWN PAPER

A Sunshine WEEKLY

TRY OUR NEW CUSTARD PIES!

The MYSTERY PRIZE

" Yum-yumikins!" said Harold Hare when he saw some new custard pies in the Grocer's Shop. But although the pies *looked* nice, they *tasted* horrid. "UUUUUGH!" spluttered Harold. "I'm not buying any of those!"

Harold's little friend, Dicky Dormouse, tasted the pies, too. "They really are horrid!" he gasped. Harold squirted soda water into his mouth to take away the taste. But Mr. Bunny, the Grocer, had a problem.

(Please turn to back page)

Jack and Jill

When this comic arrived onto the market, it really brightened the newsagents' shops with its colour gravure printed bright cover. *Jack and Jill* was published by Amalgamated Press in 1954, and swiftly became one of the most popular comics for tots of both sexes. The front cover of a 1956 copy of the comic shows *Jack and Jill* (not the nursery rhyme), two modern children who appear to be twins. They are playing on the beach, and below the four pictures are rhyming couplets. In later issues, the children were sometimes shown in one large picture, or panel, combined with a puzzle. The characters were featured in the very first issue, and continued right through to the last issue, in 1985. Amongst the artists who drew the illustrations over the years were Hugh McNeill, Antonio Lupatelli and Eric Stephens. (See Chapter 5).

The back page of *Jack and Jill*, headed 'Jolly Jingles' is a rhyme about Tom Cobley, again, not the famous song. Colour inside the magazine is reserved for the centre pages, which feature a double page picture of an extraordinarily bustling scene of children taking part in a sports day. The heading is 'There Was An Old Woman Who Lived in a Shoe' and many of the children are in slightly old-fashioned dress – the girls in long skirts and aprons, while the boys wear short jackets and Eton collars. Various objects such as a teddy bear and a dolly are hidden in the picture, so it was a test of observation for a child (and for the parents), as it is quite difficult to find the items, hidden as they are amongst the playing children!

Inside, the black and white strips are arranged four pictures to a page, which makes for good clear images. Amongst the strips are 'The Happy Days of Teddy and Cuddly the Baby Bears', 'Fun in Toyland', 'Flipper the Jolly Penguin', 'The Wonderful Adventures of Jerry, Don and Snooker' (Snooker was a rather strange cat), 'The Funny Tales of Freddie Frog' and 'The Fun and Frolics of Harold Hare'. Obviously, *Jack and Jill* didn't hold with short, snappy titles. Some of these characters became exceedingly well loved, appearing in other magazines or books too. One creature, Flipper the Penguin, drawn by various artists, Fred Robinson, Walter Bell, Walter Booth and A. S. A. Newark, was a firm favourite in the early years, making his appearance in the very first issue. He voyaged the ocean in a barrel, which he called, 'The Little Nipper', visiting all kinds of creatures and later meeting up with children Peter and Poppy, who had many adventures with him. 'Teddy and Cuddly', two delightful bear cubs, were brothers who had lots of adventures in the woods with the other creatures who lived there. Drawn by Hugh McNeill and Bert Felstead, the escapades of the little bears as another cartoon picture strip that had appeared in *Jack and Jill* since the very first issue. They continued to entertain little ones until 1969.

Harold Hare, by Hugh McNeill, was a crazy hare who lived in Leafy Wood with his friends Happy Hedgehog and Dicky Dormouse. As he was a March hare, he was allowed to be 'mad', and his friends accepted him for what he was. Harold had originally appeared in an Amalgamated Press publication called *Sun*, making his debut in 1950, before transferring to *Jack and Jill* in 1954. He later became something of a star and went on to have his own *Harold Hare's Own Paper*, in 1959, and then popped up again in the 1980s, in *Playhour*. There were also books and annuals written about him.

Jack and Jill was beautifully designed. Each picture had a short block of clear, large type printed below, a far cry from the tiny print of *Chicks' Own* and *Rainbow*. A comic such as this positively encouraged young children to read. There was also a short letter from the children Jack and Jill, which this week – still referring to the 1956 copy – began, 'Have

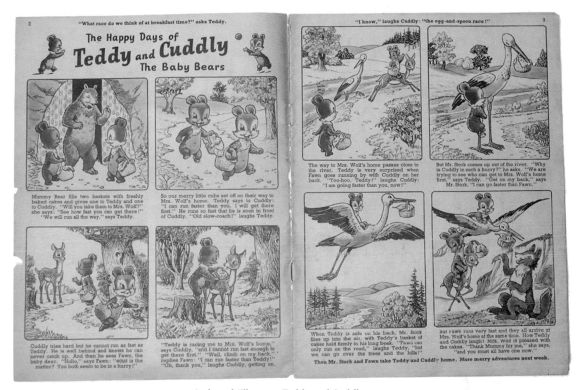

Jack and Jill pages, Teddy and Cuddly.

you got a doggie, and does it like ice-cream?' The *Jack and Jill* comic continued till 1985. Along the way it had incorporated *Teddy Bear*, *Candy* and *Playbox*, and during its life span produced some excellent characters, many of which are still fondly remembered today.

Little Star

Little Star, a D. C. Thomson production dating from January 1972, was a tot's comic sub-titled 'The picture paper specially for little girls and little boys'. Its covers were attractive, with bright graphics and a large colourful cartoon-type drawing against a fairly plain background.

Inside a 1975 edition, the full-colour centre-page spread is given over to a strip cartoon of 'Baby Crockett' who had come across from the *Bimbo* comic, which had ceased in 1971 – in fact, *Little Star* was more-or-less *Bimbo* with a name change. Later, 'Baby Crockett' became a *Beezer* regular. Also in colour are strip stories 'Pip the Penguin', 'Tim' and 'Tom Thumb', as well as 'Trumper-Time' which is a mix of poems and things to do. Other picture strips include 'Freddy, Teddy, Joe' (adventures of a polar cub, a teddy cub and a koala cub) and 'Curly' (Mary Smith and her little pet lamb). 'Goody Gumdrops' is a story about a little girl who lives in a 'sweet' town and 'Pinkie and the Princess' is a delightful and different kind of series telling the tale of a little girl living in China. The back page is devoted to a set of 'cut out and keep' snap cards.

The *Little Star* would have been a good value (at 5p) read for small children; it was attractively designed and contained lots of lively artwork. Sadly, though, it lasted for just four years before disappearing.

Magic Comic

D. C. Thomson subtitled their *Magic Comic* 'For young children', and the first issue appeared in the newsagent in January 1976. Costing 8p every Monday, this was a typical mix of picture strips and things to do. Interestingly, it contained tributes to both *The Beano* and *The Dandy*, with 'Cuddly and Duddly', nephews of Biffo the Bear, and 'Copycat', who was a nephew of Korky the Cat. Amongst other strip cartoons were 'Bobby in Blue and his Sister Sue', who were two young children on police patrol in a pedal car, and the wonderful 'Flying Flapears' – a bunny with overlarge ears which allowed him to fly. The most innovative of them all was a series called 'Spaceship Lollipop', which told of a circular spaceship in which two children and their father travelled the universe. Many of the other stories had, as may be guessed from the title, a magical theme, notably 'Peter Poppin' a young boy who had a magic pop-up book. *Magic Comic* ceased publication in 1979.

Pippin

This was a comic for little ones with a television tie-in. Issue number one of *Pippin* was published on 24 September 1966 by Polystyle, and contained stories about the 'Pogles', 'Woodentops', 'Titch and Quackers', and 'Camberwick Green' amongst others. As the issues progressed it embraced such favourites as 'Joe', 'Trumpton', and 'Sooty and Sweep'. The first issue came with a free gift of a Punch glove puppet, and it cost 7d. Its sub-title was 'The coloured picture weekly for the very young viewer'. *Pippin* proved surprisingly popular and seems to be one of the fondly remembered comics and featured in many nostalgic reminiscences, so must have made an impact on its young readers at the time.

Taking a peek into a 1975 issue, the centre-page spread colour-strip is occupied by a classic Rupert Bear tale, 'Rupert's Deep Sea Adventure', while other colour pages go to favourites 'Andy Pandy' and 'Bagpuss'. Stories 'Chigley and Trumpton', 'Mary, Mungo and Midge' and 'The Herbs' have the black and white pages. There are also puzzle and postbag pages. The front and back colour covers are devoted to 'Barnaby', a strange-looking little bear, originally dreamt up by French writer Olga Pouchine. Just over a year after *Pippin* began, Polystyle issued a similar comic, *Playland*, which proved to be another successful title. The two comics ran side by side for several years before merging in 1975, becoming *Pippin in Playland*. In the 1980s the comic was incorporated into *Buttons*.

Playbox

The Amalgamated Press comic, *Playbox*, was originally intended for small girls, with a distinct bias towards the fairer sex by way of using girl heroines in several of the cartoon strips. However, it didn't really work and it wasn't long before the boys muscled in to make it appeal to both sexes, though it still had more than its fair share of girl characters. The comic started in 1925, a sort-of counterpart to *Tiger Tim's Weekly*, but *Playbox* had 'The Hippo Girls' with Tiger Tilly. Looking at an April 1950 copy, I see that *Playbox* was a mix of picture strips and all-text (surprisingly small print) stories. The front page had a 'busy' masthead, with 'Playbox' in large fat blue letters, and an Easter picture of various animal characters playing with Easter eggs on a slide, while a cat seller of hot cross buns spills her wares. The comic cost 3d. The full-colour front page starred Twizzle, a cute long-eared rabbit-like creature who constantly changed colour, even achieving magnificent stripes. Inside, there is a picture adventure called 'Wendy; Tales of Her Adventures', which tells of Wendy and White Rabbit in Wonderland, while others include 'Snowdrops Zoo', 'Tuffy and His Magic Tail' and 'Bright Eyes', which is about 'a little film star'. Included too was a never-would-be-allowed-now strip called 'Sambo the Speeder'. The centre-page spread and the back page were printed in red and black. There were four long all-text stories, amongst them a serial called 'Pets of Mine', and also a page of 'Easter Fun with Uncle Ben', including a crossword, join the dots, riddles, and ideas for Easter games. *Playbox* kept going till 1953. It later became incorporated into *Jack and Jill*.

Play-Group

This 1984 IPC publication, *Play-Group*, was fairly short-lived. Using the photogravure technique, it was an A4-sized comic, mainly concentrating on television-based characters and puzzles. An early copy – a free sample copy it says on the front – showed assorted characters including *Magic Roundabout*'s Dougal, Florence and Brian, Sooty, a couple of Mr Men and Little Miss people, and three *Willo the Wisp* favourites – Mavis Cruet, Willo himself, and Twit the bird. Most of the magazine is given over to simple puzzles – colouring, join the dashes, solve a maze and odd one out. There are cut-out frogs to make 'a game to play with mummy', a colourful tiger mask to make and a picture of *Fraggle Rock* to paste onto card and cut into a jigsaw puzzle. Strip stories include 'Sooty and Sweep', 'The Magic Roundabout' and 'The Moomins'.

In 1985, *Play-Group* amalgamated with *Robin*, and an issue from July is entitled *Play-Group with Robin*. Inside are still a good variety of puzzles – join the dots, colouring, spot the changes, counting and others – there was certainly plenty here to keep a pre-schooler entertained for quite a while. Picture strip stories include 'Robin', 'Jenny and Ginger', 'The Moomins' and 'Sooty and Sweep'. The comic ceased in 1986.

Playhour

Originally known as *Playhour Pictures*, which began in 1954 as an Amalgamated Press follow-on to their successful *Jack and Jill*, it changed its name the following year by dropping the 'Pictures'. *Playhour* was a comic for pre-schoolers, and appealed to both girls and boys as it featured many television characters. This probably helped to give the comic extra appeal to its young readers, because familiar television favourites are always a way of attracting interest and attention. A look through a 1968 issue reveals an inviting comic, with attractive illustrations and interesting stories, such as 'Sonny and Sally of Happy Valley', who visited a hobbies show and bought a rug-making kit. They tried very hard, but they ended up with sore hands, so they made a small rug for their pet lamb's basket instead, rather than the large rug they had intended. The magazine is in photogravure style, so is bright and cheerful, and other stories include 'The Magic Roundabout', 'Rolf Harris and Coojeebear', 'Bunny Cuddles', 'Pinky and Perky', and 'Num Num and His Funny Family' (kittens who occupy the colourful centre-page spread). Also inside are 'Mr Toad' and a series based on Leslie Crowther and Peter Glaze, who feature on the 'Crackerjack Fun' page as well.

One of the earlier, much-loved characters, not appearing in this issue, was Gulliver Guinea-pig, a great explorer who travelled the world, undergoing lots of fantastic adventures in the nursery rhyme and fantasy worlds. Often, rather like Rupert Bear, his adventures were told in rhyme. Gregory, a colourful strip, painted by Philip Mendoza and Gordon Hutchings, first appeared in *Playhour* in 1958, later transferring to *Jack and Jill*.

Seventeen years later, 'Sonny and Sally' were still going strong, but the other stories have been replaced by new characters, including 'Pinkie Puff the little elephant with the long trunk', 'Willo the Wisp', 'The Mr Men' and 'Pickles' (a puppy owned by a little girl named Pat). 'The Dolly Girls', appeared in a colour strip illustrated by Rosemary Brown. This strip had come across from *Bonnie* (a short-lived little girls' weekly which ran from 1974-1975), and told of five dolls who lived together in a dolls' house, with Dolly keeping the other three (plus baby) in line. It appeared in *Playhour* from 1975 until it ended. The old favourites 'Teddy and Cuddly' were also featured, having come over from *Jack and Jill*, which had ceased in 1985. Amazingly, during its run, *Playhour* engulfed no less than ten other publications, among them *Chicks' Own*, *Tiny Tots*, *Play-Group* and *Jack and Jill*. The comic finally closed in 1987, becoming incorporated into *Funtime*.

Rainbow

Another Amalgamated Press classic, *Rainbow*, although it appealed to both sexes, definitely had a male slant. I'm including it here, though, because I know that it was one of the most popular comics for both girls and boys in the 1940s. *Rainbow*, which from 1940 also incorporated *Tiger Tim's Weekly*, was, like so many of the Amalgamated Press comics at the time, a tabloid newsprint comic with a full-colour front cover, and with a red and black back cover and centre page. The comic was first issued in 1914. The centre page, in a 1952 issue, was given over to picture strips; 'Marzipan the Magician', 'The Brownie Boys', 'The Two Pickles', 'Our Dolliwogs' and others, while the strip on the back cover, 'New Captain' is a series about a submarine featuring the, seemingly obligatory, 'Sambo' black boy. The comic also contained four longer text stories with very small print, a 'Tiger Tim's Birthday Club' section, which had a competition to win a bicycle, and 'Tiger Tim's column' with riddles and things to make and do. *Rainbow* ceased in 1956, a victim to changing styles and to more vibrant publications, though, by becoming incorporated into *Tiny Tots*, held on a few more years.

Robin back pages.

Robin

One of the classic children's comics, *Robin* dates from 1953, one of Hulton's big four – the others were *Eagle*, *Girl*, and *Swift*. A typical issue of *Robin* – this one is from the 1960s – features Andy Pandy and his friends on the front page, in full colour. Andy is making a necklace for Looby Loo, using coloured beads. Not to be outdone, Teddy makes a necklace

too, only he threads together the peas he has been shelling for dinner. The first two inside pages, which are monochrome, are given over to Bizzie Beaver and his friends who attempt circus tricks using barrels (and one wonders how many of today's children will ever get to visit a circus) before we turn to the adventures of Richard Lion. Richard Lion's tent was knocked down by a goat when he and his friends were camping in a field. This page is shared with an adventure entitled, 'Mark, A Boy Who Knew Jesus'. Here we discover that Jesus and his friends were coming to celebrate Passover at Mark's home, and that Judas was preparing to betray Jesus. In this multicultural age, religion would probably not be a chosen feature of a mainstream comic title, but it played an important part in Hulton titles.

'The Twins', two angelic looking children, Simon and Sally, feature in the following double-page spread, before we return to full colour with the centre-page spread which tells of the 'Funny Adventures of Nutty Noddle', a squirrel, and his Aunt Scofalot (who lived up to her name). Next comes a picture adventure serial, 'The Magic Crown of Jewels', set in what seems to be medieval times, and tells of Jason, Linda and their Uncle Odo who is a court magician. It includes plenty of necessary ingredients such as a giant, a castle and precious jewels.

We then reach two pages of 'oddments' – a short text story (just one illustration) about Tubby the Odd-Job Engine who was finding flies a nuisance until Neddy, the donkey, whisked them away with his tail. Underneath the story is a selection of reader's photos, with their ages and brief details of their favourite stories in *Robin*. On the opposite page is 'Chimp's Page of Fun', a selection of puzzles – join the dots, a maze, a memory test, an 'odd one out' group and a picture to colour. The final double page is given over to Woppit, created by Ursula Moray – Woppit was a character bear who rather resembled a piglet (but see Chapter 11) – and 'Learn to read with Bill and Ben'. The latter is a strip cartoon depicting the Flower Pot Men, with simple, widely spaced text underneath.

The comic reverts to colour for the back page, which is a charming full-page illustration of children shopping in a market, and it contains hidden items, such as a one-pound note and some onions, for readers to find. Other snippets in the comic include riddles along the mastheads of many of the pages, a short letter from The Twins, and the winners of the birthday club's cake. There are no details in this issue of how to join the club or receive the badge (see Chapter 8), although they had appeared in the previous week's issue. *Robin* was retired in 1969. However, that wasn't quite the end of the story, because IPC tried reviving the *Robin* comic 14 years later, but it wasn't particularly popular. With stories such as 'Pixie Fun', 'Rabbit Tales' and 'Nutty Noddle', there was nothing new or exciting, and it wasn't long before it was combined with *Play-Group*.

Teddy Bear

A friendly, photogravure style tots' comic, which, as IPC boasted, was 'The Best Picture Paper For Young Children'. Dating from 1963, it managed a 10-year run, and was an attractive publication with a bright and cheerful cover. The cover featured a large Henry Fox picture of teddy bears pursuing various activities, such as, in a 1972 issue, having a musical interlude. The bears are sweet-faced, and, while the boy plays his blue toy piano, the little girl bear is singing lustily, accompanied by her pet cat. This is also a puzzle picture, with four musical toys hidden around the picture. Inside is a story about Teddy and his family. This week he is buying a doll for his friend's birthday. Then there is 'Silly Billy – The little boy who makes you laugh', and in this issue pretends to be a doll so he can ride in a little girl's dolls' pram. Another favourite is 'Nurse Susan and Doctor David', which tells the adventures of two children who like to dress up and then pretend they are caring for patients in their dolls' hospital. This Nurse Susan and Doctor David strip was illustrated in line and wash by Roma, and made the transition across from *Teddy Bear* to *Jack and Jill* when the former closed.

The centre-page colour-spread was taken up by 'Out With Mummy', another regular series. In this issue, Mummy's car is stuck in the snow and she and the children have to spend the night at a school where a rescue centre had been set up. There were a couple of other picture stories, as well as a short text bedtime story, and there were puzzles and a picture of the 'Wallpaper Shop Man' to colour. The back, colour, cover was a story featuring 'Paddy-Paws the Puppy'. When *Teddy Bear* ended in 1973, it was incorporated into *Jack and Jill*.

Tiger Tim's Weekly

Tiger Tim, an anthropomorphic character created by Julius Stafford Baker, had a chequered career. An Amalgamated Press character who originally appeared in a magazine supplement in the early 1900s, he was later given his own monthly paper called *Tiger Tim's Tales* in 1919. This then became weekly, and a year later the comic was renamed *Tiger Tim's Weekly*.

Tiger Tim's Weekly was a nursery comic, rather like *Rainbow*, but a smaller size. Later, it switched to tabloid like its more famous companion, and became very successful. Amongst the characters in *Tiger Tim's Weekly* were 'Tiger Tim And The Bruin Boys', 'Bobby Dare' and 'The Bumpty Boys', drawn by Freddie Crompton. Tiger Tim himself was something of a thorn in his teacher, Mrs Bruin's, side. Although the comic was successful, it was merged with *Rainbow* in 1940, a time when many other comics closed due to wartime paper shortages. *Rainbow* was then subtitled 'Tiger Tim's own picture paper'.

Strictly speaking, *Tiger Tim's Weekly* could be regarded as a boy's comic, but of course, small girls loved it too. A look at a copy dated 26th January 1936 reveals a mix of picture strips and text, using a very small font. The cover, which is full colour, has a large picture of Tiger Tim, Jumbo and friends making a snow bed for a polar bear, while around the edges is a strip cartoon of the Bumpty boys. Inside is a long text story featuring those naughty 'Bruin Boys', two other stories – 'Plucky Pip' and 'The Lost Football' – and various picture strips including 'Mrs Tabby and her Tibbies' and 'The Tiny Boys of Toy Town'.

Tiny Tots

This early favourite had a long run of just over 30 years, and was an Amalgamated Press comic in the Chicks' Own/Rainbow/Tiger Tim style. Founded in 1927, it proved a popular choice for parents to buy for their tinies, and, together with *Chicks' Own*, was an experiment in hyphenated text. Parents were told that the hyphenated style made it easier for children to learn to read, and that fluent reading would be of enormous benefit later on. This tabloid-sized comic was attractive with its full colour strips on the front and back covers, and its light blue Tiny Tots masthead, decorated with small drawings in the familiar Amalgamated Press pre-school comic fashion. This overview is from a 1953 edition, and fittingly, in coronation year, features a soldier on sentry duty on a castle wall, standing proudly by a Union Flag, alongside the masthead. The front-page story, 'Tiny and Tot's Ball Goes Into the Sea' features the boy and girl twins playing on the beach with Nursie and their dog, Dumpty. Both the speech balloons and the longer picture captions are hyphenated, as they are throughout the comic. This story covers six large pictures. Underneath is a narrow, four-picture strip featuring Frisk and Whisk, two small dogs. At one time, Tiny and Tot were characters in *Chicks' Own*, but were then given their own comic. They were created by artist Freddie Crompton, who worked for many of the Amalgamated Press comics, but were later drawn by other artists and lost their endearing chubbiness.

Of the eight pages of the comic, three are given over to all-text stories – 'Jingles and the Giant', 'Monty Mouse and the Magic Toyshop' and 'The Story of Little Tom Thumb', though each has a small black and white picture. The pages also bear short verses, join-the-dots, riddles, 'Uncle Jack's Jolly Page' (which is actually a third of a page), a strip cartoon about the Comical Cats and a picture headed 'Jack-ies won-der-ful toys make sug-ar sand-castles'.

The centre pages, in red and black, contain a mixture of cartoon strips and story strips, amongst them 'Toddles, Susie and Babs' (three children at the seaside) and 'Peter and Peggy in Jungleland' (featuring two children and the familiar Amalgamated Press jungle creatures). 'Teddy and Greta' tells how Grandpa and Marjorie are on holiday and find toys the image of Marjorie's beloved Teddy and Greta in a shop. Of course, they really are Marjorie's toys that had arrived there after a series of adventures. The most interesting picture strip, which would almost sit as comfortably in a child's comic today, is 'Little

Snowdrop'. Little Snowdrop and her friend Jim are visiting a lighthouse when they notice the lighthouse keeper is looking after some seagulls. He explains that not only do the gulls become injured on the lantern, but that many others become trapped by patches of oil, and he tells the children that it's important to warm the gulls and feed them, before cleaning them using 'one of those soap-less washing powders'. Later, the children find more gulls, which they clean up. The strip ends with Snowdrop suggesting they set up a place on the beach to tend oiled seagulls. That was written over 55 years ago, and it's heart-warming to find that someone writing in a child's comic at the time was quite so clued up with conservation.

Tiny Tots continued on, determinedly sticking to its large format, speech balloons and text written under the pictures, right to the end. It was finally incorporated into the glossy, more modern-looking *Playhour* in 1959.

Toby

With its boy's name, you would be forgiven for thinking that Toby was a boy's comic, but it was really intended for both sexes. The sub-heading was 'A New Comic For Little Children' and it was published by IPC in 1976. *Toby* cost 8p every Friday, and though, with just 16 pages, it was a little short of reading matter, it was a calm, restful read for a small child. *Toby* depicted a peaceful world always showing, as one regular picture strip maintained, 'One day when the sun was shining'. Toby himself was actually a dog, in the anthropomorphic style of Rupert Bear, and he featured on the front page, in colour, in adventures such as 'Toby and the Rainbow's end'. An early issue from April 1976 reveals several female characters, amongst them 'Grandma Next Door' – children Pam and Paul are lucky enough to have their Grandma living close, and she has plenty of bright ideas to entertain them. Also there was 'Patty and Her Magic Puppy'; magic things happen when Poppy the Puppy wags her tail, and 'Fun at School with Miss Muddle' – Miss Muddle is a teacher at Jolly Towers School. Other girlie features include 'Mummy's Bedtime Story', which is a mainly text tale about a yawning pixie, and a beautifully colour-illustrated serial, 'Beauty and the Beast'.

Toby ran for around two and a half years before becoming incorporated into *Jack and Jill* in October 1978. During its short lifetime, *Toby* was able to incorporate the short-lived comic *See-Saw*, which it did in July 1977.

Twinkle

One of the most popular comics for little girls growing up in the seventies and eighties, was *Twinkle*. Certainly it is one which seems to evoke plenty of nostalgia when women recount their memories of the comics they once read. *Twinkle* made its debut in 1968 and came from the doyen of the comic world, D.C. Thomson. Issue one featured a free bracelet bearing a St Christopher medallion, 'Wear a pretty bracelet just like mummy does'. The white cover showed a drawing of a small pony-tailed blonde girl in a bright red cardigan, white top and blue trousers.

Why was *Twinkle* so special? Well, for starters, this really was a girls' comic – in fact under the Twinkle masthead was the legend 'The picture paper especially for little girls'. Most small girls at the time still enjoyed playing with dolls and prams, wearing pretty dresses and acting like mummy, and the comic reflected this. The stories were gentle and delightful. A look at an early issue, from 1971, has picture strips such as 'Nancy the Little

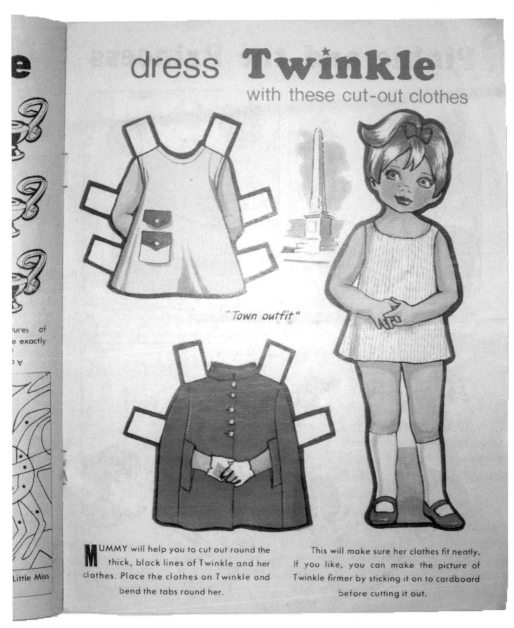

dress Twinkle
with these cut-out clothes

"Town outfit"

MUMMY will help you to cut out round the thick, black lines of Twinkle and her clothes. Place the clothes on Twinkle and bend the tabs round her.

This will make sure her clothes fit neatly. If you like, you can make the picture of Twinkle firmer by sticking it on to cardboard before cutting it out.

Twinkle paper doll.

Nurse'. Nancy and her Grandad, Mr Jingle, run a Dollies' Hospital, but one day the children who were in the waiting room with their toys which needed mending, were becoming bored. So Nancy told them to arrange their chairs like a train, and they passed the time playing. This was a black and white strip, as were several others including 'Betty Bright', who made bunny faces to sew onto her young cousin's slippers, and 'The Three Pennys' – three girls with the same name who held a dog show in the garden. 'Nancy', 'The Three

Pennys', 'Sally Sweet' and 'Betty Bright' were all regulars; they appeared in earlier issues too.

'Patsy Panda' and 'Sally Sweet of Sunshine Street' were both in full, bright colour, as was a fable, retold as a tale about a squirrel called Sammy who left his toys out in the rain. The comic was priced a 3p, and featured a bright cover showing a small girl – Twinkle – vacuuming a carpet by a doll's house. The child is sweet-faced, big-eyed and wearing a typical 1970s' tabard over matching shorts, decorated with large flowers. By contrast, the drawing of the Twinkle girl in the following decade, though still large-eyed, has a slightly older look. Artists used in *Twinkle* included Spanish artist, Trini Tinture.

Twinkle was an excellent choice of comic for a small girl, because there was plenty to look at and to do amongst its twenty pages. As well as the various picture stories, there was a club page (see Chapter 8), a page showing assorted artwork which children had sent in made from buttons, and a page of various puzzles. The back page was 'Norma's Nature Notebook', a factual read about otters, in colour, with a beautiful painting of otters that asked readers if they could find the hidden fish. Finally, inside the comic was a full-page colour advert showing characters from another pre-school magazine, *Bimbo*. Thirteen years later, a 1984 *Twinkle* reveals that 'Nancy the Little Nurse' is still going strong, there are even more things to do in the comic, and that there is now an illustrated four-page story with quite a bit of text. There is also a cut-out doll to dress, and a couple of pictures to colour in. The price had increased to 18p, in line with inflation, but this was still a great value-for-money read for little girls. Sadly *Twinkle* couldn't hold on forever, and on 5 June 1999 it stopped shining forever.

CHAPTER THREE

Golden and Silver Ages

The pre-war period and right into the 1950s, 60s and 70s, saw a wealth of classics such as *Schoolgirls' Weekly*, *Girl* and *School Friend*. Some comics, for instance *The Beano*, *The Dandy* and *Topper*, though perhaps boy-inclined, were popular with girls, too. They featured characters such as Minnie the Minx and Beryl the Peril. *Buster* was a big name comic, too, but was very boyish. Not that it stopped girls reading it, of course. One interesting point is that, certainly in the earlier decades, male writers dominated the

Old comics.

girls' comics industry, but wrote under feminine names. For instance, John E McKibbin, writing as Elise Probyn, was a prolific writer for The Amalgamated Press publications. He had several other pseudonyms, too. A classic example was Charles Hamilton who, as Hilda Richards, penned the early Bessie Bunter tales.

It's easy to see why this phenomenon occurred – in the early part of the Twentieth Century, comics were mainly slanted towards boys, and men wrote stirring tales for them. When the publications for girls were introduced, it fell to the men to turn their hand to girls' stories. Sometimes this was successful, though often men failed to grasp what kinds of tales girls really enjoyed, even in comics such as *Girl*; although 'Kitty Hawke and her All Girl-Crew', which recounted the adventures of a rather military-looking set of girls was popular. It was only once the cover was switched to the 'Wendy and Jinx' stories (set in a girls' school), and later, to 'Susan at St Brides' (a nurse), that sales really rocketed.

Golden Age Classics

Some comics seem to stick in our minds more than others. Many times, of course, the comic which we will most fondly recall is the one we read as a child, but a child would not have been loyal solely to one comic for the whole of her childhood, because children grow up. A comic that is a firm favourite with a four year old, would be deemed babyish by the age of seven, while a seven-year-old's tastes would be infantile to a 10 year old. A 12 year old is almost an adult and needs a more sophisticated read, and a couple of years later, if a girl is still buying a weekly publication, she is much more likely to opt for an adult fashion, gossip or hobbies magazine. Also, along the way, that girl will have read different comics at her friends' homes, or will have had others bestowed on her. Therefore, our memory banks will contain several titles, probably spanning infant to teen.

My own comic memories are rich with titles; some comics I bought or was given regularly, others were comics I tried out for a while and rejected for various reasons. My earliest-remembered comics are *Chicks' Own*, *Tiny Tots* and *Rainbow*. I then graduated to *The Dandy* and *The Beano*, and was also reading my cousins' *Jack and Jill* and *Robin*. My mother regularly bought *Enid Blyton's Sunny Stories*, or *Enid Blyton's Magazine* for me. At the age of 10 I became hooked on *Bunty*, and, later, *Judy*. I was also sharing my friend's *Girl* (her mother wouldn't let her have comics she deemed 'common' such as *The Beano*, so she read my copy) and I often bought *School Friend*, before graduating to *Cherie* and *Boyfriend*. I then progressed to musical papers *Disc*, *NME* (New Musical Express) and *Record Mirror*, while, being a rather strange child, I also took *Fur and Feather* and *Cage Birds*, joining the 'Junior Bird League', which boasted a beautiful, enamel kingfisher badge. This was a fifties/sixties childhood.

Those girls born in the 1960s/70s would have fond memories of *Twinkle*, graduating to *Jackie*, *Misty*, *Debbie* and comics of that ilk. By the 1980s the character comics had set in – *My Little Pony*, *Care Bears*, *Barbie* and *Buttons*. Gradually, comics became more character-themed, especially those for the pre-school market. Another popular idea was the 'part work' (see Chapter 7).

According to renowned comics' expert and writer, the late Denis Gifford, the 1960s' decade saw no fewer than 63 new weekly comics being launched in Britain. As was usual, by far the majority were boy-orientated, but amongst them some girl-friendly gems stand out. *Judy*, *Diana*, *Jackie*, *Tina*, *Mandy*, *Cherie*, *Sally* and *Twinkle* were all created during the 1960s, and many of them are still remembered with great affection. Some, such as

Jackie, were new, innovative and, maybe, a bit controversial (to the parents, anyway), while others, such as *Twinkle*, were sweet and aimed at the younger girl who still, in those days, loved dolls, dolls' houses, kittens and puppies. The other 'biggie' was *Judy*, another D. C. Thomson publication and companion to *Bunty*. This *Judy* was nothing to do with a much earlier kind of comical magazine, also called Judy, which had been launched as a rival to *Punch* in the late 1800s.

As well as the various comics, in all their shapes and layouts, there were newspapers especially for children. Of these, the most renowned was the *Children's Newspaper*, which was founded by Arthur Mee in 1919 and was published by Amalgamated Press (later Fleetway). It was to prove such a successful publication that it ran for an amazing 2,397 issues. The *Children's Newspaper* was a tabloid, 12-page paper, which originally cost 1½d , and its stories were those which it was thought would be of interest to children. It was an excellent publication resembling an adult's newspaper in miniature, using the same kind of paper and font, and with a black and white picture on the front page

When the *Children's Newspaper* began, the First World War had just ended, and there were thousands of children eager to read simplified versions of the current topics. The *Children's Newspaper* enabled youngsters to keep up to date with current affairs, which were explained in a simplified form. Not only did this publication allow children to feel grown-up, it meant that they could take part in adult conversations and also helped with schoolwork. It would, no doubt, have increased vocabulary and made the child more articulate and confident. Certainly the *Children's Newspaper* was an important addition to many families, though maybe the appeal was more middle class at the time. It is certainly remembered with affection by many adults today, and, especially, amongst the ladies, for those stories centring on the young princesses, Elizabeth and Margaret Rose, and, later, Prince Charles and Princess Anne. In its heyday, the *Children's Newspaper* sold 500,000 copies a week. It ended in 1965, when it merged into the Fleetway publication called *Look and Learn*. *Look and Learn* was, in a way, a kind of part work, but didn't build on just one topic. It was an encyclopaedia-type publication which began in 1962, and which covered a variety of topics. The first issue included features on King Charles I, The Grand Canyon, Rome and children in Tokyo, and also contained a chapter from Jerome K. Jerome's novel *Three Men in a Boat*. It later incorporated a few comic strips, including the French 'Asterix'. Unfortunately, spiralling costs forced the magazine to close in 1982.

Beano (The), Dandy (The), Beezer (The), Topper (The) and others

The Beano, *The Dandy*, *The Beezer* and *The Topper* were comics which were letterpress printed, and the first two titles are still issued today by their original creators D. C. Thompson. *The Dandy* came first, with issue number one being published just before Christmas 1937, while *The Beano* made an entrance in July the following year. Perhaps regarded as more for boys than for girls, nevertheless they were popular with both sexes, and mascot characters such as Korky the Cat (*The Dandy*) and Biffo the Bear (*The Beano*), which appeared week after week, soon became instantly recognisable to readers and non-readers alike. *Topper*, which dated from 1953, was another favourite, as was *The Beezer*. Both girls and boys appreciated the slapdash, often outrageous humour of the characters, and all the comics have had good long runs. *The Beano* and *The Dandy* are still around today, and though their format is different, many of the early characters are still featured.

Beano and Dandy classic comics.

Beryl the Peril die-cast vehicle, Lledo.

Comics such as these were true 'comics' in so far as they really were comical, they made children laugh with their crazy humour and slapstick happenings. It was fun to see *The Beano*'s Minnie the Minx, *The Dandy*'s Swanky Lanky Liz (from Lord Snooty's Gang) and *Topper*'s Beryl the Peril getting up to all kinds of pranks, and behaving far more badly that we would ever dream of doing. Of course, like all cartoons, whether static types in comics or moving in animated films, when children read or watch them, they instinctively know that it is all pretend. Just because the characters hit each other with hammers, squirt cream, trip each other up with strings of sausages or tip paint/ink/baked beans over the head of their victims, it doesn't mean it is normal, approved behaviour. It's just fun, which is what comics are all about. Bill McLoughlin from D. C. Thompson informed me that; 'All Beano ideas are done in house and illustrated by freelance artists. In fact 99.5% of ideas used in *The Beano* are staff ideas.'

The Dandy was something of a revelation, changing the way in the appearance of comics: this comic was the founder of the modern comic, instantly making its rivals seem dated and unattractive. Previously, children's comics contained little colour. They were also rather unmanageable for small hands as they were broadsheet-sized. Although the content was fine, compared to *The Dandy*, *The Beano* and others of that ilk which followed *The Dandy*'s lead, the older broadsheets appeared old-fashioned. The smaller size wasn't exactly innovative, but it was new in the comic field; story papers had used the size for a long time.

Beano and Dandy featured girl characters.

Probably the most notable transformation appearing in this new comic was the use of speech bubbles or balloons, as opposed to the traditional text-under-the-picture format. To us, with our modern eyes, it is nothing exceptional – but back then, it must have been exciting and different. Therefore it isn't surprising that youngsters were fascinated by this colourful, innovative upstart from D. C. Thomson and it became exceedingly popular. It was also unsurprising that the company promptly followed up with a similar comic, *The Beano*, which was to become even more of a smash hit.

Of course there were (and are) plenty of other comics which girls will read, even though they are very much slanted at boys, such as Fleetway's *Whizzer and Chips* which had 'Fuss Pot' as a token girl character, *Buster*, *Cor!!*, *Sparky and Wizard* (another D.C.Thomson winner). Girls also read their brothers' *Eagle*, *Lion*, *Teenage Mutant Ninja Turtles* and *Hotspur*, just as today they will read *Bob the Builder*, *Thomas and Friends* and *Dinosaur Attack*.

Swift

The heading on the top of *Swift* said the comic was for boys and girls, and certainly it included girl characters. Many girls read it, and were given the annuals too, yet it always had more of a boyish feel and was really a junior version of *Eagle*. Even so, it should be included as it certainly tried to attract girl readers and was a valuable 'fill in' before a girl graduated to the *Girl* comic, which was aimed at the slightly older reader. *Swift* first appeared in March 1953, and was edited by the Rev. Marcus Morris who founded the *Eagle* dynasty. Much of the artwork was superb, as with the other comics in the group, and amongst the artists were Frank Bellamy, the *Eagle*'s Dan Dare artist, John Ryan and Reg Parlett. Stories included 'Koko the Bushbaby', 'Sally of Fern Farm', the 'Topple Twins', 'Sir Boldasbrass' and 'Educating Archie'. Educating Archie was much loved, as it was a popular radio programme at the time featuring ventriloquist Peter Brough with his dummy Archie Andrews, and also starred Benny Hill and Beryl Reid. In addition *Swift* included educational and instructional features. After ten years, in 1963, *Swift* became amalgamated with *Eagle*.

For The Girls

By contrast to *The Beano* and *The Dandy*, comics such as *Girl* or *Bunty*, though still not without humour, also had plenty of adventure or mystery stories, or perhaps told tales of historical events or true drama, all depicted in strip picture form. These comics, though, were definitely girl-orientated as opposed to the unisex *The Beano*, *The Dandy*, *Topper* and others. I can remember reading a long adventure serial in *Bunty* that focussed on the life of Pocahontas. I had never heard of the Indian Princess in those days, and was intrigued by the way the story unfurled, with Pocahontas hurling herself in front of John Smith as he was about to be killed by her father. Maybe it wasn't historically accurate, but it was entertaining and at the same time provided an insight to the way of life of the American Indians. Picture comic strips are an ideal way to introduce history, general knowledge, geography and other subjects to children. By introducing drama or humour facts tend to stick in the brain far longer when accompanied by a cartoon strip. Though years since I read the comic, I can still vividly recall the drawing depicting Pocahontas pleading for the life of John Smith!

Memories

Sometimes our memory can play tricks: it's often difficult to recall just which comics we read as youngsters, and also when we bought them, but a lady called Anne McAndrew has very helpfully kept a diary from her schooldays. She explains: 'I have been writing diaries since 1962, all quite boring really, but I noted down a lot of what was happening. I found I had recorded each comic received. I took *Bunty* on Tuesdays and *Judy* on Thursdays. I sent in a poem and a dress design for the *Bunty* cut-out doll during 1962. A book on ballet came free in *Bunty* dated 18th September 1962, and a friend gave me a lot of *Romeo* comics at the end of December that same year. In January 1963 I dropped *Bunty* and took *Romeo* instead, which came on Tuesdays. I was fourteen when I received a free bangle inside *Judy* on the 17th January 1963. Shortly afterwards I changed from *Judy* to *Boyfriend* which came on Fridays at first, but changed to Wednesdays later in the year. By 1964 I was taking *Boyfriend* and *Jackie*, but later dropped *Boyfriend* followed by *Jackie*. I am pretty certain one of these two comics was discontinued that year. Things changed quickly after that, and I took *Woman* probably for the knitting patterns, starting work at sixteen.'

What a shame that my diary in those days wasn't as detailed as Anne's. I do have a photo, though, showing me as a teenager against my bedroom wall, which is one mass of pin-up pictures taken from comics such as *Boyfriend*. How I looked forward to those pop magazines; it was so exciting to discover that the pin-up inside was one of my favourites – and such a let-down when it depicted a star I loathed. Most of the comics from that era featured a pin-up poster or full-page picture of some kind; those from Boyfriend were special, because they were in full colour, on shiny paper, and most of the others were black and white on regular paper. It didn't really matter though – if the picture was of a favourite, then I felt duty-bound to tape it to the wall. A look at the picture really brings the memories back; there is me, young and slender, showing off my Helen Shapiro hairdo (which most of the young girls featured at that time). I'm wearing my sage green jacket made from a 'mail away kit' from a magazine over what looks suspiciously like my school uniform summer frock – pale blue with a white Peter Pan collar. All those stars adorn my bedroom, amongst them Cliff Richard, Billy Fury, Adam Faith, Mark Wynter, Elvis Presley, Bobby Rydell, Helen Shapiro and so many others, while below them is a montage of numerous Mark Wynter columns cut from *Cherie*, all lovingly fixed to the wall. Goodness, my parents must have been lenient to allow me to decorate my bedroom wall in that way. (See Chapter 6)

Girl

Girl was a classy comic, it was the one which the swots read, or those girls who had ambitious mothers. It looked good with its bright colours, utilising the photogravure method of printing, and the characters inside tended to be grammar school girls, as well as the usual ballet dancers. It cost a bit more than other comics, which is why many of us couldn't afford it, and we would eagerly borrow it from our more affluent friends, lending them our *Beano*s or *Bunty*s in exchange. This was in the 1950s and early 1960s – later, *Girl* became more trendy and attracted more of the hoi polloi, because she had to compete with the numerous other excellent reads on the market. Produced by Hulton Press, *Girl* was

Letttice Leefe Pelham Puppet.

stablemate to the hugely successful *Eagle*, as well as *Robin* and *Swift*. *Robin* attracted young readers of both sexes, it was aimed at the pre-school market, while *Swift*, as we have seen, although billed as a unisex title, was definitely boy-orientated. *Eagle* was for boys – though, of course, girls read it too. Telling a girl that a comic was 'just for boys' was like holding a red rag to a bull.

Girl was launched on 2nd November 1951, and emblazoned across the cover was the legend: 'The New Super-Colour Weekly for Every Girl'. This was one of the comics edited by the Reverend Marcus Morris, acting on his tirade in a 1949 Sunday Dispatch. (See Chapter 1.) That first issue of *Girl* sported the daring 'Kitty Hawke and her All-Girl Air Crew' on the front cover, a kind of girly equivalent to the *Eagle*'s Dan Dare. The story was illustrated in thrilling style by Roy Bailey. Starring Kitty, daughter of the owner of Hawke Airlines, the first story sees the girls coming into land after a freight delivery in Wales, and as they loop their plane, we see the classic comment, 'Kitty Hawke is the only pilot who can roll in a Tadcaster.' That remark really set the scene, showing as it did all the (male) ground crew diving for cover as the plane swooped in. Later Kitty says, 'Well, here we are again gang with one more job chalked up to the all-girl crew – to prove to Dad that we can operate his planes as efficiently as the glorious male.' Kitty is obviously a bit of a militant, an early supporter of women's lib. Along with her cronies, Winifred 'Windfall' White, Navigator Patricia D'Arcy and the Radio Officer Jean Stuart, Kitty Hawke wanted to prove to her father that the girls could operate the planes as proficiently and as capably as the male aircrews. That first instalment has Kitty thrilled to bits after learning that she is to be entrusted to fly a film unit to Africa.

The early issues contained other exciting tales too, drawing very much on the *Eagle* tradition, and also looking at the profiles of heroines such as Joan of Arc. However, it was discovered that – surprise – girls were different to boys, and they didn't particularly want to read sterling tales of bravery. Girls liked to read about girls like themselves who enjoyed hobbies such as ballet and horse riding, and attended schools with bossy prefects and homework. Soon *Girl* changed track, and put less emphasis on the *Eagle*-like adventures and more on the sedate tales girls loved.

Girl was something of a first, in that it was a comic full of picture strips aimed at girls, rather than the pre-war titles containing acres of small print and only a few pictures. It didn't take long before other comics took up the challenge, notably *School Friend* (Amalgamated Press) which was revamped from all text to a picture strip format, and which became very popular. Sadly, though, the same format didn't work on *Girls' Crystal*, which curled up into a ball and died quietly after a couple of months. The *Girl* comic has become almost legendary amongst those of us brought up in the 1950s and 60s, and it's not difficult to explain why. The stories were interesting, with a good range of characters, which seemed to have more depth than those from some of the rival magazines – you could almost imagine they were real. The printing method helped too – the shiny paper intensified the colours, while the bright yellow masthead with red lettering, soon changing to the more familiar red square on the left-hand-side of the page containing yellow or white 'Girl' lettering and white girl's head logo, was eye-catching.

For much of the 1950s, the honour of the front-page spot fell to 'Wendy and Jinx', who were best friends at Manor School. Wendy was a brunette and Jinx was a blonde, which made them easy to identify. The adventures were school based, though frequently taking the girls away from school – on holidays, excursions and trips to town – and the school, of course, was a boarding school, with a social life alien to that led by most of the state school pupils. Schools are ideal settings for girls' stories, as not only do they provide a good excuse for gathering together a group of children, there is also plenty of scope for unfriendly and sinister, or kindly and helpful schoolteachers. Wendy and Jinx had their form mistress Miss Brumble, known by the girls as Bumble Bee.

A look inside a 1956 copy of *Girl* shows Wendy and Jinx on the cover, this time trying to clear the name of a pupil's father suspected of forgery, and it takes place at a point-to-point meeting. Interestingly, the writer's and artists' names – 'Story by Stephan James; drawn by Ray Bailey and Philip Townsend' – appear at the end. Most comics don't list the contributors, but this was a regular feature in *Girl*. Other stories inside – many are serials – include 'Susan At St. Brides', which was another long-running series about a student nurse. (See Chapter 5 for Susan and several other *Girl* characters.) 'Vicky and the Vengeance of the Incas' told of how Vicky and her father, a professor, were searching for Inca gold, while 'The Pilgrim Sisters' was a history drama set in Cheapside, London, in the 1600s. 'Belle of the Ballet' was a very popular character. She was a pupil at the Arenska Dancing School, and had various adventures. Belle was so well-liked that Pelham's Puppets made a puppet in her honour. (See Chapter 11.)

Also included were three longer all-text stories, reader's letters, competitions, details of the Girl Adventures Club (see Chapter 8), and a club section, 'Adventure Corner', which this week showed a reader's ballroom dancing photos. A large colour picture of 'The First

Easter', painted by Eric Winter, together with some verses from St Luke was in the Girl Picture Gallery, while told in a colour picture story format was 'The Story of Guiseppe Garibaldi'. The regular 'Cookery Corner', had an excellent recipe for a Dutch Apple Tart, and the very popular 'Mother Tells You How' this week explained how to make pretty Easter birds from glass balls, feathers and twigs. Last, but by no means least, was Lettice Leefe, 'The Greenest Girl in School', who was making poor Miss Froth's life chaotic as usual. Lettice was a popular character, and was also made by Pelham Puppets in puppet form. (See Chapter 11.) There was plenty of reading in *Girl*; the larger pages allowing more features, and the glossy colour, which was used for several inside pages as well as the cover, made it a feel-good comic. So many excellent artists drew for *Girl* that there is no room to mention them all, but Gerry Haylock and Harry Lindfield's 'Belle' and 'Mamie' certainly deserve a mention.

No wonder it is so warmly remembered today – even if many of us still sneakily preferred *Beano*. *Girl* comic is one of those girl 'classics', one which girls from the 1950s and 60s especially remember with affection, and its many much-loved characters, especially 'Wendy and Jinx', 'Belle of the Ballet', and 'Lettice Leefe' are still discussed today on the internet. The comic finally ended in 1964, a shadow of its former self, and was incorporated into *Princess*.

One time *Girl* reader, Tricia Smith, recalls, 'I have some of the 'Mother Tells You How' sections from the comic – I loved handicrafts even at that age and used to cut them out every week. I have kept several of them, though I did have a clear out and destroyed some when I moved house. They are so deliciously old-fashioned, but the makes were really innovative and I made up quite a few, including a 'petal' hat made from broderic anglaise in the shape of a star which press-studded together to form a hat shape and was sewn to an Alice band. I made it in white and wore it to church in the summer months! I didn't realise that there were other *Girl* items [collectables to be found from the comic, see Chapter 11] – the doll is the only one I have ever come across. It is amazing what is still out there to be found.'

Interestingly, some of the stories from *Girl* appeared in a French comic, called *Line*. *Line* even copied the familiar red masthead, and at first glance the comics looked very similar. Avid collector of UK comics, Steven Taylor, writes, 'The generally accepted view in France (and Belgium) is that two publishers, Dargaud (Paris) and Leblanc (Brussels), decided to create together a comic paper for girls in 1954. They came up with the format that would become the highly successful publication *Line*, which was published weekly in both capitals simultaneously. *Line* ran from 1954 until 1963, by which time it had mutated into a pop culture magazine with articles on the popular icons of the day. It is also true that a character called 'Line' was developed by Françoise Bertier – a typical teenage adventuress – but this was very much after the fact. I hate to burst anyone's bubble, but if you take a look at the *Line* logo, what you will see is the logo of *Girl* comic. In fact in the beginning you would be forgiven in thinking that *Line* was the French-language version of *Girl*.'

When *Line* started it featured such favourites as George Beardmore's 'Belle of the Ballet' (Belle du Ballet), Ray Bailey's 'Wendy and Jinx' (Mad et Gloria), and John Ryan's Lettice Leef (Charlotte). Other UK features were 'Three Sisters called Kat', 'Vengeance of the Incas' and a wonderfully incorrect translation under the generic title 'Nos Histoires Vraies' (Our True History) which featured, amongst others, 'our' Dickens and 'our' Great Fire of London. *Line* was also distributed in Switzerland and Canada and was available in hardback editions (and occasionally in soft-cover) comprising of 20 or 26 consecutive weekly issues. Several hard-cover *Line* books were also produced based on the 'Wendy and Jinks' and 'Belle of the Ballet' stories.

Although *Girl* ceased to be, in 1964, years after Fleetway acquired Hulton Press, a new series of *Girl* was launched. This 1981 version was far different to the original, and might just as well have been a brand new comic – it owed little to *Girl*. It was more a magazine than a comic, and later combined with *Tammy*.

Girls' Crystal

A 1948 copy of *Girls' Crystal* and *The School Friend*, Amalgamated Press, is interesting to analyse: an insight to what young girls, presumably those born in the 1930s, would have been reading then. The actual publication measures 11 by 7½ in, and is printed on a very cheap paper. This would no doubt be due to the wartime economy – although the war had been over for two and a half years, Britain was still fettered by restrictions, we were a poor country with many supplies limited or on ration. *Girls' Crystal* first appeared in 1935. It

Girls comics from the 1940s and 1950s.

incorporated *The Schoolgirls' Weekly* in 1939 and *The Schoolgirl* in 1940, and ran for 23 more years before finally becoming incorporated into *School Friend*.

This 1948 issue of *Girls' Crystal* cost 3d. It was published every Friday and had been running for 13 years – we were up to volume 25. The lead story, a serial, was 'The Girl Who Put Fame First', and was written by Enid Boyten. It featured a girl with the exotic name of 'Silver Dawton'. Silver was mad about horses, and was hoping to get permission from her headmistress to enter a Fourth Form team in a forthcoming riding carnival. Naturally, there were plenty of obstacles to overcome, not least a teacher who disliked horses and a girl who was jealous of Silver.

The main illustration – which depicts Silver riding a horse with three ponies in tow, surrounded by an admiring crowd of schoolgirls – only utilises the colours blue/grey, red and brown. All the front and back cover text in the comic is printed in blue/grey, while inside text is black. There are 12 pages, which contain, as well as this horse-related serial, two other serials (one set in Egypt, the other another school type), a detective mystery and a story set aboard a liner travelling to Australia. A few small line illustrations decorated the pages, but basically it was minute text. Value for money, the comic would have given a girl a jolly good read though – much more than a modern comic. This is the most noticeable thing about early comics; the amount of reading matter they contain. Publications such as *The Girl's Own Paper* and *The Schoolgirls' Own* would have continued to entertain the average reader almost to the time the next issue was due. Compared to a modern comic, which can be read by even the slowest reader in a few hours, many of these pre-1950s

Girls' Own Paper 1890s.

publications were much more intensive reads for the older girl. It depended what a girl wanted from a comic, because even before the First World War it was possible to find them with more illustrations and far less text.

In 1953 *Girl's Crystal* was transformed into a comic rather than a story paper. A 1956 copy, still 3d, now has a full-colour cover with a picture story 'Secret of Bear Glacier', set in Switzerland, though the back cover and all the contents are in black and white. Particularly noticeable in this copy is the story, 'The Return of the Hooded Helpers', which features a secret society, founded by Wyn Lester and Jenny Marsh from the fourth form of Castle School, who wear long, monk-like robes with cowl hoods and black masks. The picture strips for the Hooded Helpers were supplied by Saxon studio, illustrating the story by R Fleming.

Other picture stories include 'Moira and the Masked Rider' – what is this fascination with masks and gowns? – 'Ella and the Mississippi Showboat' (which also involves disguise), and a tale called 'Wildflower of the Rockies' about an American-Indian girl. The comic also has three longer text series ('Kathy the Camera Girl' by Elise Probyn, 'Carol of the Circus' by Doreen Gray and 'Trixie's Diary' edited by Ida Melbourne) as well as competitions, quizzes and a club page.

Just over three years later, a 1959 copy of *Girls' Crystal* has the cover story 'Bridget All On Her Own in London'. Bridget was an Irish orphan who had come to London to stay with a wealthy uncle from America, but had been tricked by an impostor who hoped the uncle would bestow some of his wealth onto her instead. Littered with as many Irish phrases and exclamations as the writer could come up with – 'Sure 'tis', 'Begorra', 'To be sure', ''Tis meself' and a bevy of convoluted sentences – the story unfolds as the wicked Sandra, who, of course, has stolen Bridget's identity locket, plots to keep Bridget from her uncle. It's surprising how often the identity locket theme recurs – but then, naturally, the locket is important. After all, how else could a heroine prove she was really the missing daughter or heiress or stolen-by-the-gypsies baby?

Amongst the 20 pages are five further picture-strip stories, two small-print, mainly text, stories plus assorted adverts and a club page (see Chapter 8). The other stories revolve around 'Jackie of the Circus', 'Sheila and the Masked Swimmer' (still with the disguises!), a school story (Moorvale School) and one set on a lonely island. There is plenty of reading in this issue, and, more importantly, most of the stories finish on a cliffhanger, ensuring that a girl will want to buy the next issue to find out what happens. The price was now 4d, just a penny more than the issue of 11 years before. In 1963, *Girl's Crystal* was incorporated in to the more popular *School Friend*, a sad end to a much loved, long-established girls' comic.

Girl's Own Paper

Not really a comic at all, the *Girl's Own Paper* was a monthly magazine which would have been read by young ladies mainly from the middle classes, certainly in its early years. Dating from 1880, the *Girl's Own Paper* was published by The Leisure Office, a part of The Religious Tract Society. Although their aim was to enable poorer people to have access to upstanding literature, few of the poor would have been able to spare 6d to splurge on a magazine. From the modern viewpoint, the *Girl's Own Paper* is a daunting read, with its 36 pages of minute text, only occasionally broken up with a small line drawing. Much of it is fiction, with a sporadic poem, recipe, useful hint or feature to break things up. Features include such items as 'Archaeology For Girls', 'Some Special Points of Female Beauty' or 'The Etiquette of Card-Leaving' (in an 1895 issue). This latter article began, 'It is an undeniable fact that the whole universal creation within our mortal ken, or stretching away into invisible, and almost illimitable space must be ruled by certain laws'. It discusses the formality of the ritual, pointing out that 'The habit amongst ill-informed if not vulgar persons usually below the circle of upper-class society, of omitting the prefix of 'Mr' or Miss' is inadmissible amongst thoroughly well-taught and highly-bred persons'. Other items include pages and pages of 'problems' although just the answers are given, which makes reading them most frustrating.

Best of all from today's point of view are the adverts, such as those for 'Wonderful Velveteen 2/- a yard', 'Bumsted's Table Salt as supplied to her Majesty the Queen' (Victoria) and 'The Dermathistic Corset', which began at 4/11d and warned 'Beware of Worthless Imitations'. Other ads explained 'Not a rub in the tub. Venus soap does the work – not you' or 'To obtain health, strength and happiness, and to throw off all feelings of languidness and depression, there is nothing in the world like a short spin on a Rudge-Whitworth cycle'. In the earlier years, the *Girl's Own Paper* featured a plain blue cover with a black and white drawing, normally of a girl in classical dress, reading or writing, plus a long list of contents, but as the magazine progressed and technology improved, the covers became more attractive. By the 1930s it had become friendlier to younger readers, adding school stories and adventure fantasy tales to its repertoire. Many famous authors contributed over the years, including Noel Streatfeild, Angela Brazil and Richmal Crompton. The magazine went through a few name changes and take-overs over the years, but it wasn't until 1956 that it finally closed.

School Friend

This originally appeared in the early 1900s as a fiction (mainly text) magazine, but was re-launched in 1950 by Amalgamated Press to cater for schoolgirls, and seemed to have captured the late primary/earlier secondary school market. The very first issue appeared in May 1919, not long after the end of the First World War, a time when young women had tasted independence and were becoming more worldly and aware of other matters outside the home. Amalgamated Press were aiming to duplicate the enormous success they had achieved with *The Magnet*, which was a story paper for boys dating from 1907. *The Magnet* was particularly famed for its Greyfriars School stories, especially the main character Billy Bunter. These stories were written by Charles Hamilton, one of the classic names in school-based fiction.

In *School Friend*, Amalgamated Press introduced Cliff House School, and one of the pupils there was Bessie Bunter, Billy Bunter's sister. The stories were written by Charles Hamilton, make believing he was his own sister and using the pen name Hilda Richards. Later, other writers also wrote the stories and they too used the name Hilda Richards. Bessie had already appeared in *The Magnet*. Later, in 1929, *School Friend* was renamed, and appeared as *The Schoolgirl*, remaining in this guise for 18 years.

On the 20 May 1950, *School Friend* was re-launched, and it caused an enormous frenzy of buying. Amazingly, it sold over 1,000,000 copies of a single issue, and the brightly coloured cover featured 'The Silent Three' illustrated by Evelyn Flinders. People tend to think that it was boys' comics that sold the most, but *School Friend* outstripped the *Eagle's* sales, which only managed 900,000 copies of a 1950s' issue, and which just proves how girls know a good thing when they see it! This new series of *School Friend* went on to run for nearly 15 years; especially loved for its series of The Silent Three girls who formed a society at St Kitt's Boarding School. This group of investigative (nosy?) schoolgirls (see

Chapter 5) first featured in the first 1950 issue in a tale called 'The Silent Three at St Kitt's', which ran for twenty issues and showed how the girls sometimes dressed in sinister gowns with masks and pointed hoods, rather reminiscent of the Klu Klux Klan. The Silent Three – Peggy West, Betty Rowland and Joan Derwood – were perhaps *School Friend*'s answer to *Bunty*'s The Four Marys and the *Girl*'s Wendy and Jinx; the stories were written by Enid Boyten and drawn by Evelyn Flinders.

A 1958 issue of *School Friend* reveals it as an interesting mix of picture strips and of longer text-based stories. There was certainly plenty of reading matter in its 24 pages. Costing 4d, the front page featured a colour strip story entitled 'Romance at their Alpine School' which centred around Gwen Edwards and Zoe Burns who were spending a term at a school in Switzerland. Their lives were saved by a handsome Swiss Mountain Guide, who was due to marry one of their teachers, but had recently been denounced for cowardice by the villagers. The strips inside were in black and white and amongst them were a story about a sheepdog on trial for sheep-worrying (could Nona save his life?), a boy in the jungle is captured and taken to the Hill of Doom (could Janet save his life?), while a millionaire's daughter is under threat from Jarvis, sinister secretary to her father (could Sylvia save her life?) This comic really ripped your nerves to shreds. It was exactly what girls wanted to read – a mix of drama, mystery, suspense and humour but with 'girlie' themes.

As well as the four longer, all-text stories, there was the regular favourite 'Dilly Dreem The Lovable Duffer' who provided a bit of light-hearted relief. Dilly was illustrated by Dora Leeson. There was also a photo in the 'School Friend Star Parade' series; in this 1958 issue it showed ice-skater Gloria Nord, presumably the picture was to cut out and collect. The next issue promised to feature Arthur Askey; nowadays it seems odd to feature a (even then fairly old) comedian in a girls' magazine as a pin-up. Interestingly, this issue doesn't contain a story featuring those inquisitive Silent Three, who must have gone off on a top-secret mission. In 1963, *School Friend* incorporated *Girls' Crystal*. An issue from this alliance, a *School Friend* and *Girls' Crystal* dated 18 January 1964, features 'The Silent Three and the Secret of the Singing Birds', so things were right with the world once more!

This issue also contains a ballet serial and several adventure stories, while Bessie Bunter, suffering from a bad attack of hiccups, is amazed when brother Billy Bunter offers her a doughnut. As if to demonstrate the war was still a relatively recent event (it had ended just 19 years before), a new text-only serial by Renee Frazer had just begun, entitled 'Mamse'selle X – Fighter for France', telling of the adventures of a wartime agent. The full-colour front cover featured a picture strip story called 'My Friend Sara' by Wendy Lee, and favourite Dilly Dreem adorned the back cover of this copy of *School Friend* and *Girls' Crystal* in 'Dilly Dreem's Schooldays'. (See Chapter 5.)

In 1965, *School Friend* merged with *June*, to become known as *June and School Friend*. Nowadays, *School Friend* is one of the most fondly remembered of the girls' comics. It had been a popular title in its time, and was particularly loved in the 1950s, alongside *Girl* and *Girls' Crystal*. *School Friend* is definitely one of the classics.

Schoolgirl (The)
An Amalgamated Press girls' paper first issued in 1929, *The Schoolgirl* ran for 11 years, absorbing *The Schoolgirls' Own* in 1936 before finally being incorporated into *Girls' Crystal* in 1940. The paper had actually made a brief appearance several years earlier, in 1922, lasting for just over a year.

Looking at an issue of *The Schoolgirl*, which dates from October 1939, just as the Second World War began, it shows that it is very similar in style to *Girls' Crystal*. Incorporating *Schoolgirls' Own*, the front cover is a full-page illustration, showing a schoolgirl clinging to a windowsill after the ladder she was climbing had broken. A brief text explains that the story is 'The Tomboy in Peril at the House of Mystery', and it is taken from a story featuring Barbara Redfern and friends from Cliff House School. As with *Girls' Crystal*, the text is in blue, as is that on the back cover. Internal text is black. The price was 2d, and it was published each Saturday.

Inside, though, besides the stories, are other sections, such as a hobbies section and a feature on keeping younger children amused (try 'cutting out', making scrapbooks or taking them for a walk). There is also an intriguing piece written by 'Patricia' who is a kind of big sister. In this issue she explains ways of helping with the war effort by knitting for evacuees, or by rolling bandages (for a neater roll it is better to use a sardine key rather than a pencil). Patricia also shows how to make a pretty collar and cuffs set from an old chiffon scarf, and how to remodel an old coat using a scrap of velveteen. In addition there is a rather solemn letter from the editor, who warns that wartime shortages mean that paper supplies are limited, and so it is very important to fill in the form which will tell your newsagent that you would like *The Schoolgirl* each week. Items such as these give this comic a much more friendly feel. The text is very small, and has just a few black and white drawings to break it up. It also is interesting because it contains some adverts. (See Chapter 8.)

Schoolgirls' Own (The)

This attractive paper, with its blue and orange cover, first came to light in February 1921, and was to continue for 15 years. *The Schoolgirls' Own* was an Amalgamated Press publication, and cost 2d each week. It was published on Tuesdays. Sister paper to the boys' *The Magnet* comic, the girls' version was (to modern eyes) a wordy, small print, text paper with just an occasional black and white drawing. Looking at a 1928 copy, the cover shows three schoolgirls wearing the typical long, belted gymslips, white blouses and dark stockings of

Pre-war schoolgirls' comics, plus boys' favourite, *The Magnet, which* featured Bessie Bunter.

the period, with short shingled or bobbed hair. The background colour is a shade of light orange, while the drawing and text are dark blue. The title, The Schoolgirls' Own, is written in script, while above it, in large capitals is the legend, 'A WEEKLY TREAT FOR EVERY SCHOOLGIRL!' This was constantly changed, with slogans such as 'You are sure of good stories if you take –', ' The best-story paper for girls of all ages' and similar sentiments appearing each week. Below the picture is the caption 'Friends again, thanks to Naomer! An appealing incident in the splendid long complete Morcove School Story inside'. The back cover features an advert for the Schoolgirls' Own Library, a series of single-story publications.

Inside the 34-page paper (which incidentally measured a trim 9½ x 7 in), were four long stories. In this issue they were, 'The Case Against the Captain' by Marjorie Stanton, 'With Sunny to Shield Her' by Renee Frazer, 'Greta of the Mountains' by Joan Inglesant, and 'Who Spoiled the Picnic?' by Joan Vincent. There was also a page of Cookery Hints – this week's hints explained that beetroot should never be used in the same salad as tomato as the two colours clashed, and explained how to use a freezing machine – a container with a handle, which is then packed around with ice and salt – to make ice-cream. The editor, who was depicted as a smart, pipe-smoking young man industriously bent over his desk, pen in hand, in his den, had his own page, in which he mentions the foibles of 'Cuthbert the office boy', as well as discussing the latest issue of the magazine. Finally, there was Birthday Club page, with prizes of annuals if you were lucky enough to have your own birth date listed.

This delightful girls' paper, The Schoolgirls' Own, continued virtually unchanged, though the cookery hints and birthday club pages were dropped to make even more story room, until May 1936, when the paper was amalgamated with The Schoolgirl.

Schoolgirls' Weekly (The)
The Schoolgirls' Weekly was another Amalgamated Press publication for schoolgirls, slightly larger than its sister papers The Schoolgirls' Own and The Schoolgirl. It first appeared in 1922, and had, like many other papers at the time, very small print, which meant it contained lots to read. It crammed serials, features, short stories, adverts, competitions and pictures inside each weekly issue, and became very popular. Perhaps one of its most favourite characters was a young lady detective called 'Valerie Drew'; detective stories were very much in vogue at the time. The Editor wrote a 'Notes In Class. Your Editor Chats to His Readers' page in each issue, and, typical of its time, it was stilted and formal, though probably sounding no less friendly to those young readers, than the modern in your face enthusiasm we find in today's comics. One such page, in the issue dated 16 February 1929, began, 'My Dear Readers' and continued, 'I expect by the time you turn to these notes that you will have already have read the opening chapters of our splendid new school serial, "Her Handicap at School!" I should be very pleased if you will drop me a line telling me what you think of it. I am sure that you are all intensely interested in Nellie Benson and are wondering how she is going to fare in her career at Craymoor College.' Later on we find, 'I know you will all be pleased to learn that Miss Louise Carlton has written next Wednesday's splendid long complete story, under the title of "In Spite of All Her Setbacks!" And this, together with the second enthralling instalment of our new school serial and long instalments of "She Kept the Home Fires Burning!" and "Pen – Looking After Herself!" will form the main features of next week's issue.' Note all the exclamation marks.

Further down the page is a 'Personal Column', which frustratingly contains many answers but no questions. Thus we read, 'To Eton Cropped (Ely) – I am sorry I cannot agree to your suggestion, dear reader, as it is strictly against office rules. Thank you very much for it, however, and also for your compliments!' while the reply 'To A Regular Reader (Burton-on-Trent) – Yes, I should be very pleased indeed to hear from you again, dear reader, and when you write you must tell me what you think of our present programme of stories. Best wishes!' Those exclamation marks again!

Looking through an issue from 1934, the main story is 'Winnie's Amazing Waxworks', which took up 6½ pages, in very small print, with just a few illustrations to break up the text. It was an exciting and intriguing story, though. Valerie Drew 'the famous girl detective and Flash her Alsatian assistant' starred in 'Flowers of Fortune', written by Adelie Ascott and illustrated by C. Percival. Other stories include 'Patsy Never-Grow-Up' by Rhoda Fleming, and Margery Marriott's 'Autograph Anne's Ambition'.

Schoolgirls' Weekly seemed aimed at the older girl, as it contained career advice and features intended to help a girl when she left school. Many of the stories were adventures or mystery, and centred on topics such as school life, girl guides, the War (First World War), and included plenty of the stirring 'girls overcoming adversity and becoming heroines' themes. These were stories not only to entertain the schoolgirl reader, but with strong morals for her to live up to. In 1939 *The Schoolgirls' Weekly* was amalgamated with *Girls' Crystal*. Also, the page content varied over the years, as with the sister papers.

Sunny Stories

This little magazine, which measured 7 x 5½in, was a perfect size for smaller hands, yet it didn't really seem to be aimed at the youngest children. Introduced by George Newnes Ltd in 1926, it was originally named *Sunny Stories for Little Folks* but in 1937 was shortened to *Enid Blyton's Sunny Stories*. When this happened, the magazine began once more, at issue one, and arguably, *Enid Blyton's Sunny Stories* is a different, separate publication to the earlier *Sunny Stories for Little Folks*.

In the 1950s, the title was shortened again, this time to *Sunny Stories*. Not a comic as such: the stories were mainly just text with black and white line illustrations, and maybe a game or a competition. For almost 15 years the magazine was edited by Enid Blyton, and because she was such a prolific writer, she more or less wrote the whole of the magazine. A copy from 1952, with the familiar orange/red background and border on the cover, bears an attractive drawing illustrating one of Enid's stories (in this case, two children bottle-feeding a lamb, in shades of blue, red and grey), begins with a letter from Enid, headed 'Green Hedges'. Green Hedges was the name of the house in which she lived, in Beaconsfield, and in this letter she tells of forthcoming stories. There is plenty of reading in this 26-page magazine; apart from one picture strip (just four pictures long, featuring Josie, Click and Bun at Christmas), there are three long stories, line illustrated, plus a serial 'The Adventurous Four'. This copy cost 2d.

However in 1953 Enid Blyton resigned, and an issue dating from June 1953, just after the Coronation shows Crawfie, one-time royal governess, as Editor, and contains an article about 'Our Dear Queen' telling how she and her sister, Princes Margaret, once made a toy farmyard. Enid had left *Sunny Stories*, as she was peeved that Newnes would only advertise the books of hers which they published. She wanted to promote her other books, too, as well as her various associated merchandise. A year later, the role of Editor was taken over by popular children's author Malcolm Saville.

When Enid left *Sunny Stories*, she founded the rival *Enid Blyton's Magazine*. Similar in style, with the same red cover and a drawing on the front, the masthead showed the name Enid Blyton written in her own hand, while underneath was written – perhaps as a reminder to readers of *Sunny Stories* – that the *Enid Blyton's Magazine* was 'The only magazine I write'. The *Enid Blyton's Magazine* was slightly larger than *Sunny Stories*, measuring 8¼ x 5½ in, and at forty pages, contained even more reading. Enid's letter had spread over two pages in this edition from 1957, and the price was 4½d. There was now a club page (See Chapter 8), and news from other clubs which Enid and the readers supported, such as the PDSA Busy Bees. The magazine also contained competitions, adverts and a letters page, plus the stories – two serials, one of which was a Famous Five adventure, a four-picture strip featuring 'Rumble and Chuff', a Noddy story and a story about a brave cat. This cat story states, quite matter-of-factly, that the six kittens which have been born to the mother cat, were running around the house and causing so much trouble, that if homes couldn't be found, they would be drowned. Hopefully, things are more humane today, and presumably, there would be something of an outcry if similar sentiments were expressed in a modern comic. There was also a picture headed 'Country Code' showing two girls walking on a path through a field, and a note explaining how important it was to keep to the path when crossing farm land. *Enid Blyton's Magazine* ceased publication in 1959, due to her ill health.

Beryl the Peril, Topper.

CHAPTER FOUR

More From the Silver Age

What's in a name? Comics named after girls were in vogue – *Judy*, *Bunty*, *Mandy* and *Diane*. *Jackie* was different – modern, zingy and a bit more grown-up. Not all comics, of course, had girls' names; sometimes the publishers capitalised on a name which girls would latch on to, something trendy or fashionable. A classic example is *Blue Jeans*. Others are *Pink*, *Cool*, *Mates* and *Oh Boy!*

Dr Mel Gibson of Sunderland University writes, 'During the 1950s, producers started to look to both the growing teenage market and working class girls for sales, due to the shifts in education taking place at this time, rather than focusing on the middle-classes; although they continued to offer an aspirational model tied in to middle-class norms for all readers. There was also a drop in overall sales that resulted in a shift in approach at the end of the 1950s and into the 1960s. Comics for younger readers were launched that used short snappy versions of girl's names for titles. *Bunty* and *Judy* (1960) from D. C. Thomson, a Dundee publishing house with a Scottish Presbyterian origin that took a strong moral line, were the first titles in the field. These were followed by *Tammy* (1971) and *Jinty* (1974) from IPC (which took over Amalgamated Press in 1960). Cheaply produced on newsprint rather than the higher quality paper used for *Girl*, these publications also had roots in the story papers and emphasised stories over activities, although even *Bunty* included, famously, a cut out doll.

Girls' names used as the titles of comics.

'What differed was that their basis was in story papers largely read by working-class girls in their late teens and early twenties, rather than a middle-class audience. Developed to serve the increasingly literate population emerging after the Education Acts, Amalgamated Press titles *Girls' Friend* (1899–1931), *Girls' Reader* (1908–1915) and *Girls' Home* (1910–1915) influenced the comics aimed at working-class pre-teen girls in the 1960s. They told stories 'from the viewpoint of the skivvies, shop-girls and factory hands' (Mary Cadogan, *You're a Brick, Angela* 1986) and Cinderella figures working in laundries or shops were often central characters. Alongside these stories were ones about schoolgirls as well as romances for older readers. Thus, the schoolgirl story links turn of the century changes in education, a widening experience of school in the late 1950s and early 1960s and the fictional boarding school for girls of all classes.

'The accounts in these comics were not of exuberant adventures or activities that could be characterised as middle-class, but of lonely children fighting against the odds, trapped, misunderstood and exploited. Equally, the figure of the schoolgirl often differed from those in the middle-class papers in that many of the stories focused on the working-class outsider struggling with the snobbery of both staff and pupils in private schools. This double-edged theme made the reader aware of the possibility of this type of education, whilst presenting it as a nightmare.'

Mel Gibson, *Remembered Reading: Memory, Comics and Post-war Constructions of British Girlhood*

Ladybirds and Scottie dogs

I was 10 when the very first issue of *Bunty* was published, on January 18 1958, and I still remember the thrill of the free gift – a lucky ladybird ring. The ring was well made, featuring a sturdy, red ladybird with black spots, and I was so enamoured with it, that I still have it today, a prized childhood possession. Most of my friends bought a copy of the comic, too, and so we all sported our rings. The front page of that first issue was in a different style to the later comics, because instead of featuring a few drawings featuring *Bunty* (a young blonde accident-prone girl), the whole cover announced in colourful red and blue text, 'No. 1 of a great new picture paper for girls', while underneath was emblazoned, 'Ladybird ring free inside!' Two girls, a blonde, presumably Bunty, and a brunette, were shown admiring their rings, and a black Scottie dog – the *Bunty* comic's club mascot (who later acquired the name Haggis) – was shown in the top right-hand corner. There was also a note that the comic was published every Tuesday, price 4d.

Actually, the big bold colourful text on the white cover was clever marketing – the issue instantly stood out from the other comics of the counter displays of the newsagents of the time. Certainly, our local shop, Forbuoys, in Welwyn Garden City, must have done a brisk trade that day. *Bunty* continued with the uncluttered look of the comic for some time – the adventures of Bunty on the cover were invariably shown in just a few pictures, rather that the long cartoon strips which most other comics put on their covers. The masthead, reading Bunty in blue on a white background usually took up a third of the page. However, when other free gifts were given – such as the 'dainty doggie ring' in 1960 – the cover strip was removed in favour of large text, and a small drawing of Bunty with her gift. There was also a close-up picture of the free gift, thus ensuring that all comic buyers would realise that *Bunty* was extra good value that week.

Bunty went on to become one of the classic girl's comics, and it retained its sweetness and light even when other comics became notably more racy in the 1990s. Stories in *Bunty* included 'The Four Marys', which ran throughout the life of the comic. This strip told of the exploits of four schoolgirls, Mary Radleigh, Mary Cotter, Mary Field and Mary Simpson. The Four Marys picture strip was set in a girls' boarding school known as St Elmo's. In earlier decades, and right through to the late 1960s, the boarding school was a common setting for girls' stories, both in comics and books. Thousands of girls attended such schools, admittedly, usually those from more affluent families, but they were ideal for the setting of adventure stories, as there would not be the tiresome home-time which would have curtailed many of the evening activities, not to say the midnight feasts. Later, some of the girls' titles switched to photo stories, using posed photos, amongst them *Jackie* and *Bunty*. Often, models used in the romantic strips were young stars such as George Michael and Hugh Grant.

Blue Jeans

A kind of cross between a comic and a magazine, in a similar mould to *Jackie*, *Blue Jeans*, from D. C. Thompson, hit the news stands in 1977. Aimed at the young teen, the covers featured photos of teenage girls, often with their boyfriends. The issue for 15 September 1979 reveals a couple of romantic serials – one is photo illustrated, whilst the other is a traditional drawn picture strip. There is also a photo strip serial telling of an adopted girl trying to trace her birth mother. The rest of the comic is given over to fashion, beauty, readers' letters and a problem page. There's a centre-page spread pin-up photo of David Essex, while the back page, labelled 'Back Pocket' is a mix of recipes, tips and best buys. As well as all this, there is long text-only reader's true-life story.

Blue Jeans was a lively publication containing plenty to entertain and amuse an adolescent girl, with a great mix of features and stories. The comic survived for 14 years before finally succumbing in 1991. It also published a large number of separate full-length story magazines.

Bunty

Of all the girls' comics published over the years, *Bunty* is the one which most girls seem to remember and which sends them into realms of nostalgia, even more so than the *Girl* comic. It's difficult to understand why, but it held us all enthralled. Maybe because, when it first came out it was so different from anything that had come before. Though many competitors – and stable-mates – appeared using the same format, *Bunty* was the first, and so had already acquired a following.

When D.C. Thomson published that very first issue of *Bunty*, on 18 January 1958, the white cover, as previously described, bore an eye-catching message; 'No. 1 of a Great New Picture Paper for Girls' all written in large red and blue text, beneath a bold Bunty masthead. The cover also informed us that magazine was published every Thursday, price 4d. Best of all, free inside was the 'Ladybird ring'. (See Chapter 8.) This shrewd marketing – vivid graphics plus two girls with rings to provide the 'I want one of those' instinct (and the ring was a pretty trinket) – ensured huge sales. Many of the characters went on to become firm favourites, notably The Four Marys, Lorna Drake, Moira Kent, Bunty herself and, much later, Luv Lisa. The *Bunty* cover appearance proved so successful that it hardly varied until

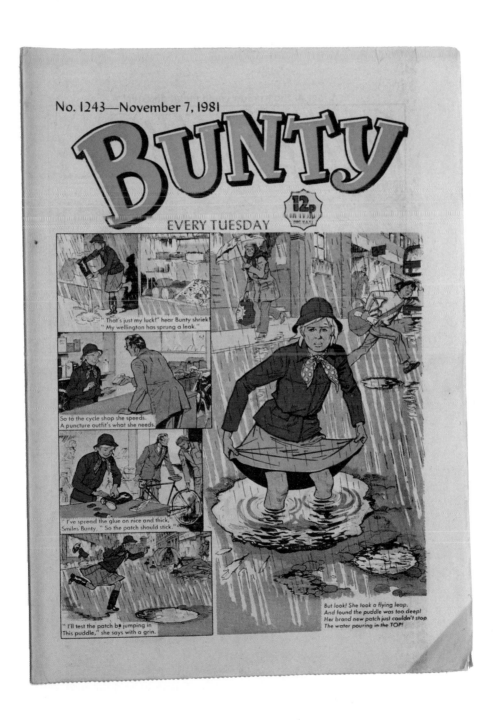

the late 1980s when the comic suddenly went modern with a complete overhaul, in the process losing its individuality

The Four Marys were schoolgirls, probably aged 14 or 15; it was hard to judge. Their ages weren't mentioned – ages were rarely mentioned in the comic strips, for fear of alienating any older readers: they might feel babyish and stop buying the publication. The girls were Lady Mary Radleigh, known as Raddy, the posh blonde one. Her father was an Earl, and had inherited Radleigh Hall, the setting for some of the stories. Mary Cotter, or Cotty, had long dark hair and was rather shy. She was very artistic, and quite a contrast to Mary Field (Fieldy), who had short hair and was very sporty. Fieldy was the lively energetic one, who won plenty of trophies. The final Mary was Simpy, Mary Simpson. Simpy was the one we all had sympathy for, because she was more like us. She didn't have a wealthy family, and it was her aptitude for mathematics that had won her a scholarship place to St Elmo's. Naturally, she was accepted completely by the Four Marys, but some of the other pupils were rude to her, looking down upon her because she wasn't of the same social level. During their time at *Bunty* The Four Marys were drawn by various artists; in the 1960s it was James Walker.

In *Bunty*, 19 September 19 1970, there was a recap of the early The Four Marys, with a story about the day the girls met, on their first day at St Elmo's. Mary Simpson was worried that she wouldn't be accepted by the other girls in the school because she had won the scholarship, and because her father was a grocer. The other girls came from rich families. The Four Marys spanned from 1958 right through to 2001, even though, towards the end, the series was looking rather dated. (See also Chapter 5.) Bill McLoughlin from D. C. Thompson says, 'All the ideas for the "Four Marys" were conceived by the staff of the *Bunty*. The synopses were then sent to an author and written before being sent to the artist. Artists didn't come up with ideas. Because a number of strips were long running it was common to have them scripted by different people. As for the change of artist, this came about due to various factors; illness or unavailability, and as the original artist retired we had to find others'.

A look at a 1960's issue of *Bunty* shows that, once again a free gift is being given – another delightful ring. This time it is a 'Dainty Doggie Ring', a metal ring with a plastic Scottie dog affixed, presumably based on the *Bunty* mascot of a Scottie dog, or 'terrier' as the comic refers to him. The cover depicts *Bunty* admiring her ring, a close-up picture of the ring, and, in huge, colourful letters, 'Free Inside for you to wear! Dainty Doggie Ring'. Inside this issue is the Lorna Drake serial, a favourite regular, illustrated by Tony Thewenetti, 'On the lonely road of a ballerina'. Lorna's dream is to become a ballet dancer, just like her father Antony, but the teacher at her dancing school is very strict and unpleasant – unsurprisingly as it was Antony who caused an accident, which led to her giving up her dancing career. Then there is 'Leap-Along Lesley', an unusual serial set in Warsaw, Poland, at the outbreak of war. Lesley's father hides plans for a new aero-engine inside her pogo stick, and Lesley's mission is to get them to the British. Other picture strips include 'Little Miss Sureshot', based on Annie Oakley, 'Fame at Her Fingertips' which recounts 'the struggle of a cripple girl to become a famous concert pianist' and 'Katy O'Conner Student Nurse' which is set in St Christopher's Hospital, London.

Additionally, there are two full text stories, one featuring a junior reporter named Jill, and the other telling of Sue Anderson, young matron of a children's home. The 'Cosy Corner' letters page gives readers a choice of prizes for their letter as well as awarding each a *Bunty* scarf, there are details of the Bunty Club (See Chapter 8), and a rather strange one-page illustrated historical story in rhyme, 'The Banished Daughter; from the ancient ballad Catskin's Garland'. Finally inside there is the 'Adventures of Toots', a humorous short picture strip based around one of the *Bunty* favourites, a young girl called Toots. (See Chapter 5.) The back cover features 'School Badge Corner' – colour pictures of school badges – and the ever-in-demand *Bunty* paper doll with her cut-out wardrobe.

The *Bunty* doll appeared for many years, and is the bane of collectors searching for uncut issues of *Bunty*! *Bunty* cut-out dolls were usually featured on the back cover and are fondly remembered by many ladies who read *Bunty* in their youth. The idea was to paste the doll onto a piece of cardboard before cutting it out, and the paper outfit could then also be cut out and attached to the doll by means of fold-over tags. A tremendous selection of outfits appeared over the years, so it was possible to amass a super collection of dolls and doll's clothes, Amongst them were party clothes, shopping outfits, dancing outfits and casual get-ups. Other series of cut-out dolls included costume dolls and uniforms. Paper dolls were very popular at the time, and other magazines occasionally featured them as well, such as *Twinkle*, whose doll could be dressed (as with the *Bunty doll*) with paper outfits with tabs to hold them on to the doll.

Says Sharon White, 'I was started out on *Twinkle* but I remember avidly getting *Bunty* every week because of the paper dolls on the back. I spent ages cutting them all out and gave them all names and they lived in a suitcase under my bed that was stuffed full of them. I'm not quite sure what became of them. I also remember reading my sister's *Jackie* and loved all the make-up advice! I then progressed to *Look-In* and used to collect the pop star posters and covered my bedroom wall in them.' Another *Bunty* fan is Kathy Martin who says, 'I loved *Bunty*! And I also remember *June* and *School Friend* but they might have belonged to my older sisters because I think they were a bit before my time. When I got older I was mad about *Jackie*, of course, and I used to get *Look and Learn* on a regular basis.'

Ten years after the 1960's *Bunty* issue previously mentioned, a copy dating from 1970 has inside free gifts of two Tip-Top-Knots (hair-ties). Now, the all-text stories have been discarded and the comic consists mainly of picture strips, apart from 'Cosy Corner'. The Four Marys are still included, though the one in this issue is, as mentioned earlier, an interesting look-back to the day the girls met. There is also a competition with a chance to win a transistor radio or Polaroid camera, and various picture strips based around ballet, school, a talented swimmer, a talented singer and a girl who rode a cow in a gymkhana!

By the 1980s, the Four Marys still reigned supreme, though they were more updated in style. Stories still revolved around talented girls – ballerinas, gymnasts and ice-skaters – and Toots was still there. 'The Incredible Adventures of Mini-mum' told of Helen Spears' mum who had unwittingly drunk a 'reducing liquid' making her just a few inches tall. Unsettlingly, there was a rather scary picture strip from the 1980s entitled 'Hannah in the House of Dolls', which featured Hannah, a young girl disguised as a 'cripple', not a term usually found today, who was working in a doll shop. Hannah discovered that the shop's owner, Mrs Scradgett, was removing the 'life force' from certain small girls and transferring it to dolls. The dolls, once they had the girls' brains, could steal goods from the homes of the children they belonged to and at night return to Mrs Scradgett in the shop, to deliver the stolen items. The dolls were made by small girls who were starved and cruelly treated, and were hidden in a secret room. It was certainly a creepy story, and rather unsettling, but with *Spellbound* magazine now ceased, perhaps it was decided to try to attract more older, or worldly-wise readers, by including a few edgy stories in *Bunty*.

Bunty Cut-out dolls.

SCHOOL BADGE CORNER

MOSELEY PRIMARY SCHOOL (COVENTRY)

ALNWICK SECONDARY MODERN SCHOOL (NORTHUMBERLAND)

GIGMILL COUNTY PRIMARY SCHOOL (STOURBRIDGE)

ALTON PARK JUNIOR SCHOOL (CLACTON-ON-SEA)

BARNSTAPLE GIRLS' COUNTY SECONDARY SCHOOL (DEVON)

DALE GIRLS' SECONDARY MODERN SCHOOL (LEICESTER)

GREEN ROCK PRIMARY SCHOOL (WALSALL)

OAKDALE JUNIOR SCHOOL (POOLE)

BEESTON ROUNDHILL SCHOOL (BEESTON)

ST ANTHONY'S ANNEXE SCHOOL (CHIGWELL)

GRANGE COUNTY PRIMARY SCHOOL (RUNCORN)

BONAR BRIDGE JUNIOR SECONDARY SCHOOL (ROSS-SHIRE)

PITCORTHIE PRIMARY SCHOOL (DUNFERMLINE)

Stop Here For Hours Of Fun With

Bunty's CUT-OUT WARDROBE

HOW would you like to dress up Bunty? Here is how to do it. Paste the figure of Bunty on to a piece of cardboard and cut round the black outside lines. Then cut out her three smart outfits—taking care to include the white tabs, too. Then simply by folding the tabs over Bunty's shoulders and waist you can fit on the lovely clothes. And watch out—there will be more of Bunty's pretty clothes for you to cut out and fit on, NEXT WEEK.

Printed and Published in Great Britain by D. C. THOMSON & Co., Ltd., and JOHN LENG & Co., Ltd., 12 Fetter Lane, Fleet Street, London, E.C.4. Registered for transmission by Canadian Magazine Post. © D. C. THOMSON & CO., LTD., 1960.

Bunty, back page.

In the late 1980s the format of *Bunty* changed; it became a colourful glossy, and, as well as the drawn cartoons, began to include some photo-story format strips, with youngsters acting out the adventures. Perhaps the best remembered was 'Luv Lisa', which ran for sometime and featured a girl and her younger brother. The girl, who, for some reason, invariably wore her sweater sleeves covering her hands, would be depicted writing in her diary as the page header, and then her adventures – or, actually 'domestic situations' might be a better term – would be acted out. Lisa lived with her family, which included a rather bossy mother, an elder sister called Alison, a younger, quite dopey, brother, Martin, and a fluffy black dog called Gnasher (presumably a tribute to the dog owned by Dennis the Menace). 'Luv Lisa' was a fixture for several years, but a disadvantage of photo-strip serials is that the characters grow up and, unlike the drawn cartoon strips, don't remain constant. So Lisa might be intended to still be acting as a 14-year-old, but could be 18 in real life – and it showed. In 1987 *Bunty* amalgamated with *Suzy*, and the 20 June issue was entitled *Bunty and Suzy*. The cover depicted Bunty and Suzy toasting their merger in orange squash at a tea party.

The issue of *Bunty* dated 22 July 1995, selling at 50p, featured – as was the *Bunty* norm – a colour photo of a young girl. Unlike the hand drawn covers of earlier years, which always featured the same blonde youngster, the photo covers showed a different girl each week, chosen from a variety of ethnic backgrounds. The brunette on the cover of this issue clutches a glass containing a soft drink, as a tie-in to a free gift which is an 'Angel Delight Crazy colours colour changing swizzle stick'. Inside the magazine, which still featured the intrepid Four Marys, now in colour and more updated, and wearing jeans and casual wear, is also another favourite school series, 'The Comp', which had switched to *Bunty* when *Nikki* folded in 1989. The series 'When Harry Dumped Sally' demonstrates how the comic is moving with the times by accepting that many comic-readers also had boyfriends, while 'The Change in Cheryl' features a family who fosters a teenage girl – again, story themes are becoming modernised. There is not a whiff of ballet or pony riding in this issue. Also in the comic are letters pages, a pen pal page and puzzle pages. The back page contains a pin-up picture of Boyzone. Interestingly, although the most of the characters depicted are well into their teens, the ages of the children writing into the comic averages nine years old, with the eldest being just 12.

Bunty managed to hold on for another six years, but finally, in February 2001, it breathed its last. It had acheived a run of just over 43 years, a proud achievement by any standards. *Bunty* had paved the way for countless other British girls' comics, daring to introduce stories about comprehensive schools rather than posh grammar and boarding schools. Although it did feature ballet, horse riding and other middle-class activities, it also made a point of including stories about working girls and those in one-parent, foster or otherwise broken homes. It was one of D. C. Thomson's stars, more so than even its popular stable-mates *Judy* and *Mandy*, and is unsurprising that *Bunty* is one of the most remembered and best-loved comics of the sixties', seventies' and eighties' generations.

Debbie

Debbie was a D.C. Thomson publication, which ran for 10 years from 1973: a mixture of picture strips, photo strips, text stories, letters, puzzles and recipes. The first issue, priced at 3½d, contained a free gift of a 'cameo beauty brooch', which was 'for trendy girls'. To modern eyes, it doesn't seem in the least bit trendy, in fact it looks most old-fashioned –

but it wasn't – because in the early seventies, there was a craze for Victoriana fashions, with long skirts, chokers and leg-of-mutton sleeves being very much the in thing.

An August 1980 copy of *Debbie* reveals a black and white publication, with the first story, 'Beaver Girl', about a 'crippled girl' who was tending a pair of beavers, much to the annoyance of local landowners. Amongst other picture strips are 'Trixie's Treasure Chest (a girl who inherits a chest of magical objects), 'Singalong Sal' (a girl with a pure singing voice which could shatter glass) and 'Dina's Desperate Days' (a swimmer who is blackmailed by her coach). A photo strip, 'Bad Times for Brenda' is a moralistic tale of a young girl who plays truant from school to meet up with a boy at a fairground where he works. The boy persuades her that she will have a much better life if she returns to school and passes her exams. There is a feature on life at the Royal Ballet School, a letters page, a text story and a colour pin-up picture of an Alsation dog! *Debbie* ran for ten years, engulfing *Spellbound* along the way, and finishing at the beginning of 1983 when it was incorporated into *Mandy*.

Diana

Another 'name comic' was *Diana*. Diana was a popular name at the time, and the *Diana* comic was begun by D. C. Thomson in 1963 – long before we associated the Diana name with royalty. *Diana*, a large colour rotogravure publication, cost 6d in the 1960s, and the first issue showed a happy young girl ice-skater. Free inside was a 'lovely golden chain bracelet'. In format and style, it could have been trying to compete with *June* or *Princess*. The attractive, full-coloured cover of a 1969 issue featured a youngish girl (still wearing socks, so not old enough for stockings) daydreaming, with the comical happenings shown in a series of pictures. According to a letter in this issue, the average age of readers fell into the 7-12 age group, though many readers were older. It was the kind of comic a girl could turn to when she tired of *Bunty* or *Judy*, as it dealt with other topics without being too 'poppy'.

The *Diana* comic was a varied read, with plenty of stories (which were sometimes a bit dark and scary), a page devoted to pop stars and a double page 'Spotlight' spread with letters, queries, readers pictures, problem column, cut-out picture of a ballet dancer and a lot more besides. Some of the stories were quite quirky, notably the serial 'The Spaceship in Our Kitchen', which centred on a family with a mini spaceship plugged into the kitchen light socket, manned by the JinJees who came from a tiny planet. When anyone displeased them, they 'supercallifrated' them with a ray gun. The back page featured 'Our Gang', a story revolving around the humorous adventures of a band of dogs. And sometimes, the comic contained a column written by a cat called Candy. *Diana* also often included a page which, when cut and folded, turned into a mini booklet. These booklets were on all kinds of subjects, including Eyes, Ballroom Dancing, and Glass. This was one of the first girls' magazines to incorporate general knowledge articles as well as the more usual girlie topics. *Diana* kept on going until 1976 when it merged with *Jackie*.

Emma

Emma was one of the later, 1970s, D.C. Thomson's girl comics, and inherited the popular notion of giving comics girls' names. It followed the *Bunty, Judy, Mandy* and *June* format. According to the first issue, dated 28 February 1978, and which featured a majorette – majorettes were very much in vogue at the time, and all over Britain young girls were

TOP OF THE CLASS FOR SUPER STORIES!

9p

Debbie

EVERY MONDAY

No. 393 AUGUST 23, 1980

Inside-
8 STORIES
- READERS' LETTERS
- RECIPES
- PUZZLES
- YOUR STARS
AND A
- PRIZE X-WORD

WIN A MUPPET!

FREE GIFT INSIDE

emma

FREE INSIDE

Lesley of *Blue Peter* shows you how to make Christmas gifts to keep everyone happy

emma
NO.2

emma

FREE GIFT INSIDE

emma

THE SKY'S THE LIMIT FOR...
WHERE IT'S ALL HAPPENING FOR GIRLS!

training as mini baton twirlers – Emma stood for 'Excitement, Mystery, Marvellous free gifts and Action'. The first 'marvellous free gift' was 'your very own initial brooch', which came with a set of initials so that it could be personalised. Emma's scenario was that she was a TV Reporter, thus giving the magazine the excuse to investigate current television shows, interview pop stars and have an 'Emma Magazine' in the centre of the comic featuring reader's letters. There was also a strip cartoon feature, The Emma Report, which saw our intrepid heroine tackling various activities and occupations – she investigates the police, rides a police horse and finds a lost child. Emma also helps an injured ballet dancer through synchronised swimming lessons, goes deep sea diving and tries hot air ballooning. Later that same year, the magazine underwent a facelift, featuring a full colour photographic cover (rather than a colour drawn cover). Interestingly, back in that first issue, the full colour photo technique was in use, but had been relegated to the back. It featured photos of the Muppets together with an article of Emma meeting them – though Emma herself was shown as a black and white drawing. One of the longest-running characters in Emma was Sue Spiker. Sue was a feisty girl from a children's home, whose main talent was playing volleyball. Rude to her teachers and to most adults, and constantly fighting with her peers, she was a problem. Sadly, Emma was very short lived, running for less than 18 months before being swallowed up by *Judy*.

Jackie

This was the one that the girls of the seventies and eighties gravitated to, after they had grown out of the picture story schoolgirl/ballet/pony comics. *Jackie* was feisty and a bit daring, it was a comic which many mums frowned upon, which made it even more desirable. It discussed fashion, make-up and, most of all, boys! Amongst its staff was the now-famous Jacqueline Wilson, who for many years has claimed the *Jackie* magazine was named after her. She says that when she was working for D.C. Thomson, she used to contribute to a, as yet unnamed, comic and one day the men in charge of the teen department informed her that the new comic would be out soon, and would bear her name.

However, according to Bill McLoughlin from D.C. Thomson, 'There has been this consistent claim about the origins of the *Jackie* name, but as *Bunty* and *Judy* predated *Jackie* it is likely the girls' name theme continued. The naming is, I suspect, a coincidence. Simply there is nobody here now who was about at the launch so it is impossible to say one way or the other.'

Jackie was launched on 11 January 1964, a zingy, forward-looking magazine/comic right from the start, and, to prove its excellence, was to run for almost 30 years. Filled with romantic picture strips, pop star features and fashion tips, this was one for the trendy young teens to be seen with, a world away from *Bunty* and *Mandy*.

The cover designs were bold and striking, sometimes drawn, later photographic, and with the title emblazoned at the top in large letters. Costing 6d every Thursday, *Jackie* provided a lively, but not too taxing read and was a good way for any modern young girl to keep up with the latest trends. Inside a 1978 copy, we find just two picture strips, featuring light romantic stories. The rest is given over to fashion, pop, beauty and problems (See Chapter 9). There is also a confessional feature of a girl who cheated in her history exams and a light-hearted piece on how to get on with your, mum, dad, brother and sister. Lots to read, and, best of all a double page spread called 'Dressing Up' featuring delicate fashion sketches of long floaty dresses from Laura Ashley, C&A and Dorothy Perkins. Three years later, the 13 March 1981 issue of *Jackie* contains a free gift of a 'Jackie alpha-belt', two photo strips, a long text story and an unmissable feature called 'The Path of True Love; All About Boys', which every reader would have consumed avidly.

Jackie had a reputation for being daring, for tackling subjects other girls' comics wouldn't mention. Mothers were upset, partly because they thought their younger daughters would get hold of it, borrowing it from their elder sisters. They probably did – but it wouldn't have done them much harm. More likely, as innocence was still widespread at that time, anything they didn't understand would go harmlessly over their heads. Certainly, compared with the images, words and articles found in magazines and newspapers today, *Jackie*, far from being a comic to be feared, was really a pussycat. *Jackie* had an outstanding, 30-year run, blazing a trail for other pop/fashion/teen publications, with great illustrations and plenty of innovative ideas. Amongst the artists who worked for *Jackie* was Norman Lee who also drew for *Romeo*. Along the way, in 1976, *Jackie* incorporated *Diana*, before abruptly ceasing publication in July 1993: without being incorporated into anything else. Presumably, the folk at D.C. Thomson deemed the time was right for *Jackie* to end. So it did.

Jinty

This comic, dating from 1974, was a little different from the usual run-of-the-mill comics. It dared to experiment a bit with various genres, although the very first issue included the usual expected free gift, this time a bracelet with a 'smiley' attached. A 1977 copy of *Jinty* included 'Battle of the Wills', which involved a scientist making a duplicate of girl, allowing her to train both as a ballerina and a gymnast. In a final showdown, the scientist ruthlessly eliminated the ballerina. Another story, 'Cursed to be a Coward' told of a schoolgirl swimmer, Marnie, who has been told by a fortune-teller she will die in 'blue water'. The fortune-teller later tried to murder Marnie by pushing her under the water of the school swimming pool. It was an unsettling, if exciting story.

Other story strips include one about a girl with second sight, a really scary tale about a girl haunted by a devil woman whose face had appeared in a mirror, and a couple of humour-based strips to provide a bit of light relief. *Jinty* also contained a pop page, a letters page, an astrology column, assorted cartoons and a strip of 'Alley Cat'. In this issue there was a competition to 'Win an Angel!', which was actually an Angels' Nurse doll from the BBC TV series *Angela's Angels*. The first-prize winners won a fully fitted model ward and a patient as well!

The *Jinty* masthead was blue, with Jinty written in yellow script, and it was published each Wednesday, price 8p. The front cover picture was a colour drawing from a story, or of something else which could be found inside, together with exciting text to hook customers into buying – 'Life must end for one of these girls but which one?' or 'Stage Fright; Linda loved playing the clown but tragedy was coming her way'. On the back cover was an excellent craft page with a coloured drawing and detailed instructions for that week's make. Amongst the crafts featured were producing various pretty scarves by utilising delicate fabrics or open-weaving, creating ear-rings from beads or feathers, and fashioning an ethnic-type headband from felt or suede.

Jinty ran for over seven years before it ceased publication. It was incorporated into *Tammy* at the end of 1981, but not before it had earlier absorbed two very short-lived comics, *Penny* and *Lindy*. It was sad that *Jinty* couldn't hold out any longer, but times were changing.

Judy

This was another from D.C. Thomson, of the same ilk as *Bunty* and *Mandy*. The first issue was published on 16 January 1961, and the comic was to run for 31 years – not as long as *Bunty*, but even so, an impressive span. Free inside was a flowery bracelet. The earlier issues of *Judy* followed very much on from the *Bunty*-style, with black and white strip stories, a text only tale, a 'Busy Bea's' letters page and a club page (See Chapter 8), while the early covers had one main picture. Later covers showed a colour strip story, such as the late 1960s' 'Bobby Dazzler', which continued on the back page.

'Sandra and the Stranded Ballet', drawn by Paddy Brennan is one of the serials in a 1968 copy of *Judy*, priced at 5d. Sandra Wilson was a member of the Imperial Ballet Company, and when the plane carrying them to Moscow crash lands in Greenland, the girls continue to practice in the snow. Amazingly, they don't seem to freeze in their tiny costumes and ballet shoes. Sandra's adventures regularly cropped up in *Judy* in the 1960s, she seemed

to be one of the favourites. Another story is about 'Spender Sue' who has inherited a vast fortune – but there is a catch; she must spend one half of it in a week, not as easy as it sounds. Some of the serials were exciting, thriller types such as 'The Girl From DORSET' which stood for the 'Department to Overcome Rebels, Spies Enemies and any other Threats', with the characters using James Bond-style equipment such as a pencil radio receiver, tracking bugs and a watch, which dazzled people by emitting a blinding light. Marion, nicknamed 'Maid Marion' was the heroine, and she took her instructions from the DORSET's chief, a woman known as 'Mother'. Other stories include a historical series set in 1837, two school-based stories, a horse-riding story, and, unusually, an account in pictures of the early life of impersonator/comedian Mike Yarwood.

Ten years later, *Judy* has altered quite a bit – gone is the strip story cover, this May 1978 issue features a picture of singer Les Gray from the pop group Mud, and costs 7p. Inside, the stories are quite strong – these aren't centred around ballet schools or boarding schools, instead we have a story set in 1890 on a world trading cruise, another in Australia in the 1850s and a third set a century before in western America. One excellent, progressive series, 'Follow-My-Leader Lil' has a girl confined to a wheelchair as the heroine, determined to stop a local builder from building on wasteland used as a play area. Intriguingly, four pages are devoted to cartoon-type humorous strips. There is a club page (see Chapter 8), but the 'Busy Bea's' letters page has now been replaced by a 'Laugh 'n' Chat Spot', and the back page has been given over to a page dealing with pop facts and pictures. A 1979 change saw *Judy* joining forces with *Emma*, and the masthead read, Judy and Emma. Some *Emma* features were incorporated too, notably 'Sue Spiker' and the *Emma* magazine pages. The stories continued to be strong, 1979 issues featured such serials as 'The Frightening Fours' (a sinister cloud descended on Earth, and four-year-olds suddenly developed adult brains and minds, becoming Cloud Soldiers who used other children as slaves. The intent was to build machines to poison Earth's atmosphere.) Another series, 'The Fish Twins' was the story of strange sea-children who battled to save a coastal community threatened by alien sea creatures, caused by atomic waste dumped in the Arctic. In 1991 *Judy* was amalgamated with *Mandy*, at first being known as *Mandy & Judy*, but soon it was abbreviated to *M&J*. (See *Mandy*, this chapter.)

June

Fleetway Publication's *June* first appeared in 1961, containing a free flower bracelet. This was another comic for the late primary and early secondary school readers. The first issue included an Enid Blyton text story 'The Mystery of Banshee Towers', and a Pat Smythe story 'The Three Jays Ride Again'. There was also a feature by naturalist Gerald Durrell on 'My Zoo Friends', a school story and an article on cookery, so it provided a good all-round read for a girl for just 4½d. The cover featured a photo of a young girl admiring her 'lovely floral bracelet', and the logo of the *June* rose appeared in the masthead alongside the bold *June* title, in blue. Also inside this first issue was a feature called 'Diana's Diary' which this week focussed on a girl hoping to dance in a display but who trips over her brother's bike and sprains her ankle – will she be able to dance? There was also a strip featuring a sweet little girl called Jenny who was intent on playing hospitals with her daddy, and a pattern to make a felt sausage dog.

In 1965, *June* amalgamated with *School Friend* to become known as *June and School Friend*, which appeared in the masthead in large red and blue letters. By then it boasted

'44 pages of Stories, Fun and Features' and cost 7d. One of the legacies that *School Friend* brought along was the picture strip of the adventures of the tubby favourite Bessie Bunter, sister of Billy. The comic was a good mix of stories and features in 1965; amongst the strips were the humorous 'Vanessa From Venus', 'Life At St Luke's' which told the story of Nurse Jenny Jones, 'Holiday Princess' – a princess from Lichenburg who donned peasant clothes to visit her subjects and 'Lucky's Living Doll'. The features included a 'Star Special' insight with singer Francoise Hardy, the 'True Story of Madame Curie', a 'Date With Donovan', a fashion feature on petticoats (girls still wore them in the sixties) a page of readers' letters and a club page. (See Chapter 8.) *June and School Friend* continued to thrive, along the way engulfing the short-lived *Poppet and Pixie*, right into the next decade, before merging with *Tammy* in 1974, and finally becoming known as *Tammy and June*.

Mandy

D.C. Thomson obviously had a thing about 'name' comics. *Mandy* arrived in 1967, following the *Bunty* and *Judy* format, and the cover featured Mandy, a short-haired brunette. That first issue contained a 'lovely rainbow ring', and the eye-catching cover had a white background with huge text proclaiming the issue was 'No. 1 of a new picture paper for girls'. There was plenty of reading matter, including two text stories and around ten picture story strips. Browsing through a 1970s' copy reveals the stories include 'The Gentle Giant', a shire horse called Big Tom, owned by Jill. In this issue he supported a fallen beam on his back, saving the people in the forge from being trapped. 'Friend of the Lonely' stars Susan Holmes, a 'clerkess' in Midwich Welfare Department, who helped lonely people in her spare time, while the Carmen Bernardo illustrated strip, 'Very Important Pupil', tells of Lynne Williams who was caught in the rays of an exploding meteorite, receiving terrific energy, rather like a superhero. Another, alien series is a humorous story featuring 'Thingummy', representing Klork one of the planets of Mars, at the Olympic Games. Other stories include 'Fay Nightingale' a junior war nurse in Kharhiri, 'The Mystery of Mavora' which is a mermaid-shaped rock responsible for many tragedies, and a tale set in an island school. *Mandy* also contained a letters and jokes page and a text only story, this issue's one being 'June in the Jungle; an old Mandy favourite returns in a super new story.' There were an excellent variety of stories in this comic, from the wacky to the more thought-provoking kind.

On looking at a *Mandy* 15 years on, the magazine still seems to be the same format, with the same mix of stories. In 1991, *Mandy* became *Mandy & Judy*, and later the comic was renamed *M&J*. A 1992 copy of *Mandy & Judy* reveals a transformation; for a start, the magazine is slightly larger and has switched to the gravure style of printing, as opposed to the earlier letterpress. The cover is bright and colourful; it still features artwork rather than photos, but the pictures are realistically painted, with plenty of depth. It shows two, modern girls – presumable Mandy and Judy, looking much older than when depicted in the original *Mandy and Judy* comics. On turning the pages we see lots more colour, and there is a lively feel to the magazine. Several photos appear, on the Pen Pal and letters pages, and there is also a selection of photos on the back cover, of children who are 'Best Friends'. The magazine is crisp and inviting, and the stories are interesting, such as one involving an animal-loving girl keeping pets in an orchard near her house, until her animal hating father decides to buy the land. 'Nola Knows' recounts the problem of a girl who can see into the future, 'Margie In the Middle' is a light-hearted story of a girl whose two friends

hate each other, 'Strange Neighbours' is a series about a girl much older than she seems, while 'The Many Faces of Moppet' is a series set around a strange mascot doll with hidden powers. There are also mock 'diary pages' from Mandy and Judy, a Starscope, and a classic story reprinted from a 1968 edition of *Judy*. Really, *Mandy & Judy* was more like a new comic than a mishmash of the two singles.

The more trendy-sounding *M&J*, from 1993 was altered again, though not as drastically as before. Perhaps the most obvious change was the cover, which now not only featured a large red M&J logo, also had a full-colour photo of a young girl. The story mix is still good, and includes 'Penny's Place' which, although a school story, also featured a café run by Penny's parents. Penny's family isn't particularly well off, while her best friend Donna comes from a family of seven, with another on the way, so has hardly any money. Some of their other friends, though, have wealthy parents. The series is thought-provoking, and the people seem real. 'Penny's Place' proved such a popular series, that when *M&J* finally ceased, it moved across to *Bunty*, and was restarted from the first episode. (See Chapter 5.) Particularly scary was 'Skeleton Corner', which cropped up from time to time. In the issue dated 17 April 1993, the skeleton overheard a young girl, Janie, wishing she could fly like a bird. He caused a robin to show her how. The girl loved flying, until the robin told her she must fly forever. The story finished with the skeleton explaining that Janie was still up there, a streak of white in the sky, serving as a reminder to everyone to be really sure that what they wish for is something that they really want. *M&J* finally ceased in 1997, though the *Mandy* annual lived on.

Mates

Mates, from IPC, was a mixture of picture strips and features as so many of the *Jackie*-style comics were. First issued in 1975, this was a weekly publication, mainly black and white but with a colour pin-up and a few other colour pages. The three picture strips were drawn, as opposed to photo strips, and were mainly romantic stories. Other features included letters pages, problems' pages, pop news, recipes, fun quizzes and a makeover section. In 1981, *Mates* was merged with *Oh Boy!*

Misty

The 1970s saw the mystical genre appear for girls, spearheaded by the now cult comic *Misty*, published by IPC, and the slightly less scary D.C. Thomson's *Spellbound*. *Misty*, which had first appeared in 1978, bore warnings emblazoned across the front, such as 'stories we dare you to read' or 'stories not to be read at night' and some of the stories were, quite frankly, terrifying. Certainly they were more than enough to give susceptible readers nightmares, or at least a good scare, and all praise must go the publishers for having the courage to experiment with this new genre. *Misty* was probably inspired by *Jinty* or *Tammy*, which both used the dramatic 'cry and scare' story genre to great effect but *Misty* made its tales even more scary. However, it probably owed some of the idea to *Spellbound*, which had been issued a couple of years previously. Coincidentally, *Spellbound* closed just a month before *Misty* emerged.

With its themes of the supernatural and horror, *Misty* was a welcome addition to the girls' comics market, a different genre which appealed to those girls who wanted something more than school stories. The stories in *Misty* – and in *Spellbound* too – gave girls something to discuss in the school playgrounds, something which they could chew over and use as a basis for discussion. The stories were strong and thought provoking, and it was quite fun to scare yourself a bit, in the company of other girls. Though, sometimes, reading the comics on your own at night could be a bit frightening. That very first issue, which contained a free lucky charm bracelet, had a cover design of two young girls, obviously terrified at something they had just witnessed, holding up a candle.

An issue of *Misty* from 1978 has a story about a butterfly collector called Betty, a rather horrid girl who has no sympathy for the butterflies she kills. All she wants is a rare Purple Emperor butterfly – but while out butterfly hunting one day a monstrous butterfly captures her instead, in a net. The story finishes with the girl incarcerated inside his killing bottle. One of the serials, 'Moonchild', illustrated by John Armstrong, and told by Pat Mills, revolves around a girl with the power of telekinesis, with an episode ending on a cliffhanger when, in the night, the door bolts open by themselves and the girl's long dead grandmother bursts through. A note on one of the pages indicates that *Misty* was intended for the 7-12 age group, though some readers were much older, and it seems odd that some seven year olds were reading this when others would still have been at the *Bunty/Mandy* stage. I would have expected this comic to appeal to girls in the early years of secondary education. Looking back, the oddest – and most clever – thing about *Misty* was although it had power to scare, unlike traditional horror comics, there was very little frightening stuff to see. Girls weren't shown covered in blood, or disembowelled; instead, subtle hints, expressions, nuances in the text hinted at horrors far worse than a young girl could possibly dream of. And that was *Misty*'s strength – it made girls use their imagination, and in the process scare themselves silly. The artwork was always very strong in *Misty*, which added to the dramatic appeal.

However, *Misty* was surprisingly short-lived, and one wonders if, in part, it could be due to the fact that there were no regular characters, apart from Misty herself. The nature of the stories meant that the featured heroines were constantly changing, so there was no anchor. Girls seem to like familiar characters that appear each week; the familiarity adds a friendly, comforting air – even in a scary comic. *Misty* melted away in 1980, after just two years, and was absorbed into *Tammy*. (See also Chapter 4.) Recently, *Misty* has become something of a cult comic, and in September 2009, a *Misty Classics* comic special was sold.

Nikki

A short-lived comic, which began in February 1985, and was presumably aimed at the 'last years of the primary school, first years of the senior school' age group. *Nikki*'s main claim to fame was 'The Comp', written by Anthea Skiffington and illustrated by Ron Lumsden, which was an excellent picture strip centred around Redvale Comprehensive school and made a change from the endless stories of grammar and boarding schools, beloved by so many comics. 'The Comp' has become something of a cult picture strip, with its fans still reminiscing about it. Amongst the characters were Laura Brady, who was very much into sports and later became captain of the girls' football team. Rosalind 'Roz' Cummings, was an American girl who lived in Britain with her English father, who was divorced, while twins Becky and Haley Sinden were almost opposites; one hating sport, the other a tomboy who thought sport was the bee's knees. Claire Carter suffered from impaired hearing, and could lip-read which often proved useful in plot lines, Pippa Cragston and Morag Gordon were the school bullies, while Freddy and Hodge were two of the boys who were regularly featured. The headmistress was very strict and known as 'Grim Gertie'.

Having said that featuring a comprehensive school made a change, *Nikki* still kept up tradition by including other school stories, such as in an issue from December 1985, 'Tom Came Too', about a girl at boarding school and her horse. The comic also contained a problem page (see Chap 9) as well as pages of puzzles, things to make and do, and a letters' section. This latter page contained a letter from a disgruntled parent complaining that when *Nikki* began it was excellent, and seemed to be aimed at encouraging a wide range of interests for girls around the eight to thirteen age group. Now, the writer was accusing *Nikki* of turning into a carbon copy of other boring teenage romance comics on the market. She said that now her daughter was going right off it, and so was she! The Editor had replied by asking girls to write in to see if they agreed. *Nikki* finally ended in September 1989, after a run of just over four and a half years, merging with *Bunty* in the same month, and taking 'The Comp' with it.

Oh Boy!

Dating from 1976, *Oh Boy!* was another of the comic-strip-cum-pop-fashion magazines which surfaced during the 1970s/80s. An IPC publication, *Oh Boy!* was published weekly, every Thursday, and cost 14p. An issue from 1978 contains a double page colour picture spread pin-up picture of actor Mark Hamill. Reading through, the impression is that the comic was intended for a slightly older age group, maybe 16-plus. For instance, the photo strip story tells of a young girl having an affair with a married man, and wishing she could 'just lie there naked at his side' forever. There are also two drawn picture strips and a short, text-only serial in which the girl speculates on what will happen if a would-be pop star boyfriend gets her alone in the bedroom. Letters, problems, pop pages, fashion make-overs and fun quizzes plus a send-away freebie of lipstick and perfume, made for a very readable comic which was surprisingly good value. However, presumably not everyone thought so, and in 1985 *Oh Boy!* was amalgamated with *My Guy*.

Pink

This IPC publication first appeared in 1973: a mixture of fashion, stories, pop and advice. *Pink* included several picture strips featuring older teens rather than school kids. A 1976 copy (which incidentally bears a colour photograph of singer Linda Lewis) shows that at the time it cost 12p and consisted of 30 pages. Inside are three picture strips – 'Patty's World' which tells of a girl whose mother is rushed to hospital after collapsing and the effect it is having on her love life, while 'Don't Leave Me Lynne…Not Now' is about a girl at a football match who is enlisted by the star player to smuggle him out of the ground. The third story, 'Sugar Jones' centres around Sugar, who 'seemed to be one of the trendiest, kindest stars on TV. Only Susie, her assistant, knew that Sugar was mean – and forty years old!' (Goodness, forty years old must have seemed ancient to those 1970s' bright young things.) With a colour page pin-up spread of Flintlock, fashions, letters, problems, quizzes and features on dating, this was the perfect read for the young teen. The quality was impressive too, it was printed on thick, matt paper. *Pink* finally amalgamated with *Mates* in 1980.

Pixie

Pixie was a sweet, wholesome read for young girls, presumably aimed at the under-tens. It was the kind of comic the most staid of great aunts would be happy to give to the small girls in the family circle. Published by IPC, it first appeared in June 1962, and sadly was

destined to run for only six months. This comic was colourful and attractive, and printed on a quality matt paper. It featured classic writers such as Enid Blyton with 'The Naughtiest Girl in the School' and illustrated by Tony Higham, as well as 'Milly Molly Mandy' by Joyce Lankester Brisley and Frances Hodgson Burnett's 'The Secret Garden'. Other stories included 'Marion of Sherwood', 'Tutankhamun and I' and 'When Black Beauty was young'. There was a puzzle page, a page with a beautiful illustration and a poem and a page of cartoons.

The covers of *Pixie* were charming, with, typically, a photo of a young girl with a pet puppy, kitten or budgie, or maybe surrounded by dolls. The masthead featured the title in large lowercase letters. Above, it read 'Every girl's very own favourite'. Maybe it was too sweet, too twee, just too 'nice' for its young audience. Whatever the case, this delightful magazine was amalgamated with *June* in January 1973, after a total of just 30 issues.

Princess
Princess was a Fleetway publication, which first emerged in 1960. This publication was a cross between a comic and a magazine and, in a way, was like *Girl* in that it seemed to have some upper class appeal. Even the cover was a bit posh, with a glossy colour photo of a girl in a party crown about to eat a slice of cake. A gift of a plastic daisy flower bracelet was given free with the first issue, and the comic cost 5d. Stories included 'Lorna Doon' and 'Circus Ballerina'.

The issue dated 10 June 1967 featured Francis Marshall's painting of 'Princess Marianne' on the cover, wearing a very smart green dress with frog fastenings and a stand-up white collar, watching a cavalcade of horse guards outside Buckingham Palace. At the time *Princess* cost 9d, making it a little more expensive than some of the other comics of the day, and the beautiful full-colour cover was subtle, rather than garish. The back of the cover was devoted to stories from the ballet, in this issue it concentrated on Ondine, told in colour picture strips, though the pictures were more like beautiful paintings, and were by Severino Baraldi. It's easy to see why even the cover alone would win over many girls. It was so attractive.

Inside, the 30 pages contained a mix of picture strips, photographs, paintings, text-only stories, competitions, cartoons, fashion and factual articles. It was a varied interesting read and would have kept a girl busy for some time, unlike many of the basic story-strip titles. In this 1967 issue, it was good to find an old friend, Lettice Leefe from *Girl*, only here she was just Lettice by John Ryan, and wasn't in a school environment. It was the same old Lettice, though, still getting things muddled. Three years before, *Princess* had merged with *Girl*, and obviously Lettice had found a new home. After the two comics combined, the first few issues were called *The New Princess and Girl*.

The green dress featured on the cover is advertised inside *Princess* as being made from cotton twill with a smart white collar and insert pleat, and made by Popchicks in navy, pink or green. The prices ranged from 56/- to 64/- depending on size. Picture strips include 'Annette's Secret' which is set during the Civil War, and 'Alona the Wild One' (two friends have been attempting to row the Atlantic, but have been overtaken by a violent storm, and now one girl is unconscious, and the other has lost her memory). 'On Stage' (Mary is engaged to Pete, a photographer, and has just bought her wedding dress – a trendy ethnic mini – and a peignoir, while 'The Mystery of Melham Castle' is a story set around a film company. 'Lyndy of Latymer Grange', a student studying ballet at a Dancing School, bears more than a passing resemblance to *Girl* comic's 'Belle of the Ballet'.

A strip telling the story of Mary Stuart, entitled 'The Ill-fated Queen' occupies the full-colour centre-page spread; once again the pictures are beautifully drawn with masses of detail, especially seen in the elaborate costumes. Another excellent colour feature is 'Animal, Vegetable and Mineral', written and drawn by Eric Tansley. This week he looks at a Saffron crocus, a Goldcrest, a Painted Lady butterfly and a piece of rock containing pyrites or 'fool's gold'. During its lifetime *Princess* featured many excellently drawn stories and articles, such as the very popular strip 'Happy Days', which was drawn by Andrew Wilson and written by Jenny Butterworth.

Even so, all good things must come to an end, and in 1967, *Princess* merged with *Tina*, forming the new comic *Princess Tina*. Many years later, however, in the 1980s, IPC tried to reuse the *Princess* name, but the new comic, a completely different format, folded after just six months, being swallowed by *Tammy*.

Princess Tina

Princess Tina was an amalgamation of *Princess* (see above) and *Tina*. *Tina* was a very short-lived comic from Fleetway, running for just six months in 1967 before combining with *Princess*. It did, even so, have a good reputation for originality with some excellent storylines, notably Jane Bond, illustrated by Michael Hubbard. The *Princess Tina* comic ran for six years, and was a mix of stories from the two comics. The cover was more grown-up than that of *Princess*, often illustrated by Walter Lambert, and with a 1970 edition featuring a stunning, lively painting by Manfred Sommer of bikini-clad teens against a seaside background. This attractive picture would have stood out against the more sedate, dare I say, old-fashioned and tired same-y covers which appeared in the newsagents' shops each week, no doubt attracting a whole new readership. Incorporated inside were the usual readers' page with letters and notes, a fashion article and a natural history feature. The Trolls were still in evidence (carried over from *Tina*), as well as Barbie the Model Girl and Willy the Wily Wolf. With stories such as 'Sister to a Soccer Star' it was clear that *Princess Tina* was aiming to appeal to modern girls, although it still played safe by including a Student Nurse series. One of the best girls' strips was 'Patty's World', written by Phillip Douglas and drawn by Purita Campos. It was so liked that it was carried over into other comics such as *Pink*, *Mates* and the later *Girl*. It was reprinted all over Europe, and was especially popular in Holland and a huge hit in Spain, though there, Patty's name was changed to Esther. It is still popular in Europe today. Unfortunately, all this wasn't quite enough to save *Princess Tina*, and in 1974 it became incorporated with *Pink*.

Sally

This rather short-lived comic was an IPC creation. *Sally* first appeared in 1969, but was only produced for 21 months. Although a rival publication, *Sally* followed the *Bunty/Judy* format, even to using a girl's name as a title. The front cover featured a masthead showing the name Sally written in red script, and the head of a girl with her blonde hair cut into a bob, and in issue one, she was admiring her 'lovely free cameo ring'. A 1970 copy of *Sally* has a humorous colour strip on the front cover, 'Maisie's Magic Eye', which featured a girl with a rather useful brooch which glowed and made people do what she said. Other stories include 'Mandy's Secret Diary' (a boy Mandy likes is accused of theft), 'The Ghost Hunters' (a series billed as 'spine chilling tales of mystery and imagination'), 'Cat Girl' (she turns catlike when she dons her magic cat suit) and 'Thunk' ('The funny 'Thing' from outer space'). There was also a double page 'Sally Calling' problems/star signs page. *Sally* ceased publication in 1971.

Sandie

Another short-lived IPC comic which was, nevertheless, surprisingly popular, at least if the amount of copies still around is anything to go by. *Sandie* appeared on the newsagents' shelves on 12 February 1972, together with the obligatory free gift, in this case a styling comb. Free gifts appeared for the next three issues, as was the norm at the time. Issue three contained a pretty daisy-print 'dolly purse'. The comic was published weekly, every Monday, and cost 3½p. At 40 pages, it was quite a substantial read. Very much of its time, *Sandie* was full of ballet, school, horse and gymnast tales, all presented in a picture strip format, and boasted, 'It's the best girls' picture-story paper there is!' One of its most well known characters was Wee Sue, a scholarship pupil at Blackhurst School, and a champion athlete. This later transferred to *Tammy*. A look inside an issue dated 29 April 1972 reveals mainly black and white picture strips, plus a pet care page (pigeons), readers' letters and a double page (red and black) full of jokes, puzzles and cartoons. Stories include a gymnastics-based series 'No-one Cheers for Norah', 'Sandra Must Dance' – a girl injured in car crash is able to use a 'unique psychic bond' to transfer her dancing skills to her twin sister – while 'Silver is a Star' tells of a girl with little money struggling to keep her horse from being sold.

Standing out amongst several school-based stories is the exciting 'The School of No Escape', which centres on a school in which the evil headmistress, Miss Voor, turns out to be an alien from a planet called Esora. With scenes showing her about to stab pupils, give them memory-loss injections and planning to kill a pupil and leave her body 'lying at the bottom of a quarry', this was quite a scary read, no doubt giving plenty of schoolgirls bad dreams! The *Sandie* covers were full colour and attractive, and very distinctive, featuring a blue masthead with the Sandie heading in yellow, while the cover was divided into three each containing an illustration from one of the stories inside. *Sandie* was incorporated with *Tammy* on 27 October 1973.

Spellbound

Spellbound, by contrast to *Misty*, was not quite so scary – it was slightly more upbeat, although even so, stories about mummies and ghosts were not for the faint-hearted youngster. It was issued by D.C. Thomson two years before *Misty* made its presence felt. *Spellbound* arrived in the shops in September 1976, and instantly stood out amongst the other girl comics. No sweetness and light on the cover here! Issue number one featured a girl with a candle (rather like the idea which the later *Misty* used), and the chosen colours were blacks, purples, gold and blues. Free inside was a Mystic Sun Pendant, and the first series included such strong stories as 'When The Mummy Walks', 'I Don't Want To Be a Witch' and 'Lonely Lucy'.

Many stories were set in times past, such as one revolving around a scarab ring which had a terrible power and had to be destroyed to allow a young girl to live. *Spellbound* had a 'Spooky Spot' letters page, in which readers sent in their ghostly tales. Some of them were really

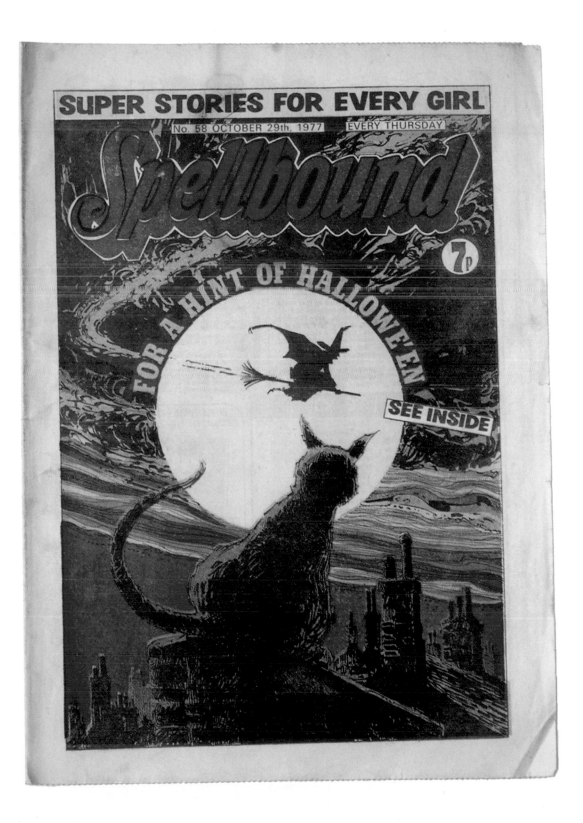

frightening, made more so because they were real, not made-up stories. Inside a November 1976 copy is a continuation of the picture strip 'When the Mummy Walks – Terror in a Quiet London Street'. Jenny Hunt, trainee curator at the Granville Museum and her friend Bob were on the trail of the Mummy of the Goddess of Manaton. The Goddess was a terrifying, staring figure seeking revenge on those who had violated her tomb in Egypt. She was controlled by the sinister Head Curator, and had been ordered to 'silence' Jenny. Amongst the other tales, there is a text story in this issue, too, called 'No Morning Tea, Thank you', which works quite effectively as it is so simple. A young girl goes to stay at a guesthouse with her parents, and next morning her tea is brought to her by a schoolgirl, together with a newspaper. The schoolgirl is pale, and doesn't speak. The newspaper headline tells of bombers battering the town in 1942, and the young guest realises that the schoolgirl was killed in the raid. The schoolgirl turns out to be the daughter of the lady who ran the guesthouse.

A year later, in an issue dated 29 October 1977, which featured a particularly attractive cover of a black, slightly long-eared cat, sitting on the rooftops, silhouetted against the moon and watching a witch fly past on a broomstick, the 'Mummy' series has ended. Instead, there is 'Vengeance of Vampirene – Irene, the Vampire Princess'. The vampire is actually Princess Irene in disguise, and she is trying to rescue her father who has been imprisoned. 'The Ghost of Greystones' is also about a girl in disguise, this time as a ghost hoping to catch a thief, while 'Marina' is a gipsy girl with the gift of second sight. A series called 'The Music Master' features The Supercats, who were regulars of *Spellbound*. The Supercats consisted of four girls from Moonbase 4, who 'had been chosen from all corners of the galaxy for their courage and very special powers'. In this adventure they are drawn towards a planet that seems to be emitting music. The Supercats discover that an ageing 'Dee Jay' is playing music, which puts people in a trance. He captures the old people (everyone over 30!) and hides them away, so that the planet seems to be populated by beautiful youngsters. The stories in *Spellbound* were tamer than those found in the later *Misty*'s, yet they still provided food for thought, and were certainly different to those in the other comics emitting from D.C. Thomson, such as *Bunty*.

At 7p, *Spellbound* was a penny cheaper than *Misty*, and both were unusual, lively reads for a girl tired of ponies and ballerinas. *Spellbound* continued until January 1978 – a run of 69 issues – and the very next month, IPC's *Misty* appeared, presumably picking up the readers who had previously enjoyed *Spellbound*. Sadly, *Misty* too, only had a short run, of under two years. It's probable that parents played a large part in the eventual downfall of both these comics, as they were much more likely to go for the traditional types of comics for their girls rather than the new-fangled ones with rather dubious story lines. It was, nevertheless, a great loss – *Misty* and *Spellbound* had been imaginative and original publications, bringing a new dimension into the world of girls' comics. Maybe, though, the majority of young girls were just not ready for them, and really did prefer their cosy worlds of schoolgirl and sports stories.

Tina

Launched by Fleetway in February 1967, the first issue of *Tina* came with a free 'Lovely gold-plated Troll brooch'. The Troll characters (a popular craze at the time) were to become associated with both *Tina* and the later *Princess Tina*, featuring regularly in picture strips. *Tina* contained a mix of picture stories and features; particularly notable was Jane Bond and Willy the Wily Wolf. (See Princess Tina.)

Tammy

Tammy, an IPC comic, first appeared in the newsagents' in 1971, and was to run for 13 years. It proved so successful that, apparently, it was second in the sales' stake to *Bunty*, almost from the start. The comic was dreamt up by writer Gerry Finley-Day, who had an understanding of what really appealed to girls. Realising that they enjoyed sad stories, he ensured his heroines underwent many hardships and cruelties, making them suffer – the sadder and more dramatic he made the magazine, the more girls loved it. The first issue of *Tammy* contained not one, but two free gifts – a ring and a bracelet – thus immediately giving it a sense of one-upmanship against other comics, which only ran to one free gift at a time! This first issue, which cost 7d (3p in the new-fangled decimal money which had just been introduced) was packed with picture strips (mostly black and white) while the coloured back page was designated as 'Pets' Page', with this first issue being given over to the care of cats and kittens. Issue two would feature guinea pigs.

The front cover depicted a happy-faced young girl wearing her free ring and bracelet, with the heading Tammy in red daisy-encrusted lettering. The comic announced that free inside issue two was to be a 'two in one wallet' which contained fold out pages with information and spaces for personal notes. Picture strips included 'The Secret of Trebaran' – a girl goes back in time only to find she risks being burnt at the stake as a witch for having a tape recorder on her which played 'The House of the Rising Sun'! 'No Tears for Molly' featured the ups and downs of a 1920's servant girl, and there was a school series "The Girls of Liberty Lodge'. Of course, there was also an obligatory ballet story, in this case, 'Betina at Ballet School', illustrated by Dudley Wynne. There was a Club page too. *Tammy* quickly became a firm favourite with girls.

A 1977 copy of *Tammy* certainly shows why it was so popular, even though the price had more than doubled in just six years; for 7p a girl would find nine reasonably long story strips, as well as the usual letters and adverts for other IPC products. The cover of this issue features a 'readers' cover idea' – a colour drawing of a blonde girl with her hair in pigtails, presumably Tammy herself, as she featured regularly on the covers at this time – reading a copy of *Tammy* while playing tennis. At the top of the comic it said 'A Smash-hit that's Tammy'. This logo was changed each week to tie in with the cover idea, others included 'Always first on the menu', 'A cut above the rest' or 'It's a knock-out'. The back issue of this week's comic featured a 'Melonmania' competition, with prizes of Sportel colour video games, Audiotronic radio cassette players and Newporter skateboards, for completing a limerick.

Amongst the stories are: 'Time Trap' a series centring on a young girl called Leonie Page, who somehow found herself back in the Middle Ages and under threat of death. The dramatic illustrations, as well as the John of Gaunt/Wat Tyler storyline cleverly combined history with an exciting read. Another story, 'Dawn's Doomwatch', tells of a girl who throws litter around, until an accident caused by a collapsing disused mine literally jolts her mind into visualising the effects which severe pollution could bring. There is the obligatory serial set in a school – the one in this 1977 issue is called 'Babe at St Wood's'. Babe is an American girl, who is the daughter of a gang boss and has been sent to St Wood's to learn refinement. This episode sees Babe outsmarting criminals who tries to intimidate the owner of a Chinese laundry. The centre pages of *Tammy* are given over to a Bessie Bunter tale; it's good to see the old girl still holding her own. Probably *Tammy*'s most favourite character was Bella the gymnast, the saga of Bella Barlow, who starred in many series of stories. In this issue there is a flashback with Bella recalling her past. The original story of

Tammy.

Bella was written by Jenny McDade, but later episodes were written by John Wagner – who later wrote Judge Dredd! – and Primrose Cumming, according to artist/historian David Roach; they were illustrated by John Armstrong. Amongst the other *Tammy* artists who deserve a mention are Jim Baikie, who worked on many classic girls' titles including *Jinty* and *June*, and the Spanish artist Rodrigo Comos. Roderigo also drew for *Valentine*.

Along the way, *Tammy* merged with *Sally*, *Pixie*, *Sandie*, *June*, *Misty*, *Jinty* and *Princess*. The mergers tended to use the lost comic's name for a few weeks before quietly dropping it, hence we had *Tammy and Sandie*, and *Tammy and June*. In 1980 the comic became called, what else, but *Tammy and Misty*. It's interesting to compare an issue of this comic with the earlier *Tammy*, and a March 1981 copy of *Tammy and Misty* reveals that Bella has made it to the front cover, as well as to three more pages inside. Bessie Bunter, drawn by Reg Parlett, is still there too, causing chaos at Cliff House school, while Wee Sue, another favourite – a girl smaller than her classmates, and her teacher, Miss Bigger – also provides light relief. Gone is the scariness of *Misty*, overshadowed by the usual school/sports/pets/swimming stories common to most girls' comics at the time. It's only slightly redeemed by 'Monster Movie; Strange Story from the Mists', a picture strip featuring a girl called Lorna Wright whose dad was an amateur movie maker, and Lorna is spooked by a monster who looms from the

water, just as she rounds a cliff out of camera shot. There is also a page of makes – creating a magazine cover or recipe folder for your mum – and a letters page, which includes the news that from 4 March 1981, the price of *Tammy and Misty* will rise to 14p. *Tammy* herself merged with the later IPC *Girl* magazine (as opposed to the Hulton original) in 1984.

Tracy

A D.C. Thomson publication, which first surfaced in October 1979, *Tracy* was to run for almost six years. The very first issue, dated Saturday 6 October 1979 had a particularly bright, fresh-looking cover bearing an attractive design. The cover painting depicted a young girl with a blonde bob, with a blue budgerigar – called Elton – perched on her finger. Budgie appeared on the cover of most issues; he was one of the important characters! With the first issue of the comic was a free badge, which featured either Korky the Cat, Minnie the Minx or Beryl the Peril, and all three designs were shown on the cover. Issue two came with a free guitar comb – 'It's Top of the Pops!' and a competition with exciting prizes to be won, including a combined TV set/radio/cassette recorder, as well as separate cassette recorders and transistor radios.

Inside *Tracy* were '10 Terrific Picture Stories Every Week', amongst them such stories as 'Tammy Smart's Schooldays', 'The Spell on Aunt Nell – And Me As Well' and 'Slave to the Beauty Queen' – all good stuff, the kind of tales young girls at the time enjoyed. Everything was depicted in picture strips. Other stories over the years included 'Tammy Smart's Schooldays' which featured the problem of bullying when Tammy secretly took the place of her brother at a boys' school, and 'The Plot Against Penny' which focused on a conspiracy to keep Penny Morgan and her dad apart. Many of the stories in *Tracy* were strong, with themes to make girls think. *Tracy* disappeared in January 1985, sadly sinking without trace!

Picture strip in Judy.

CHAPTER FIVE

Favourite Characters

Many comics featured regular characters, which appeared in each issue, and we grew to love them. Also, in the later decades, television-related comics and comics promoting certain toys began to take over the market – Barbie, Toybox, Sabrina, My Little Pony, Cbeebies, Teletubbies, Fifi and the Flowertots, Dora the Explorer and dozens of others.

Character or not?

When is a comic a character comic? This can be a tricky question, because once a comic, *The Beano*, for instance, becomes established, the subjects of many of its cartoons become well known, and so can rightly be described as famous characters. We all know, or have heard of, Dennis the Menace, Minnie the Minx, Korky the Cat, Biffo the Bear and Beryl the Peril, for example. Most of us can recognise them if we see a picture of them; the characters all have their own distinguishing features, clothing or traits. So you could argue that *The Beano* or *The Dandy* are character comics because they have been around so long that many of their featured personalities are household names. However, in this instance, the term character comics is used to describe those comics which have been created around an already established or popular media programme or toy.

There are numerous examples of character comics; sometimes well known characters such as Sooty and Sweep, the Wombles, the friends from The Magic Roundabout, Andy Pandy, Postman Pat or the Moomins feature in a picture strip in a television or media-related comic, and so that comic could be called a character comic. However, there has been a growing trend for comics to be associated with one particular character, often a television favourite or maybe a toy. Examples include the comics *My Little Pony, Sindy, Barbie, Dora the Explorer, Fifi and the Flowertots, Care Bears, Sylvanian Families, Disney, Bratz* and *CBeebies*. Some are better than others, and some are excellent. One particular comic worth mentioning is the *My Little Pony* comic which began in the 1980s. This comic, which contained attractive

Minnie the Minx by Robert Harrop.

coloured picture strips, also published various specials and a monthly extra called *My Little Pony and Friends*. *My Little Pony* ran a club, which encouraged young girls to be creative; the main way it did this was by holding a yearly competition in which members had to submit topics on various subjects. The entries were often very impressive, with lots of thought going into each one. They included thick workbooks, drawings, collages and lots of writing. By awarding prizes of top-of-the-range pony toys and holding an award ceremony with celebrities and a trip to the Horse of the Year Show, Hasbro ensured all the members wanted to win an award. Competition was stiff, which was why the entries were of such a high standard. Another character comic from the 1980s was *Sylvanian Families*, published by Marvel at 45p. This comic contained a mix of picture strips, longer text stories, activity pages and a badger family set of dolls to cut out and dress.

Over the last few decades, there has been a tremendous growth in the number of comics that are based around one particular character or programme. Inevitably, this must be

related to the fact that so much of the modern child's time is devoted to the watching of television or DVDs. Any comic launched on the shoulders of a television series is given a massive boost in terms of publicity. Children will see the comic in the shops and recognise the characters they regularly watch, and so are much more likely to choose that comic rather than one in which they don't recognise any of the figures shown in the drawings. Likewise, if the comic revolves around a favourite toy or doll, then that will take priority over an unfamiliar publication. It's possible that a child can learn to read more quickly from a character comic, purely because she will already recognise the characters and be familiar with the situations shown in the comics.

Media-related Comics

Media-related comics are nothing new. Films, music and radio all played large parts in the history of the comic, although from the sixties onwards it was the music industry which captured the largest slice of the media-based comic market; later the television-influenced comics cut in. Though many of the comics and publications appealed to both sexes, a huge quantity of pin-up types and romantic story-based comics were deliberately slanted towards the girls. They were deemed too sloppy, or too girlie for the boys. Certainly at school, a boy caught reading *Valentine* or *Boyfriend* would never live it down.

Comics such as *Radio Fun, Film Fun, TV Fun, TV Comic*, and similar, appealed to both boys and girls – and also in some cases, to more mature readers too. I recall reading both *Radio Fun* and *TV Fun* in the 1950s, loving them because they featured such people as Arthur Askey, Tommy Cooper, Charlie Chester and Norman Wisdom, people who I had heard on the radio or seen on television or in pantomime already. Films were big in the mid-1950s, with people like Diana Dors, Jayne Mansfield and Doris Day household names. Later, as more and more people acquired television sets, it was the stars from those who dominated the comics – it was those people we wanted to read about and see in their crazy adventures. Radio stars were popular too, but slowly declining – girls didn't want to read about Bebe Daniels or Molly Weir in the late fifties.

Some Recent or Current Media Comics for Girls

Current media comics for little ones – pre-schoolers and early primary – include *Cbeebies, In the Night Garden, Fifi and the Flowertots, Toybox, Fimbles* and *Tweenies*. These comics all seem to be activity rather than story based; in a way, they take the place of the traditional puzzle books. Although they don't contain much reading matter (most children have access to plenty of books nowadays), they will allow a child to pass several hours completing the various tasks. They set out to teach and inform, and certainly the recent issues of the comics I have looked at, although media led, do tend to be lively and bright, and the majority contain well thought out educational activities. It's interesting to speculate whether, one day, any of these titles, or those below, will become collectable.

Barbie

The Barbie doll is the top selling, most famous doll in the world, and so it is only right that she should have a comic. A comic called *Barbie* (what else?) was launched by Marvel in Britain on 5 October 1991, and cost 55p. Right from the start, it presented Barbie just as the owners of the doll perceived her – a girl who could do anything. In the first issue, she is seem changing a tyre on her car during an adventure called 'Girls Can Do Anything', making observations as she does so. For instance, she points out that the car must be on a level surface before the tyre is changed, the hazard warning flasher must be activated and then she checks to make sure the brake is secure and the automatic transmission is in park. She explains how the jack must be inserted into the slot on the side of the car with the flat tyre, and to pump the jack handle to lift the car up. Girls reading the *Barbie* comic learned a lot more than how to put on make-up and dress their hair. As well as two long picture stories, this high quality all-colour publication featured a cut out and dress Barbie doll and plenty of craft makes. It came with a free gift of strawberry lipgloss. A *Barbie* comic is still published, now by Egmont, and a look inside an issue from 2009 shows how comics have changed, even since the beginning of the 1990s. This is now completely activity based, the only 'story' being a very short (less than 100 words) section of text, with spaces where stickers need to be inserted. However, there is lots here to keep a young girl entertained, including two press-out dolls and their clothes. Amongst the other things to make and do are pictures to colour, mazes to follow, odd ones out, fashion designing and a sheet of stickers to use in conjunction with the various activities. The magazine comes with a free gift – in this issue it's a plastic 'magic writer' – costs £2.50, and is published every three weeks.

Bratz

The monthly D.C. Thomson publication, *Bratz*, featuring the four, rather outrageous Bratz girls whose doll personna ousted Barbie off her pedestal, had to cease at the end of 2009 following a Bratz dispute with Mattel, owners of Barbie. *Bratz*, certainly by October 2009, actually contained very few images and connections with the Bratz dolls, instead it was more of a pop and fashion magazine. It contained the usual embarrassing moments pages (called 'Bratz Blushes') and, in this issue, had a four-page feature on Miley Cyrus, the actress and songstress also known as Disney's Hannah Montana. Other features included ideas for starting a 'Best Friends Club', giving plenty of sensible advice on how to be a good friend. However, the tongue-in-cheek quiz page, which asked questions such as 'Do you ever get told off for talking in class?' and 'Are theme parks awesome?' rather depressingly concluded that, depending on the chosen answers, a girl would become 'a model, actress, TV presenter or a pop star'. It seemed the careers of yesteryear – vet, nurse, stewardess, secretary – were an absolute turn off. Amongst the free gifts with this issue of *Bratz* were a small doggy notebook, a pen, two phone charms and some sticky 'jewels'.

Sindy

Sindy, a collectable and popular doll, first starred in her own comic, also called *Sindy*, in 1986, which was published by Marvel. At that time, the Sindy doll was still manufactured by Pedigree Toys and had the original 'chubby' face. A succession of makers later, plus a change of publishers, saw the comic alter its format as well as the look of the doll featured. The issue of *Sindy* featured here is from the 20 October 2004, when the doll was marketed by New Moons and the comic was published by Panini. The cover features a photo of a Sindy doll wearing a feather-trimmed tutu, and the comic is priced at £1.75. On the front is a free gift, an attractive and durable pendant consisting of a pair of pink-enamelled metal ballet shoes on a thin plastic cord with a 'silver' chain clasp. The back of the comic shows a photo of a Sindy doll in a ballet pose; it's bright, attractive and glossy.

Inside, the magazine is packed with things to make and do, but there are no traditional picture strip stories. However, there is a story headed, 'Not So Sweet Dreams', which shows

photo cut-outs of a Sindy doll with captions set into cloud-shaped frames. Bang up to date, the captions say such things as 'On the way home, Sindy started texting Lilli and Mya. She was so worn out she didn't feel like doing anything more energetic than taking a hot bath. But she was waiting to see her best friends, so she suggested they bring a couple of DVDs over to her house and sleepover. Mum said she'd order in pizza and some delish ice cream – bliss!' It's interesting to compare this with a comic of even 20 years before, when texting and DVDs would be alien concepts to a young girl. (See also Chapter 7.)

Tinker Bell
Disney Fairies *Tinker Bell* comic, which is published monthly by Egmont at £2.50, began in 2007. Unlike the majority of today's girls' comics or magazines, *Tinker Bell* actually contains a traditional-style picture strip with text beneath. Beautifully illustrated in full colour, in the usual Disney style, the story which appears in the October 2009 issue is entitled 'The Starlight Harvest' and is an adventure featuring *Tinker Bell* and her friends. This is a particularly attractive publication, and also includes such activities as colouring, a word search, quizzes and odd one out. Additionally there are projects to make of a shell mirror and a fairy.

Totally Tracy Beaker
This character creation by Jacqueline Wilson was given her own magazine/comic in 2005. *Totally Tracy Beaker* was a G.E Fabbri publication, and it cost £2.99 every fortnight. Very much a 'things to make and do' magazine, it was adored by Tracy Beaker fans – Tracy Beaker originally featured in a series of books about a young girl who had been placed in care. A cross between a comic and a part work, *Totally Tracy Beaker* came with various free gifts which were activity inspired – inkpads, photo frames and roller stamps, for example. Also included were chats with people in various occupations such as a hairdresser, extracts from Jacqueline Wilson's Tracy Beaker books, puzzles, ideas for writing pop songs and instructions explaining how to draw 'super-cool pop stars'. Also in this magazine were animal pictures and facts, social skills including ways to make and keep friends and, above all, lots to make and do. *Totally Tracy Beaker* was a lively and upbeat read with a very positive approach to life.

Top Girls – A Few Much-Loved Characters

Most comics, even those intended for boys, feature a token girl or two. Sometimes, a character will evolve and become really popular, known to most people whether or not they read the associated comic, for example Minnie the Minx. Other characters become much loved, though only the readers of the comic get to know of them. There are far too many to list here, so I have selected a few of the most popular, and although this is headed 'Top Girls' a couple of males have crept in. The characters listed here were the ones which cropped up time and again when women were discussing the comics they once read, and so I hope that your favourite will be included.

Bea (*The Beano*)
Bea is the baby sister of Dennis the Menace, from *The Beano*. She was 'born' in September 1998, as part of the comic's 60th birthday celebrations. Dennis was wondering why his

mother was feeling sick all the time and why his dad looked unduly pleased with himself! Bea was drawn by David Parkins, who had taken over from David Sutherland, and he gave her a yellow and black stripy romper to match her big brother's jumper, and which lent itself admirably to her name, 'Bea'. A few issues later, Bea was given her own strip, drawn by Nigel Parkinson. Bea has a doggy friend called Gnipper. Dennis' and Bea's mum takes great delight in shouting, 'Bea! No!' whenever she does something naughty, providing a convenient pun on the comic's name, *The Beano*.

Soon Bea was given her own strip, drawn by Nigel Parkinson, who often draws Dennis the Menace. This very naughty, but cute, baby, whose first word was 'Mud', is becoming quite a little star, with many resin figurines, photo frames and other collectable items appearing in the shops, all featuring Bea. Bea's friend is Ivy the Terrible, who joined her in the picture strip.

Bella Barlow *(Tammy)*
As with *Girl*'s 'Belle of the Ballet', 'Bella Barlow' from *Tammy* was an orphan. She was a talented gymnast who underwent many adventures over the years including shipwrecks, kidnapping in Russia and saving the life of a fellow gymnast by breaking her fall (becoming confined to a wheelchair in the process.) She even took part in the opening ceremony at the Montreal Olympics! The Bella Barlow picture strip was drawn by John Armstrong, who seemed to particularly specialise in gymnastic drawings.

Belle of the Ballet *(Girl)*
Belle appeared in *Girl* for many years. She was an orphan, Belle Auburn, a member of the Arenska Dancing School. The strip was written by George Beardmore and drawn by Stanley Houghton, and it ran in *Girl* from 1952 until 1964. The stories then switched to *Princess*. Interestingly, the adventures in strip form were also published in France, in a comic called *Line*. Belle appeared, too, in book format in both Britain and France.

Bengo *(Candy and others)*
Bengo the boxer puppy was particularly popular during the 1950s and 60s. Created by Polish artist William Timyn, who usually signed his work as 'Tim', he starred on children's television in a series of programmes in which Tim drew pictures while telling a story about the puppy and his friends. Bengo also appeared in strip cartoon format in various comics and magazines, including *Harold Hare's Own Paper* and *Candy*. The magazine *Woman's Illustrated* ran a Bengo club for children in the early 1960s, which had an attractive bronze plastic badge shaped like Bengo's head, while numerous tie-ins were made, amongst them ceramic ornaments by Wade and other companies, as well as squeaky toys, a Pelham puppet and various books.

Beryl the Peril *(Topper)*
Dating from 1953, Beryl the Peril appeared in the very first issue of *Topper*. She was created by David Law, who also created Dennis the Menace, and so, unsurprisingly she shared many of Dennis's traits, as well as his taste for red and black. Beryl's best friend (or often, enemy) was Cynthia, and she had a pet turkey called Gobbler. Later, she was given a dog called Pearl. In the 1980s she became the front-page star of *Topper*. Her costume was changed several times, as were her facial features, and she later joined the cast of *The Dandy*. Beryl

tormented her teachers, neighbours and long-suffering parents. Interestingly, her parents looked identical to those of Denis the Menace. Even more interestingly it seems that David Lowe had a daughter, Rosemary, and she was the inspiration for Beryl the Peril. Her young playmate, Robert Fair, was constantly creating chaos, and so he became the boy behind Dennis the Menace.

Bessie Bunter *(School Friend)*

Bessie Bunter, sister of Billy, first appeared in *The Magnet* in a 1919 story about Greyfriars school, which Billy attended. Bessie was a pupil of a nearby girls' school, Cliff House School. When Amalgamated Press decided to publish a girls' magazine called *The School Friend*, which later was changed to *The Schoolgirl*, Cliff House School was a major feature, and was run by Miss Stackpole, the headmistress. Initially the stories were penned by Billy Bunter's creator Frank Hamilton, appearing under the name of Hilda Richards who was supposedly Frank's sister, however they were soon written by other authors. Bessie, an ultra-plump girl with a liking for cream buns, later appeared in *June* and *Tammy*. (See appropriate entries.) Bessie was not a particularly likeable girl, at least initially, being conceited and untruthful, as well as prone to be ultra bossy. She later softened up, becoming a more comical figure in the later comics such as *Tammy*.

Dilly Dreem *(School Friend)*

Dilly Dreem was 'The Lovable Duffer' who provided some light-hearted relief as a change from all the sleuthing in *School Friend*. Dilly was illustrated by Dora Leeson, and the strip later became called 'Dilly Dreem's Schooldays'. Bespectacled, and of a similar nature to *Girl*'s Lettice Leefe, Dilly Dreem was usually in some scrape or another.

Belle, Pelham Puppets.

Four Marys *(Bunty)*

Comprising Mary Cotter, Mary Field, Mary Radleigh and Mary Simpson, the group of schoolgirls who made up The Four Marys were stalwarts of *Bunty*, right from the start. The girls were pupils in a typical girls-only boarding school of the era. The school was called St Elmo's and all four Marys shared a study in Bee's House. Each girl had her own persona, Lady Mary Radleigh, was the posh one. She was blonde and answered

Bea from McDonalds.

The Four Marys (Bunty).

Beryl the Peril, Robert Harrop.

Bengo by Wade.

to the nickname of 'Raddy', and she was the daughter of an Earl. When Raddy was not at St Elmo's, she lived at Radleigh Hall. Mary Field was the energetic sporty one, always winning the races and the trophies. This Mary had short hair and was known as 'Fieldy'. The artistic one was Mary Cotter, or 'Cotty'. Cotty was shy, and had long dark hair. The fourth Mary was Mary Simpson. Her nickname was 'Simpy', and she was something of a misfit, because she was an ordinary girl as opposed to the other middle class girls. She was at St Elmo's because she had won a scholarship for mathematics. Her family weren't wealthy at all; her father was a grocer. Mary Simpson had short dark curly hair. When the series began, the girls were neat in their uniforms of gymslips and blazers, but by the time Bunty reached the 1980s, they were casually dressed in jeans, yet the old St Elmo's values remained.

The Four Marys is, for some reason, the picture strip story which most women today remember from reading *Bunty* in their girlhood. The series was kept on, and on, and, even though the concepts became increasingly outdated as time passed, it seemed that no one at D.C. Thomson had the heart to kill off this much-loved story, or those four girls all named Mary. (The name Mary itself became increasingly old-fashioned as the decades wore on.)

Other characters from the series included the two bullying schoolgirls, Mabel Lentham and Veronica Lavery. They were very snobbish, rather odious, spiteful upper class girls. Mabel and Veronica disliked the Four Marys, partly for their popularity but also because Mary Simpson, who they deemed common, was included in the group. The head teacher was Dr Gull, very much of the old-traditionalist schoolmistress type, as was 'Creefy', Miss Creef, the Four Mary's form-mistress. Later, Dr Gull was replaced by the more liberal Miss Mitchell. Artists changed on this long running series, but in the 1960s it was James Walker.

Ivy the Terrible *(The Beano)*
Obviously a pun on Ivan the Terrible, Ivy is a four-year-old girl, who is the bane of her parents' lives. She is mischievous and cheeky, and annoys everyone she meets. Ivy first appeared in 1985 and was drawn by Robert Nixon. She has her own regular comic strip in *The Beano*, and is a friend of Bea. (See entry.)

Jack and Jill *(Jack and Jill)*
Jack and Jill were the young children from which the *Jack and Jill* nursery comic took its name. Nothing to do with the nursery rhyme characters, these were modern, 1950s' twins, the children of Mr and Mrs Honey. They lived at Buttercup Farm. Aged around six or seven, the twins had great fun exploring the farm and the animals. Their companion was a puppy called Patch who led them into all kinds of scrapes. The children also re-enacted various scenarios they came across, such as a cowboy film, using their creativity to find various props. The children were in the comic right from the start, and were still there at the end. The illustrators changed quite a bit over the years and included Eric Stephens, Antonio Lupatelli and Hugh McNeill. These delightful, innocent youngsters remind us of a way of life now sadly lost.

Keyhole Kate *(The Dandy)*
This very nosy girl – in fact her nose was so long that it reached her goal before the rest of her did – was one of the originals in *The Dandy*, appearing from 1937-1955. She was

drawn by one of D.C. Thomson's most prolific and talented artists, Allan Morley, who was one of the few to sign his own work. Kate liked to peer through keyholes so that she knew exactly what was going on. Later, she appeared in *Sparky*. Her cartoon boasted, 'Keyhole Kate's a little sneak. See her on this page every week.' Kate wore her hair in two plaits and was rather skinny.

Kitty Hawke *(Girl)*

Kitty Hawke and her All Girl Aircrew, was the front page serial in the early issues of *Girl*, and the strip was illustrated by Roy Bailey. The strip starred Kitty, who was the daughter of

Lorna Drake.

the owner of Hawke Airlines. Kitty seemed to be an early Woman's Lib supporter, determined to show her father that girls could do things as well, if not better than the men. The first issue of *Girl* demonstrates this clearly with Kitty's classic, often-quoted remark in which she declares that she has proved to her father that 'we can operate his planes as efficiently as the glorious male'. Along with her friends, Winifred 'Windfall' White, Radio Officer Jean Stuart and the Navigator Patricia D'Arcy, the feisty Kitty was eventually replaced, as the war was becoming old-hat amongst the modern misses of the 1950s.

Lettice Leefe *(Girl)*

Star of a comic strip in *Girl*, Lettice Leefe was subtitled 'The greenest girl in school'. Bespectacled, with dark hair styled in pigtails, dressed in school uniform and with a somewhat earnest look, Lettice's good intentions invariably ended in chaos. Lettice was thought up by John Ryan, who was later famed for his children's cartoon creations Captain Pugwash and Mary, Mungo and Midge. Her long-suffering teacher was Miss Froth, and Lettice lent a dash of humour to the, often serious, stories in *Girl*. In the late 1950s Pelham Puppets created a string puppet as a Lettice Leefe character. They also produced a

Lettice Leefe, Pelham's Puppets.

now rare glove puppet. Lettice later appeared in *Princess*, without the 'Leefe', and removed from the school environment. Lettice even had some music named after her – the Lettice Leefe Hop. The French publication *Line*, similar to *Girl*, featured her, though her name was changed to Charlotte. Lettice Leefe is one of the most fondly remembered of the 1950s' girls' comic characters.

Lisa *(Bunty)*

Lisa (Luv, Lisa) wrote her diary each week in issues of 1990s' *Bunty*, telling of her everyday adventures at home and school, as well as those of her rather silly brother Martin and their big sister Alison. Lisa went through a phase of having the strange habit of wearing her jumper sleeves right down over her hands, though no one in the stories ever commented on it. The story strips were illustrated by photos as opposed to drawings, so consequently, Lisa aged throughout the series, which continued for several years.

Lorna Drake *(Bunty)*

Lorna Drake starred in a ballet series in *Bunty*, which was illustrated by Tony Thewenetti. Lorna's dream was to become a ballet dancer, but her dancing teacher, Thelma Mayne, is crippled. The accident was caused years before by Lorna's father, who was a dancer losing his sight when he accidentally dropped his partner, Thelma. Consequently, Thelma was extremely strict and unpleasant towards Lorna.

Minnie the Minx *(The Beano)*

Minnie the Minx, one of the comic world's most iconic characters, was created by Leo Baxendale, and she first appeared in *The Beano* dated 19 December 1953. She is the third longest running of *The Beano* characters, coming behind Dennis the Menace and Roger the Dodger. Minnie was later, from 1961, drawn by Jim Petrie, who penned 2,000 of the comic strips before he retired in 2001. Jim was reported as saying, 'Little Minnie has been very good to me. She has kept me in porridge all these years.' As a demonstration in how political correctness has changed the face of comics, in Jim's first strip, Minnie had pinched her mum's feather duster to make a Red Indian headdress, so that she could take her friends captive. Her father punished her with a beating from his slipper. Nowadays you cannot use the term 'Red Indians' nor show any form of corporal punishment.

Minnie's character is so easy to recognise that she has been immortalised in several ways. Perhaps her greatest achievement is to be cast as a statue decorating the streets of Dundee (where D. C. Thomson, publishers

TOP: Minnie the Minx, McDonalds.
LEFT: Minnie the Minx statue in Dundee.

of *The Beano*, are based). Here, holding her up her catapult she takes aim at Desperate Dan who is striding ahead. The statues were created by sculptors and artists Tony and Susie Morrow. Minnie has also appeared as resin sculptures by Robert Harrop, various plastic freebies from McDonalds and Burger King, and as a cloth doll by Real Beano Gear. (See Chapter 11.)

Moira Kent (*Bunty*)

Moira Kent was the earliest ballerina found in *Bunty* – she appeared in the first issue as a young girl who yearned to dance, but who needed to win over her disapproving grandfather. Her story was told in 'The Dancing Life of Moira Kent', and she featured for many years. Eventually, 'Moira Kent' was destined to become an international ballet star. Acclaimed as one of the finest ballerinas in the world, Moira was a member of the Globe Ballet Company.

Pansy Potter (*The Beano*)

An early character from *The Beano*, the title of the comic strip 'Pansy Potter the Strongman's Daughter' is actually a rhyming couplet when read in a Dundee accent! Pansy originated in 1938 and was drawn by Hugh McNeill, later with Harry Hargreaves. Pansy Potter then appeared in *Sparky*, though drawn by John Geering, before later returning to *The Beano* in the 1990s with Barry Glennard as her illustrator. Pansy was, as the title of the strip implies, the daughter of a strong man, and who had inherited his talent. Super strong Pansy was a schoolgirl able to juggle with weights and anything else that happens to be handy. She featured huge arms and her hair was spiky, rather like that of Dennis the Menace.

Penny's Place (*M&J*)

This strip began in *M&J*, and told of a girl called Penny and her family. Penny's parents ran a cafe called Penny's Place. Penny's best friend was Donna, who (class distinction here) was from a working class home and had lots of brothers and sisters. Penny, Donna and her other friends lived in the same town and attended the same school. The story was later reprinted in *Bunty*, as it had proved so popular.

Silent Three (*School Friend*)

The Silent Three were the three girls who starred in a long-running, popular feature in *School Friend*. Betty Rowland, Joan Derwent and Peggy West were all pupils at St Kitt's Boarding School. They first appeared in 1950 in 'The Silent Three at St Kitts'. The stories were written by Enid Boyten and illustrated by Evelyn Flinders. Betty, Joan and Peggy often donned long robes with hoods as a disguise, and solved various mysterious involving other pupils as well as robberies and the like, while of course, battling against their tyrannical head prefect.

Susan (*Girl*)

The picture strip in *Girl*, 'Susan at St Brides', was written by Ruth Adams and illustrated by Peter Kay. Susan was a nurse, a girl with a career who was brave, with a sense of humour and was also a little feisty. She wasn't afraid to answer back if necessary, even to the senior doctors, and became something of a role model for girls who warmed to her sensible,

Woppit.

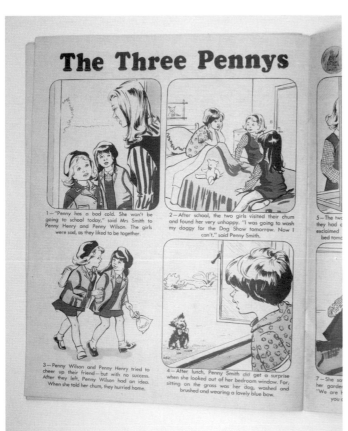

The Three Pennys.

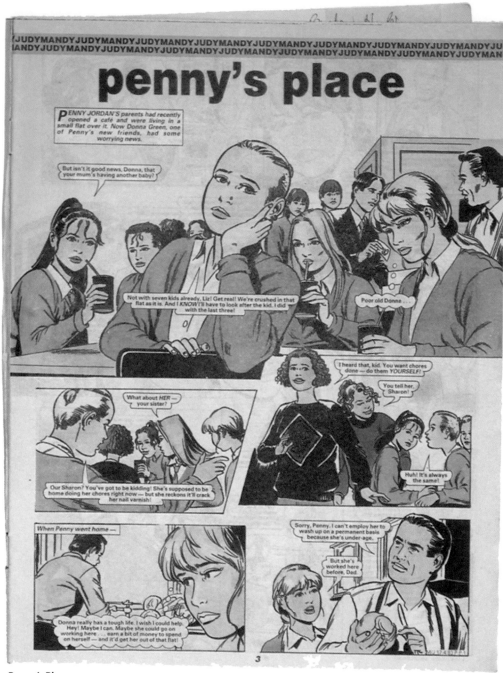

Penny's Place.

stand-up-for-herself attitude to life. From 1955 until the 1960s, Susan nursed her way through *Girl*, and is one of those characters whose personality made her stand out. At the time, nursing was a very popular career for young girls, with adverts for student nurses appearing in many publications.

Toots from Bunty.

Swanky Lanky Liz *(The Dandy)*

Swanky Lanky Liz was a member of the 'Lord Snooty and His Pals' gang in *The Dandy*, which she joined in 1950. Previously she had her own strip. Liz was originally drawn by Dudley Dexter Watkins, one of D.C. Thomson's finest artists, and was the man responsible for the cow-pie eating tough man, Desperate Dan. Earlier, the artist had created that Scottish legend, the cartoon character 'Oor Wullie'. Liz, who was extremely tall and thin, held her nose high in the air. She had long plaits and wore school uniform.

Three Pennys *(Twinkle)*

The Three Pennys were three young girls who all happened to be called Penny. There was Penny Wilson, Penny Henry and Penny Smith. Their gentle adventures were mainly centred around the home environment, with the girls acting out situations they had witnessed and were aimed at pre-schoolers and early primary school age children.

Toots *(The Beano)*

Toots is one of the few girls featured in *The Beano*. She appears in 'The Bash Street Kids', and is Sidney's twin sister. She's the youngest – and the only girl – in the class. *The Beano* tends to be very boy-dominated. Toots is a tomboy, and is sometimes a bit bossy. She is very in to music, wearing her headphones, and in later strips began to take more of a starring role, alongside Danny. 'The Bash Street Kids' picture strip was originally created by Leo Baxendale in 1954, and was known as 'When the Bell Rings'. Two years later, it was renamed 'The Bash Street Kids', and has become one of the favourites in *The Beano*.

Toots *(Bunty)*

Bunty also featured a little girl called Toots, who had her own short comic strip each week. Toots was an amiable small girl who wore a spotted dress. Her hair was short and she sported an enormous bow on top of her head. Bill Ritchie was the artist, and Toots was one of the longer-running characters, appearing from 1958 to 1983.

Wee Sue *(Sandie/Tammy)*

A light-hearted picture strip, which tells of the adventures of Wee Sue, a pupil at Milltown Comprehensive. Wee Sue is shorter than the other pupils, hence her name. Her form teacher is Miss Bigger. Wee Sue appeared in *Sandie* and *Tammy* and was a popular character who made the most of her short stature.

Wendy and Jinx *(Girl)*

Wendy and Jinx, who were best friends at Manor School, were favourites in *Girl*. Later, they took over the front cover page from 'Kitty Hawke and Her All Girl Air Crew'. Wendy was a brunette and Jinx was a blonde, and their adventures, which often involved a bit of sleuthing, were usually school based. Their form mistress was Miss Brumble, who was referred to as Bumble-Bee. The 'Wendy and Jinx' picture strip was written by Stephan James, and was illustrated by Ray Bailey and Philip Townsend.

Woppit *(Robin)*

This little bear-like creature was featured each week in *Robin*, and he soared to fame when a fluffy toy Woppit was adopted by Donald Campbell as a mascot for his *Bluebird*, in which he aimed to break the land speed record. (See Chapter 11.)

Bash Street Kids with Toots, The Beano.

CHAPTER SIX

Teens Go Pop

The pop music culture had its comics for girls, featuring plenty of 'pin-ups' and information about the stars. These comics had names such as *Boyfriend*, while for teens who wanted a little innocent romance, *Romeo*, *Roxy*, *Valentine* and *Cherie* fitted the bill.

Teen Comics

Today, many of the comics published in the 1950s and 60s and aimed at teens, are particularly sought after. It is surprising, in view of the vast numbers of these comics that were sold, how difficult it is to find some of the titles. It seems they were quick reads, which soon dated, and once the pin-up pictures had been ripped out, the rest of the comic was thrown away. Especially collected are those which feature the more popular singers and groups such as the Rolling Stones, Elvis Presley or the Beatles, and though the prices aren't excessive, first editions of many of these titles are certainly rising. The difficulty is to find them in perfect condition – not faded, dog-eared or torn.

Column written by pop singer Mark Wynter for Cherie.

Romeo and Cherie.

Cherie comics are difficult to find.

Romantic picture strip (Romeo).

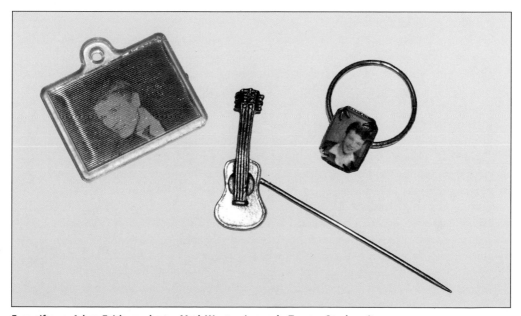

Free gifts; an Adam Faith pendant, a Mark Wynter ring and a Tommy Steele guitar.

Before the 1950s, the teenager didn't exist; or, at least, not by name. Children turned into 'young people' and, as they were usually in work by the age of fifteen, if not before, quickly grew into adults without any interim adolescent interlude. All this changed when post-war culture, mixed with cult movies such as 'The Blackboard Jungle', gave rise to Bill Haley's 'Rock Around the Clock'. Suddenly those between the ages of thirteen and nineteen were a force to be reckoned with.

Manufacturers quickly realised that here was a major untapped source of spending power. Soon clothes, shoes, books, records, gadgets and, of course, comics, appeared, to hopefully capture a slice of this new market. Young people, now officially 'teenagers', revelled in their newfound power and soon developed their own styles and crazes. At long last they didn't need to dress like their parents – there were fashions especially for them. With the music came the pin-ups; crooners, singers and musicians, and the teenagers wanted to read about them. They also needed comics and magazines to reflect their own interests; girls especially were keen to read about romance, fashion, cosmetics, pop and film personalities and to be entertained with fantasy stories that would detract from their often humdrum lives.

The publishers of comics came up trumps, and by the late 1950s and early 1960s, publications such as *Roxy, Romeo, Boyfriend, Cherie, Mirabelle, Valentine, Marty, Serenade* and *Rave* were spilling over on the newsagents stands. These comics took various forms. Some followed the traditional drawn strip cartoon format, though with romantic rather than adventure or humorous stories, while others told similar tales in a series of photographs, using models to act them out. Many magazines included stories based on the lives – or imaginary escapades – of current pop stars. Pull-out double page pin-ups featured pop artists such as Elvis Presley, Cliff Richard, Tommy Steele, Marty Wilde, Mark Wynter, Craig Douglas, Bobby Vee and John Leyton. Slightly later came the groups; The Beatles, Rolling Stones, Billy J Kramer and the Dakotas, Gerry and the Pacemakers, Wayne Fontana and the Mindbenders, Freddie and the Dreamers, The Dave Clark Five, Dave Dee, Dozy, Beaky, Mick and Titch, The Animals and many others. These pin-up photos decorated the walls of teenage girls' bedrooms the length and breadth of Britain.

Several comics employed pop stars to write weekly columns, telling the fans of the concerts they played, their latest records and of various incidents which happened to them or, in the case of *Roxy*, ran a picture story purportedly told by a star, such as one headed 'This story is told by Johnny Duncan himself!' (Who?) Or at least, the star allowed his or her name to be used, even if they didn't actually put pen to paper themselves. If a girl's favourite singer was featured weekly, you could guarantee she would stay loyal to the comic, at least till she went off him, preferring another star instead. The comic enforced this loyalty even more by the use of free gifts (see Chapter 8), often relating to the comic's pop star column writer or to other current musical favourites. These gifts could include rings, pendants, picture cards, booklets, thin plastic records that really played, brooches, combs or items of make-up. Another vital ingredient of a comic was the problem page (see Chapter 9), which gave helpful advice to those teenagers brave enough to write in regarding their insecurities, whether boyfriend troubles or spotty skin worries. Most of these comics appealed to the younger teens, perhaps up to the age of sixteen. At this age, a girl normally felt slightly above the world of comics; by now she was settled in her job in an office, shop or factory. She would graduate to buying either fanzines (*The Beatles, Rolling Stones*) or more general pop magazines (*Rave*) to pop-based newspapers; *New Musical Express* (*NME*), *Disc* or *Record Mirror*, which would provide an overall guide to the pop music scene of the day.

Author and pin-ups, 1960s

A typical magazine story of the time would feature 'Mandy' or 'Lynne' or 'Sue' yearning for 'Dave' or 'Mick' or 'Paul', telling of how she thwarted a rival by making the boy jealous (i.e. pretending she had found a new boyfriend) or had discovered her rival was two-timing, already married, a writer of malicious letters or had 'a past'. The latter was obviously something unpleasant, and was never dealt with in detail, leaving the reader to imagine all kinds of things (if she could, for most girls of the time were quite innocent). Sometimes the stories told of girls aiming to be models, film stars, stewardesses or pop singers, but invariably there was a (tall, handsome) male involved. However, this was the fifties/sixties, so the stories were invariably moral, with happy endings. The device of creating a tale around the title of a popular song of the time in pop-based comics was especially used in *Valentine* (Amalgamated Press). *Valentine* was first introduced in 1957, and was to prove one of the more successful of the romantic comics, continuing for twenty years.

Compared with many of today's comics, which are often quite explicit and are bought by children who might not even be into their teens, the stories, queries and features were harmless, and would cause little to upset even the most staid maiden aunt. Very much of their day, these romantic picture papers and pop-slanted comics are now quite collectable, especially titles such as *Cherie* and *Marty*. Considering the huge amounts that must have been sold at the time it seems comparatively few have survived, as opposed to say, *Bunty* or *Girl* comics. Perhaps, unlike the picture papers for younger girls, those intended for teens were regarded as too shallow and temporal to keep for re-reading; they were very much of the moment. Also, because pop stars had a tendency to fall quickly from favour, the comics soon dated and would then have been discarded, unless the girl stayed steadfast to her favourite. Probably, in the case of the pin-up type magazines, the middle portrait pages were detached and fastened to the wall, and the rest of the comic relegated to the bin, because there was no recycling in those days. Today, these teen reads provide an intriguing insight to those now-distant decades, revealing a world of beehive hairdos, sooty-lashed eyes, white pouting lips, dated fashions and innocence. No computers, mobile phones, BlackBerrys or iPods to be seen, just pictures of youths dancing, singing and chatting. It was a different world.

Adverts

As always with old comics, the adverts are an intriguing bonus, often mirroring life at the time with items we no longer use or require. For the princely sum of £9.19.6 (just under £10 in today's money), a girl could buy a Westminster record player, exclusive to Currys. The advert boasted the 'Latest 4-speed motor plays records of all sizes. Large built-in speaker and adjustable tone for crystal clear reproduction. Twin sapphire styli, Ultra light-weight case. Guaranteed! At a record low price!' If the girl couldn't afford one, and was really desperate, she could put down a 10/- deposit, and then pay 37 weekly payments of 5/9, giving a grand total of £11.4.7 (£11.23).

Other adverts encouraged a young girl to apply Clearasil which 'Ends Embarrassment. Starves Pimples' to her skin, to use Cuticura products – soap, medicated liquid and talcum – and to take Anadin for her period pains, which would also calm nerves and lift depression. She was urged to listen to Radio Luxembourg highlights on 208 – notably the Honey Hit Parade – and to pay for everything she needed by becoming an agent for a mail order catalogue. 'As a Day's agent you can make pounds in your spare time. No experience needed!' *Roxy* advertised duster macs and full circle felt skirts (low deposit and 9 fortnightly payments), Voxette tape-recorders (only £11.19.6), cross-over overalls, smocks and pinarettes (3 for 5/11), and 'Rock 'n' Roll guitars cash price £6.6.0', with a free coloured skiffle sash! (See also Chapter 8.)

Here are some of the popular comics and comic-type magazines from the 1950s/60s. There were other, slightly later titles, including *Petticoat* and *Trend*, which were really magazines and so fall outside the scope of this book.

Boyfriend

This bright and breezy pop publication, *Boyfriend*, by Proprietors City Magazines first appeared on 16 May 1959, and of course, even the name was an instant attraction. Now girls' could honestly say they had a boyfriend, even when they hadn't. Its gravure style set it apart from the others, right from the start, and although it contained a token one or two story strips, it was obvious that the magazine's focus lay elsewhere. This was a pop magazine; it was different and very colourful – at least on the outside – though the inside was still mono, apart of course, from the piéce de résistance, the pin-up. Inside, the centre pages were given over to one large colour photograph of a pop star or group. This move was sheer genius; all girls wanted pin-up pictures, and the centre pages of *Boyfriend* must have decorated thousands of bedroom walls throughout the country.

The issue dated 27 June 1964 has a small photo of singing duo Peter and Gordon on the front cover, alongside a message to say that they were inside in 'supersize colour'. Also on the cover was a picture strip called, 'Come On In, the Water's Dangerous', about Lucy, a girl who loved swimming but it didn't seem the thing to do on holiday – all her friends wanted to do was sunbathe. Eventually though, a boy does venture in but gets into difficulties so Lucy rescues him. He had gone into the deep water to try to impress her, even though he was a poor swimmer. Of course, it all ended happily. The other picture strip in this issue is 'If I Can't Have You This Year' and featured a girl who had her sights set on a sophisticated, slightly older man, who didn't notice her. After trying various ways to change herself and catch his attention, she realised that she was being silly, and decided to stay with her friends instead. There was also a text-only serial, 'When the Town Fell Down' but no author was listed. Most of the magazine, though, consisted of articles, such as 'Flowery But Sincere', which explained fashion and why you should be careful how you wore large flower print dresses. It included a straight shift dress, declaring, 'The colour choice is way out' – at the time this meant that it was highly fashionable. *Boyfriend* continued until 12 March 1966, when it combined with *Trend*. For a few weeks until 7 May 1966, the comic was known as *Trend and Boyfriend*. It then switched names to become *Boyfriend and Trend*, from 14 May 1966 and this title continued until 2 September 1967. There are numerous complications then, as *Trend* later combined with *Petticoat*, and so really, *Boyfriend* by then had disappeared.

Cherie

Of all the teen magazines available in the 1960s, *Cherie* was my favourite, without a doubt – not least because my favourite pop singer, Mark Wynter, had a regular column inside.

Cherie wasn't as well known as *Roxy*, *Romeo* or *Valentine*, and today it is one of the hardest of the teen comics to find. It was a D. C. Thomson publication first issued in 1960. A browse through a couple of issues from 1962 reveals there is a lot of reading packed into its 28 pages, and though, today, the paper looks an inferior quality, then we accepted it because it was the norm for so many comics, especially the teen romances. After all, comics were ethereal – no one, it was thought, would want a comic once it had been read. How wrong they were – today collectors snap up publications such as these.

This mix of stories and features includes (in issue 67, 6 January 1962) a front-page story 'Sailor Beware of Love' coloured in *Cherie*'s usual red/blue/black inks. This story tells of a feisty girl who, while rummaging under the engine of her taxicab, has her bottom slapped by a passing sailor. In his defence, he mistook her for his Uncle Seth (or so he says). She is

Inside Cherie.

annoyed, and, it turns out, runs a rival cab service, doing her best to sabotage the one the sailor is now working for, as he is deputising for Uncle Seth who is ill. As the sailor uses phrases such as, 'Hi Unky, my old porpoise' 'What happened, Sethie, old pip' and 'Cool off sweetie, give us a nice big smile', it's unsurprising he gets on her nerves. Later, he puts her over his knee and spanks her and hangs her from some railings by her dungaree straps – so I was most disappointed when she decided she liked him and would marry him! Most of the stories end with wedding bells – that's what a girl wanted in those days. The serials were 'Cindy Lee', set in a hospital and 'Paula and the Student', a girl who meets up with a student and falls in love but 'he was more interested in a gay time'. (In this day and age, it adds a different connotation to the story.) Another serial was 'Lady Catherine's Secret Lover', set in Tudor times. One of the favourite stories, 'Three Girls in a Flat', is missing from this issue, but reappears in the 26 May copy.

With letters, problems, 'Secrets of the Stars', which explained that singer Eden Kane was known in America as 'the Hully Gully guy', a feature on best fashion and beauty buys, an article on men's ties, and of course, that half-page by Mark Wynter, *Cherie* was an entertaining read for 5d. Sadly, it only ran for three years before being swallowed up by *Romeo*.

Marilyn

An Amalgamated Press publication first introduced in March 1955, *Marilyn* was probably named after Marilyn Monroe, and was quite a popular name at the time. It was the first of the teen romance comics, and opened the floodgates for plenty more. Comics such as these were perfect for the girls who had moved on from *Bunty*, *Girl* and the like and who were beginning to have thoughts about boys, romance and, of course, white lace and wedding veils. A 1958 copy features just one colour, red, on the cover, and the main picture of a front-page story shows a young man (they mostly wore smart suits and slicked back, side-parted hair in those days) aggressively demanding that a girl should go with him to the Carnival Dance. Her dilemma is that three men have asked her; who should she choose? Easy-peasy – she babysat for her sister instead, and the three men came round; two were angry but the third helped babysit, so she chose him.

Incidentally, when reading through comics such as this the change in today's attitudes is striking. As well the obvious instance of the word 'gay', which has completely changed context today and which is used extensively in these early comics in its original meaning of lively and carefree, men's attitudes towards women would not be tolerated today. Admittedly, the 'good guys' are shown as kind, thoughtful, maybe a little shy – but some of the men are quite abusive towards women. They grab them, spank them, order them around and are generally masterful, yet in many cases women accept this behaviour without question. Formality is paramount, in many case, even in the 1950s and 1960s, older friends are referred to by the titles Mr or Mrs, while men open doors and carry parcels for their womenfolk. In the story above, the man who helped with the babysitting told the girl she could go to the dance and he would stay with the children. Can you imagine the uproar today if a young man, unknown to the youngsters' parents, was left alone in the house with two small children? In the event, she didn't go, but even so it just shows how trusting we once were, and how much has been lost to us today.

Back to the comic – there were three picture strips, two serials and a longer-length text 'powerful love story' called 'My Man Martin', but the author isn't credited. An American

Romantic comics.

influence is extremely noticeable, especially in speech – 'Tab Talking', a general chat column, is packed with expressions such as 'Man Alive!', 'Y'know how it is, honey', 'We'd got the gramophone, kid. But he sure got the needle!' and 'Say, kid, get your bonnet ready'. Jim Dale (he was a pop star then, not an actor) has a column called 'Spin That Pop', discussing Johnny Mathis, Sarah Vaughan, Michael Holliday and ATV's *Cool for Cats* programme. Beauty hints, astrology column, problem page and best of all from today's viewpoint, all those wonderful old adverts (See Chapter 8) for products such as Twink perms and 'Figure flattering tapered tartan slacks', gave superb value for 4d. A rather authoritative advert in *Marilyn* states, 'When you buy Marilyn you must buy Roxy'. No doubt most girls obeyed. *Marilyn* ran for an impressive ten years before becoming incorporated into *Valentine* in 1965.

Marty

Marty was an independent comic, published by C. Arthur Pearson, and the first issue was produced 23 January 1960. Presumably named after popular singer Marty Wilde, who was featured on the front cover of the first issue, it was billed as 'the first ever photo romance weekly'. As this sub-title indicates, the stories were told using photographs of models who acted out the situations. It was innovative, and many other publications followed suit. However, the photographic trend wasn't to everyone's taste, not least the artists who gradually found themselves out of work as the fad spread. As well as the photo strips, the comic included features, a letters/queries page and pop news. *Marty* was moderately successful, with a run of just over three years. It became incorporated with *Mirabelle* in 1963.

Mirabelle

Mirabelle started out as a romantic magazine for woman, but soon changed into a typical early sixties' picture strip comic. Initially published by an independent company, C. Arthur Pearson, in 1956, it later passed to IPC. It was to incorporate romantic magazines *Marty* in 1963 and *Valentine* 11 years later in 1974. Featuring a full-colour cover, a back page pin-up photo, and several photos inside, this is much more modern looking than *Marilyn*, *Roxy* and others of that ilk. A 1964 issue reveals a 30-page magazine with five drawn picture strips, while the centre pages are given over to a free pull-out Disc-Star date birthday book. The strips are light romance, and of course, the girls look far more modern than those depicted in the more formal *Marilyn* – although the men still smoke pipes. The features are all pop based apart from a problem page. They include an article on Manfred Mann, who explained with refreshing honesty, 'We don't make records for fun, we try for a hit because we like lots of money and hit records bring in the money.' On the back is a colour portrait of the group the Kinks. In 1977, *Mirabelle* was merged with *Pink* after an excellent run of 21 years.

Romeo

Another of D. C. Thomson's excursions into the field of light romance, for a while *Romeo* ran alongside *Cherie*, though had a much longer run. *Romeo* was introduced in 1957, and boasted, unlike many other romance comics of the time, a full-colour cover. An issue dated 30 July 1960 which cost 4d, contains four picture stories and three serials, one, 'Lucille', being based on the classic novel 'Lady of the Camellias'. Three of the stories end in weddings, and they are all light-hearted. There is also an American-type cartoon strip

on the back cover called 'Pam', and another, illustrated in more of a comical-style called 'Scooter Annie and her Pal Lou'. Letters, show-biz information and fan club column provide plenty of extra reading. Eight years later, *Romeo* was still the same length of 28 pages, but there was more proper content as the show-biz questions and fan clubs had been dropped. There were even three text-only stories, 'Green Eyes' by Sheila Crowson', 'Heaven on Earth' by Anthony Finucane and the intriguingly titled 'Marriage of the Young Girl with High Boots and Silver Hair' by Barbara Nash. An article called 'Poise and Girls Go Together' explains the correct way to stand and differentiates between 'The Shuffle-Scuffler', 'The Stair-Strider' and 'The Stand-Up Sloucher' while an odd creation called 'Thumbking' comments on reader's letters. With a problem page, prize competition, crossword puzzle, poems written to pop stars, feature on The Batchelors singing duo and a back-page pin-up picture of Tony Blackburn, even though the price was now 6d, it was still a good buy! In 1973 *Romeo* changed style and became more of a magazine with lots of features and pop stars, but in 1974, after a run of over 17 years, it was incorporated into *Diana*.

Roxy

One of the earliest of the pop comics was entitled *Roxy*, and the first issue, dated 15 March 1958, and priced at 4d, gave away a silver guitar pin, 'Free with every copy. Tommy Steele's Lucky Little Guitar'; as the cover announced. *Roxy*, a weekly romance for girls was another Amalgamated Press comic, and it's possible that it took its name from the *Roxy* cinema chains, because during the 1950s and early 1960s, cinemas were the most popular places for dates. Tommy Steele introduced the story on the front page of that first issue, and each week a different star featured on the cover alongside the declaration, 'This story is told to you by (name) himself!' The covers of *Roxy* featured a black and white story strip, small photo of the star in question, and a bright green background. This unusual choice of colouring ensured that it stood out in the newsagents' shops.

With 28 pages, *Roxy* provided plenty of reading matter for teens, and was a mix of picture strips and star features. The strips were fairly long, some spread over six pages, such as 'Let's Talk It Over', from 8 November 1958, which centred on a girl running a transport café, which gets into financial difficulties. The café was saved by a handsome trucker, who also married the girl. Another story, 'Kisses Sweeter than Wine', told the story of a girl kissed by a stranger at a film club, but she didn't know who it was. How could she find out? Alma Cogan's 'Glamour School' featured beauty hints and tips, while Marty Wilde revealed the secret of 'My Two Wonderful Years'. Johnny Duncan introduced the front-page picture strip while a serial, 'Dangerous Near Him' was an exciting adventure-romance, telling of Anne, a girl who has met up with an old friend, Bruce, in South America. Bruce is about to be shot because he has defied Don Carlos the cruel dictator. Unfortunately, *Roxy* proved to be one of the more short-lived of comics. Even so, it managed to run for five and a half years before becoming incorporated into *Valentine* in 1963.

Serenade

The comic *Serenade* was an extremely short-lived comic for teenage girls, and the first issue dated 22 September 1962 contained a free gift of a record. I remember playing the record over and over, chiefly because it featured Cliff Richard telling us about the new comic, and began, 'Hi there, this is Cliff!' It wasn't a proper record, it was very thin clear plastic, so I stuck mine onto a piece of cardboard to make it more durable, and have it still.

Rare plastic free record from first issue of Serenade.

Romantic picture strip from Cherie.

Serenade was published by Fleetway Publications, and was more of a pop-based comic than a story-based magazine. It was colourful: instead of the primary colours of reds, blues and greens which most of the teen comics used, this one used pinks, turquoises and pastels too. That first issue featured a front-page colour-strip story, a photo of Cliff Richard and a promise that inside was, 'Free! A disc from Cliff'. Using the terminology of the time, the headers announced such slogans as, 'It's New, It's Great, It's Swinging', and we were promised that inside was 'fashion, beauty and showbiz'. Sadly, this lively and colourful publication ran for just four and a half months before being incorporated into *Valentine* in February 1963.

Valentine

There was plenty of reading in this 40-page comic, which first saw the light of day at the beginning of 1957. Published by Fleetway Publications, it cost 5d and was available every Monday. The covers featured a black and white picture strip with a light blue border and header. Under the title, Valentine (written in white script) was the motto, 'Brings you love stories in pictures'. And it did. Lots of them. The cover songs were inspired by various pop songs, and a photo of the artist who sang the song was pictured alongside the story. This device was also used for many of the stories inside the comic.

In the issue dated 13 January 1962, the front page is based on the song 'Best Time For Love' sung by Mark Wynter. A small photo of the singer is on the front, while the black and white drawings and captions tell of a young girl holidaying in France but dreaming of a boy called Jimmy with whom she had broken up. All ends well, of course, and the lovers are reunited. Inside the comic, further stories are inspired by *Like In Love*, sung by Edie Gorme and Steve Lawrence, *I'll Step Down* by Gary Mills, *Come With Me* (Doug Sheldon) and The McGuire Sisters' *Melody of Love*. Also inside the magazine is a centre-page spread of singing idol Bobby Vee, pages of letters and advice, and several adverts. An earlier issue of *Valentine*, dating from 1958, features fashion and several pages of answers to reader's questions about singers and film stars. Stories include those based on *Only Forever* by Dean Martin, *Heartless* by David Whitfield, *Move It* by Cliff Richard and several others whose names are now long-forgotten. There is a centre page pin-up picture of Marty Wilde, and an article about the success of Ricky Nelson, tipped to be the next Elvis. As with many other teen magazines, continental artists such as Jordi Longaron did much of the illustration. Towards the end of the 1960s, *Valentine* changed its style somewhat, including more of the magazine-type articles, and less serials, concentrating on complete stories. It now looked much more modern than when compared to its old, 1950s self. Even so, sales dwindled, and it was finally combined with *Mirabelle* at the end of 1974. However, during its run, *Valentine* had incorporated several other romance magazines, amongst them *Roxy*, *Marilyn* and *Serenade*, proving itself to have been one of the most popular of the early teen romance comics.

CHAPTER SEVEN

Part-Works

Sometimes these build into reference works, while often they contain dolls or outfits with each issue, enabling a girl to form a collection. The idea seems comparatively recent, and the current trend of gift-attached part-works probably started with *The Adventures Of Vicky*, first published in the 1980s by Fabbri, though there were earlier part-works, such as *Golden Hands*, which formed encyclopaedias, and *Discovery*.

Part-works are an interesting form of comics/magazines, and are a special, luxury read for children who enjoy building up the sets of magazines as well as acquiring the free attachments. In some titles these giveaways can be exceptionally collectable. Although nowadays many comics have a free gift with each issue, these gifts are usually ephemeral – plastic jewellery, booklets, sweets or hair decorations. However, the part-works will have dolls, dolls' clothes or teddy bears attached; items which are worth keeping. Amongst the dozens of part-works' titles are some that have appealed to girls, and these I will mention

Part-works.

as examples of what to look for. A few of the titles and their gifts have become quite collectable, notably *The Adventures of Vicky* and *Discover The World With Barbie*. At the end of this book you will find an appendix listing the various dolls, outfits and toys that came with many of the girl-orientated part-works.

Part-works lengths vary, but are typically between 30-60 issues, normally fortnightly, though some are weekly. Some part-works are much shorter, just half-a-dozen issues or so, while some can run for several years. Usually, the first issue or two is sold at a knock down price to hook the reader, and then the price will return to a much higher figure. Usually, too, the first issue will contain an extra special giveaway: a doll if the series is a doll/outfits collectable series, or a bear if the topic is teddy outfits, for example. Often, the dolls were made from porcelain, and some were of exquisite quality, notably those from *The World of Disney Princesses* (De Agostini). Other doll titles were *Porcelain Dolls* (De Agostini), *Adventures of Vicky* (Fabbri), *Dora Dress Up and Go* (Fabbri) and *Dolls of the World* (Eaglemoss).

It's as well to keep in mind that, with most of these part-works, newsagents will normally only stock the earlier issues. This is to encourage regular readers to take out a subscription. Consequently, this means that people can't buy random copies that happen to catch their eye, and so the later copies of a part-work are invariably harder to find. Many part-works, though aimed at children, are an interesting collecting field for adults, as not only do you receive lots of comics, you also can start a collection of dolls, bears or other items.

Adventures of Vicky (The)

Published by a company called Fabbri in 1991, unrelated, so I am told, to G. E. Fabbri who publish many part-works and comics, *The Adventures of Vicky* was an attractive fortnightly magazine aimed at, presumably, the 6-11 age group. It was expensive for the time, selling at £3.50, which was way above the average pocket money, so unless she had indulgent parents, a girl was unlikely to acquire a full set. Each issue was themed, falling into one of four main topics – Science and Nature, Living in the Past, Jobs People Do and Countries of the World – so the scope of the magazine was a bit muddled. Sometimes Vicky went exploring through time or investigated new careers, while in other issues she travelled the world, but whatever she did, she needed a costume fit for the occasion.

The magazine featured Vicky's adventures and seemed aimed at girls in the 6-11 age group. It consisted of plenty of advice, tips, photographs, drawings, games, puzzles, strip cartoons, and quizzes. Packed with interesting information, it painlessly passed on knowledge while the child thought she was just enjoying a good read. On the back page was Vicky's Diary, a clever idea consisting of a blank section for the child to fill in after reading the comic. This ensured that she really did read it and didn't just look at the pictures. There was also a project such as a necklace to make or a recipe to follow. Everything fitted into the theme of the issue. For instance, issue one shows Vicky dressed in a safari outfit, and the cover

Vicky (Actress).

announced, 'Find out more about: Science and Nature, Jobs People Do, Living in the Past, Countries of the World' – one of the themed topics mentioned previously.

The first issue of *The Adventures of Vicky* was subtitled 'Vicky on Safari', and was the most vital issue of the series, because it had the teen doll, Vicky, attached to the front of the magazine in a box. She wore a safari suit and had a rucksack and other accessories. All the other magazines in the series had outfits on the cover, so if you needed another doll you had to buy the first issue direct from the publishers. The doll given free with *The Adventures of Vicky* was an 11in-tall plastic teen doll, and though unmarked, is easy to recognise today with her straight blonde hair, sweetly smiling mouth, painted eyes, and distinctive freckles across her cheeks and the bridge of her nose. She was an attractive doll, though not particularly well made.

The following issue featured Vicky at the stables, so attached to the magazine was a riding outfit complete with hard hat and boots, while issue three contained a particularly pretty Tudor outfit. Amongst the subsequent outfits were pop star, ballerina, astronaut, Ancient Rome toga and a cowgirl. The outfits were well made and, often, unusual. If a girl didn't have a Vicky, then the outfits would fit a similar sized teen doll. Today, the doll has been discovered by enthusiasts who go to great lengths to search out Vicky dolls and all

Adventures of Vicky Issue 1 (Safari).

the little bits and pieces which make up the outfits. The magazines, too, are beginning to be collectable, especially if the costumes are still attached, and that very first Safari issue, complete with doll, can reach a high price. Also keenly sought after are the rare costumes dating from the later issues. As with most part-works, after a few issues had been sold in the newsagents, they reverted to being sold on subscription. Therefore, sales were more limited. (See Appendix)

Angelina's Fairy Tales

First published by G. E. Fabbri in 2003, this delightful part-work, *Angelina's Fairy Tales*, was based on the ballet dancing mouse character and her friends dreamt up by Katharine Holabird and Helen Craig. The first issue contained Angelina, a mouse soft toy, and subsequent issues came with either an outfit, or, occasionally, one of her friends. The outfits, all sized to fit Angelina, were based on fairy tale ballets, and were charming. Each issue cost £2.60 and the magazines were issued fortnightly. Inside each issue, which was themed to the costume attached, was the story of the ballet, such as Giselle, and articles on dressing up, items to cut out to prepare for a show, puzzles, games and craft makes. (See Appendix.)

Discover the World With Barbie

This part-work proved so successful that the initial run was extended. Published by Eaglemoss in 2003, *Discover the World With Barbie* featured dozens of beautiful costumes, but it never had a doll attached, not even to the first issue. Maybe they assumed that all girls had a Barbie, or similar, already. They were probably right, and if she didn't have one, well, basic Barbies were so cheap and easy to buy.

Discover the World With Barbie.

Barbie outfit from the part work
(California).

The magazine's theme was that of Barbie travelling the world, so of course she needed the appropriate costumes. Sometimes they were a take on a national costume, but more often they were glamorous outfits associated with the country or suitable to wear at a grand event there, such as a ball or visit to an opera house. Most of the outfits were well made and full of detail, for instance the Canadian set with its fluffy pink hooded coat, pink trousers and white jumper, or the creative yellow Charleston outfit, which Barbie needed for a trip to Chicago. The Hawaiian multi-coloured flower-strewn raffia skirt and the Scottish red dress with green bodice and tartan trim were attractive too. Many older girls, who might have long-stopped playing with dolls, subscribed to this series – in fact, many adult Barbie collectors did as well, often buying basic Barbie dolls in bulk, and dressing them in the free outfits. This method provided a collector with an instant, stunning doll collection. (See Appendix)

Dolls of the World

Some magazines gave a free doll with every issue. *Dolls of the World*, published by Eaglemoss in 1999 had a pretty 8in-high porcelain doll attached to the cover of each issue in a clear plastic bubble to protect it whilst it was on the newsagent's shelves. These magazines were issued fortnightly and cost £4.50. Each doll was beautifully and colourfully dressed in a national costume and so a comprehensive collection could soon be assembled. The accompanying magazine was excellent, with information regarding the featured country and the names of the garments that the dolls wore, plus articles on various aspects of doll making, but there was a slight drawback. Although perfect for young girls, porcelain wasn't the ideal medium for children to play with, while many adult collectors don't rate foreign costume dolls very highly. Even so, the idea was good, and though the dolls might not have held much appeal to the more traditional adult doll collectors, from the point of view of teaching girls about the history and customs of foreign lands, the concept was ideal. (See Appendix.)

Dora Dress Up and Go

In 2007 the youngsters' favourite, Dora the Explorer, was chosen to star in her very own magazine, *Dora Dress Up and Go*. One of the G. E. Fabbri publications, the first issue came with a free Ty Beany plush Dora doll attached to a cardboard sleeve. Dora wore orange shorts, a pink top and carried a backpack. Subsequent issues had assorted costumes, amongst them a cowgirl, surfer, pirate and ice skater. Each issue was themed to the costume given free that week. For instance, issue no. 2, 'Ice Skating Fiesta', included instructions on how to make your own tiara, as well as a pond, icy trees and a rosette for Dora. The various puzzles and pictures to colour are ice-themed, and you are even taught a few words of Spanish. (See Appendix.)

Felicity Wishes

Felicity Wishes was based on a fairy character, Felicity, who was featured in a series of books by Emma Thomson. The fortnightly part-work was published by G.E. Fabbri in 2007, cost £2.99, and each issue showed another of Felicity's career wishes coming true. Some of her wishes scattered through the 32 parts of the magazine were very unusual, and it's interesting to see how much they varied from Vicky's aspirations of 16 years before. Amongst other things, Felicity wished she was a theme park attendant, eco-worker, bee keeper, perfume designer, weather girl, shoe designer, inventor and butterfly house attendant. Even so, Felicity did have some things in common with Vicky; she too wanted to be a journalist, actress, pop star, ballerina and chef. It seems some dreams never change. The first issue of the magazine came with a pretty Felicity fairy doll, and subsequent issues had an appropriate career outfit attached. The magazine itself was full of puzzles, things to make, stories and ideas for activities. (See Appendix.)

Magic of Ballet

Along with pony riding, ballet must be one of the most loved interests of the primary school child, so a part-work magazine based on the ballet theme could not fail. Eaglemoss produced *Magic of Ballet* in 2007, an interesting publication filled with all things ballet. It contained features on hairstyles, costume, ballet techniques, stage make-up, theatrical knowledge and a ballet diary, as well as recipes, craft makes and quizzes. Each fortnightly issue had a gift attached, and these were pretty girlie things such as ballet charms, bracelets, necklaces, make-up and hair ornaments. The magazine continued for 60 issues. Subscribers were given an extra free gift of a pretty make-up tin box, which could be used to house the gifts of make-up that came with some of the magazines.

Porcelain Dolls

This part work by De Agostini entitled *Porcelain Dolls* contained plenty of interesting articles about the various doll manufactures, especially those which made bisque china. It analysed dolls and their makers, looking at the various types of doll, and the companies, for instance the German bisque factories. Each issue had a small porcelain doll or, sometimes, a traditional-looking item attached, such as a see-saw, pushchair, cradle or pram. Often, there were two items, for example issue no. 2 contained 'Sally, an Adventurous Spirit' and her see-saw, while issue 4 had baby Emma and her wicker pram. (See Appendix.)

Teddy Bear Collection

This excellent part work, *Teddy Bear Collection*, from Eaglemoss, dating from 2000, consisted of no less than 80 teddy bears. Each fortnightly magazine described the various bear companies, the history of bears, displaying bears, famous bears and bear-making techniques and cost £4.50. With every magazine came a dressed teddy bear, which was very well made with plenty of attention to detail. The bears represented all kinds of characters, and amongst them were 'Alphonse the Artist', 'Milo the Milkman', 'Sidney the Scientist', 'Giogio the Gondolier' and 'Hugo the Harelquin'. Each 9in-high seated bear bore a tag which read 'The Teddy Bear Collection' and described the bear. For instance, the tag for Alphonse the Artist reads, 'Alphonse is a two-tone bear. He is dressed in a traditional French artist's smock and beret. His paint brushes are tucked into his pocket and he carries a palette of paints in his paw.' Bob the Baseball Player has a tag which says, 'His team shirt is red and white and he has a cap to make. Make this hitter of home runs part of your team.' (See Appendix.)

Wonderful World of Sindy

When the fortnightly magazine, *Wonderful World of Sindy*, suddenly appeared in the shops in 2007, collectors were really excited – here was a magazine which was giving away a retro Sindy doll with each issue. Even more exiting, she was dressed in a copy of a classic Sindy outfit. In all, four issues appeared – and then it was stopped. Hachette, in conjunction with Pedigree, had been carrying out a trial run in certain areas, and it's to be hoped that it proved successful enough to be viable as a future part-work series. Each 16-page magazine contained information about Sindy, and also about the happenings of the relevant year in which the costume was first issued. The dolls, though not such good quality as the originals, still bore an amazing likeness. Attached to the first issue was a Royal Occasion Sindy, dating from 1977. Further issues contained a 1975 Sindy Nurse, a 1974 Sunsuit Sindy and a Fashion Girl from 1972. Although other issues were advertised the trial then stopped, but hopefully the part-work will be issued in due course.

Wonderful World of Teddy Bears

The *Wonderful World of Teddy Bears* first appeared in 2000, published by De Agostini. The magazine was an excellent read which contained such items as articles on various makers of bears, and different categories of bears such as those made famous in the literary world. Each issue cost £3.99, and was published fortnightly. It was a mixture of collectables and crafts – every fourth issue, subscribers received a bear, while the issues in between contained either a paper pattern and pieces of fabric, or items of clothing and accessories, to make each bear a themed outfit, including bride, holiday or schoolgirl. The items were

Dolls of the World.

Magic of Ballet and makeup box.

Teddy Bear Collection.

Wonderful World of Sindy.

Porcelain dolls.

Wonderful World of Teddy Bears.

World of Disney Princesses, Snow White.

cleverly chosen, so that they overlapped – with the last piece of an item, you would also receive some of the pieces required for the next bear, so you never felt you wanted to stop taking the magazine. Each bear was 9in high and labelled 'Venus Promotions'. In all there were 20 bears. (See Appendix)

World of Disney Princesses

From the collector's point of view, the *World of Disney Princesses* part-work was a winner. Originally trialled for a few issues, it appeared a couple of years later in the newsagents as a fortnightly magazine and cost £5.99. It was published by De Agostini. Each copy came with a porcelain Disney character, and the attention to detail was really remarkable. Every doll was carefully modelled to represent the character it portrayed, and it was evident that enormous thought had been put into this series. The set included many unusual Disney characters, such as Triton from *Little Mermaid*, as well as the more usual favourites. Interestingly, issues in some other countries included dolls which weren't available in the UK issues. (See Appendix)

Porcelain Dolls.

CHAPTER EIGHT

Freebies and Clubs

Free Gifts and Join the Club Freebies kept the readers happy – rings, bracelets, make-up and booklets. At one time, it seemed every comic had its own club page with a badge, list of rules and secret code or sign. Why was this so popular, and what purpose did it serve? Did it encourage loyalty to one particular comic?

Free Inside!

With a plethora of comics on the newsagent's counter, it was necessary to catch a child's eye, to make a comic stand out. This needed to be a device which would encourage her to deviate from her usual comic, or maybe, if she wasn't a regular buyer of comics, something which would urge her to buy this particular issue. Hopefully, then, she would enjoy it so much that she would continue to buy it each week. Sometimes this could be brought about by a particularly bright or attractive front cover, or perhaps a promotional price, but more usually, the ruse was to include a free gift.

New comics were often launched by a free gift, and gifts were sometimes given for issue two and issue three as well. Free gifts were also given from time to time to ensure the comic retained the readers' loyalty. Another ruse was to form an 'exclusive club', often with its own secret code or sign. A nominal payment was charged, and readers sent in their postal orders for the required amount. In turn, they would receive a badge (many of the earlier ones were often attractive, enamel affairs, though later, tinplate became more usual), a codebook and a letter of welcome from the club 'chief'. Each week, the comic would have a club page or section, which would include a 'secret message' in code, and usually a list of forthcoming members' birthdays. Sometimes there might be pictures of members, or competitions exclusive to members, or even 'lucky names' of members – it was a clever ruse to make the members feel privileged and special. Naturally they wanted to buy the comic each week in case their name was mentioned. Just think how dreadful it would be if you lapsed, your name was listed, and you missed out on a prize.

Free With This Issue!

Bill McLoughlin from D.C. Thomson explained that the gifts given away with comics were a regular thing, though generally happened just twice a year, in spring and autumn. March and September were the popular months, but, certainly in the boys' papers when a collection of cards or collectables were being given away, the push often started in February and went on through March. The frequency varied, although competitions with a manufacturer were common in the summer. He has a vague recollection of a competition for which the prize was a Moulton bicycle; at the time this would have been an amazing prize for any youngster, and most certainly an incentive to buy a copy of the comic.

Free gifts.

Rosebud Ring from Judy.

Troll Brooch from Tina.

Dainty Doggie Ring, Bunty.

Pre-war free gifts.

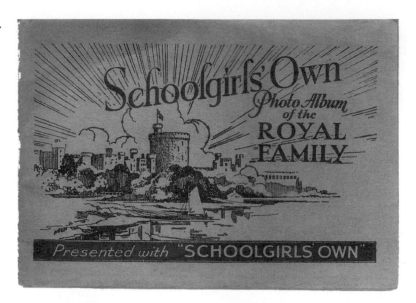

Nowadays, free gifts in girls' comics can be quite substantial, and might include dolls, dolls clothes, purses, make-up items, lockets, brushes and notebooks. In the 1950s and 60s, girls were satisfied with plastic trinkets such as bangles, combs, rings, lucky charms or headbands. Other popular gifts were embroidery transfers or small booklets. Sometimes, pop-related memorabilia was given away – *Cherie* included a lucky Mark Wynter 'love ring' in their issue dated 21 October 1961 (issue 56, cost 5d), while the first issue of *Roxy* (15 March 15 1958) contained an elegant silver-coloured Tommy Steele guitar pin, which was engraved TS on the back. Items from other comics include Adam Faith lenticular pendants, small picture lockets, pin-up posters (especially from *Boyfriend*, which featured full-colour centre-page pictures each week), booklets of pop information, song lyric sheets and sticker books. (See Chapter 6.)

Bangles made from coloured plastic were the free gift in *Blue Jeans*, 28 May 1977, while in the 1968 September 11th issue of *Mandy*, the free gift was 'The Forget-Me-Not Book for Addresses and Birthdays'. In 1962, *Judy* gave away free 'Rosebud Rings', which had a pale pink pearly stone – I still have mine!

Badges

Some of the club badges were most attractive. The majority bear the name of the comic, though some assume they will be automatically recognised and consist just of a logo. Some badges are more easily found than others; those of *Girl* and *Bunty*, for instance, would have had a much wider membership than, say, *June*. One of my favourite badges is the *Bunty* enamelled Scottie dog, dating from the 1950s to the 1960s. Featuring the jaunty little black dog, wearing a tartan scarf, who featured on most of the covers of *Bunty*, this badge is an inch high and coloured black, silver and red. The dog is seated on a plinth marked with the word Bunty. Later the badge was changed to a more basic circular white badge which showed a blonde girl presumably Bunty, and the wording 'Bunty Club'. Another favourite is the enamelled bluebird issued by *School Friend*. Again around an inch high, this delightful, flying bird badge is cryptically marked 'S.F.B.C.' – the School Friend Birthday Club, and is blue and gold. Perhaps the smallest is the diminutive badge of the *Robin* comic club, at ¾ of an inch high and ½ an inch wide. It consists of a gold robin with a red enamelled breast, and has the words 'The Robin Club' embossed beneath.

The club badge from the *Girl* comic was an inch high, gold-coloured head of a girl's profile, based on the logo of the magazine. It bore the legend 'Girl Adventurers', and like, several other badges of the period, featured a small ring on which could be hooked the plaques issued when a member renewed their subscription. Another attractive badge is the *Judy* ballerina. At 1¼in high, this slim silver ballerina is dressed in a yellow tutu, with a yellow cat by her right foot and a silver cat by her left foot. The comic's name, 'Judy', is printed underneath in silver letters on a black background,

Various other badges turn up from time to time, many of them are related to newspapers who included sections for children, or who even printed special comic supplements. These include the 'Gugnunc' badge showing the long ears of Wilfred, from 'Pip, Squeak and Wilfred' fame and the colourful Teddy Tail League badge from the *Daily Mail* which shows Teddy the mouse in a colourful, red, white, blue and pink design. There is also a similar badge from the *Daily Herald* featuring Bobby Bear. The Gugnunc badge is marled W.L.O.G. the Wilfredian League of Gugnuncs – and is blue enamel with the lettering and bunny ears in gold. The club was formed by the *Daily Mirror* in 1927, while the 1930s' Teddy Tail League, another tremendously successful club, had its own secret sign so that members could acknowledge each other. On members' birthdays they were sent a full colour card designed by Herbert Sydney Foxwell, the Teddy Tail artist. Bobby Bear's Badge was made from enamel, and was an inch in circumference. It bore a picture of Bobby Bear and the words, 'Bobby Bear Club. Daily Herald'.

The *Daily Express* is famed for its Rupert Bear badges, whilst a slightly more unusual one is the adorable Bengo Club badge, showing the mischievous boxer puppy designed by 'Tim'

Badges from clubs
run by comics.

Bunty Club Scottie badge.

Bengo Club Badge, from Woman's Illustrated.

(William Timyn) in the 1950s. Bengo starred on children's television at the time in a series of cartoons drawn by Tim, as well as in several comics and magazines, and was used on a badge produced for a children's club run by *Woman's Illustrated* magazine. The Bengo badge is made from gold-coloured plastic and is 1¼in high. A very well known newspaper club badge is the green and white tinplate 'I Spy' club badge. This club ran for several decades in the *News Chronicle*, and later in the *Daily Mail*. The I Spy club was run in conjunction with a series of small books containing pictures of objects together with places to tick them off when one had been spotted, or 'I Spied'. Points were awarded regarding the scarcity of the object. When the book had been completed, it was sent to 'Big Chief I-Spy' at the *News Chronicle* (or *Daily Mail*) who would send a coveted certificate. These booklets were wonderful for keeping children amused on journeys and visits to places of interest, and most of us who had these books can still remember quirky facts we learnt as we filled them in.

Amongst the many tinplate club badges from comics to be found is the previously mentioned *Bunty* club badge, which has a diameter of 1½in and features the head of a blonde 'Bunty girl' in a blue top, and the legend 'Bunty Club' in red. A similar size is the *Jackie* badge. This one is a photographic style badge showing a smiling brunette in yellow and red on a blue background, together with the words 'I'm a Jackie Girl', while, at a smaller 1¼in is the Diana Pony Club which depicts a horse with a girl who is dressed in a red jumper. The lettering, 'Diana Pony Club' is in yellow. Finally, the little *Twinkle* club badge, just an inch in diameter, features the head of a blonde girl and the words 'Twinkle Club'. There are many, many more badges to be found.

Club Membership

The cost of membership to one of the clubs run by the comics varied, as did the 'perks', but usually it was a nominal sum, payable by postal order. In 1968, the Judy Club cost 2/- (10p) to join, and members received a membership card and membership number, the club's secret code and 'a beautiful chromium and enamel badge'. Each comic contained a Club Page, which had such things as a crossword puzzle, with pen and pencil sets for five lucky club members who completed it. Another feature was a 'Find The Name' competition (readers use the secret code to decipher a name shown in a picture) – ten winners would receive the pen and pencil sets. There was also a competition showing a couple of singers 'disguised' with masks, and readers had to guess who they were, and a recipe for making Turkish Delight.

Nine years later, the Judy Club was still going strong, though the membership had gone up to 25p. The badge was now of the circular tinplate kind rather than enamel. The Club Page was as busy as ever, with a crossword, 'Guess the Proverbs', a word quiz and a 'Hidden Coins' game, though only one competition offered prizes, and that was by guessing the title of a well known record by looking at a drawing. Ten prizes of £1 record tokens would be awarded to members who sent in the correct answers.

Bunty, *Judy's* stable-mate, also had clubs and competitions. Initially, it cost a 1/6d postal order to join, and for that, not only would a girl receive the delightful enamel Scottie dog badge, but also a membership card and certificate, details of a secret mark and a secret code. The code enabled members to read the messages printed on the *Bunty* club page in the comic, and to enter the competitions. It was really frustrating for non-members knowing that there was a section of their favourite comic they couldn't understand, even if it was only a short message. Invariably, they felt obliged to join. It was a case of feeling 'out of things' otherwise.

Judy club card.

Bunty Club.

The *Girl* comic Adventurers Club badge turns up frequently, so was obviously a very popular club to join. In 1956, membership cost 1/6d. Would-be members were informed, rather bossily, that they must fill in the form in block capitals 'taking great care to put your full address'. Then they had to fill in a return address label, which read at the top 'Address this label to yourself using BLOCK CAPITALS'. The club appearing in the *School Friend* comic was known as the S.F.B.C. (School Friend Birthday Club), and lists of five or so birth dates of lucky readers were published each week. Reader's couldn't just claim a prize though, because, assuming their date was featured, they then had to solve a competition – in this 1958 issue it was to sort out various proverbs – and then they were imperiously told to 'write all four properly on your card'. Winners had the choice of a needlework set, Chinese chequers game, fountain pen, writing folder or stamp collector's outfit. Competitions and letters also appeared in the page, with prizes of five shillings for each letter featured, and 'mystery prizes' for competitions. A competition on the club page in a 1956 copy of *Girls' Crystal* required members to solve a puzzle-picture listing various foods, and then to write them – neatly – on a postcard. It was important that a grown-up signed the card to confirm the answers were the girl's own work. The prize was a netball. Girls could also see if they were lucky winners of another contest, which depicted a list of Christian names (a term not often used today) together with the first letter of a surname. If it matched a member's full name, she could choose from various prizes, amongst them an autograph album, a nylon hairbrush, a box of coloured dominoes, a lucky black cat brooch, a ball bearing skipping rope, a stamp collector's outfit or a book token.

FREE! in Twinkle
Specially for little girls

This Dainty Red Ring

A Super gift for a little girl.

FREE in Twinkle, issue dated September 15th.
On sale Wednesday, September 12th. Price 3½p.

60

Supercats Club

Happy Hallowe'en when it comes everybody! It's traditionally the time for witches and spooks, so we're all going to look under our beds before retiring on the 31st!

Moonbase Four are having a Hallowe'en party—we're dressing up as witches for the occasion! Remember to enter our "Bewitched" competition—the entries will maybe give us some ideas for our costumes.

And don't forget the most important thing of all—the Supercats' Club! Just look at what you'll get when you join—an exclusive pendant, a colourful sew-on patch and a denim-look pouch containing your Zodiac Code. Don't the girls look proud to be Supercats?

Here is how to join—it couldn't be easier. Simply fill in this special joining coupon and send it with a 40 pence Postal Order, crossed and made payable to D. C. Thomson & Co. Ltd., to SPELLBOUND SUPERCATS' CLUB, P.O. BOX 66, DUNDEE DD1 9LN.

SUPERCATS' CLUB

NAME ....

ADDRESS ....

....

....

I enclose a 40p. Postal Order.

SUPERCATS' SPECIAL FEATURE
HALLOWE'EN HIGH JINKS

Having a party for Hallowe'en? Here are a few tips how to make the party go with a swing.

Why not have everybody disguised (much more interesting!) wearing masks, joke noses and witches' hats? That way you can get to know everybody all over again!

Decorate your house—if your mum allows it, that is! Cut out cats, witches, broomsticks and lanterns from...

BEWITCHED

SUPERCATS' HALLOWE'EN COMPETITION

25 "SPELLBOUND" BELTS TO BE WON!

BEWITCH us with a witch! Draw a witch for us—she can be funny, spooky or even beautiful—in fact, anything you fancy! The twenty-five best and most artistic will win a "Spellbound" belt each.

Fill in the coupon below and send it with your entry to SUPERCATS' HALLOWE'EN COMPETITION, SPELLBOUND, 20 CATHCART STREET, KENTISH TOWN, LONDON NW5 3BN.

SUPERCATS' HALLOWE'EN COMPETITION

NAME ....

ADDRESS ....

Spellbound club form.

June and *School Friend* had a busy club page, and in 1965 the page was filled with readers' letters, a word puzzle and a list of lucky birthdays. Members would receive prizes from a choice of a fountain pen, lucky charm bracelet, box of embroidered hankies, writing folder, oil painting by numbers set or a guinea for their contributions. *Twinkle* 'The picture paper especially for little girls' also had a club, and in 1971 it cost just 5p to join, an absolute bargain. All a little girl (or her parents) had to do was to send a 5p postal order and a stamped addressed envelope, and a badge would be sent. *Twinkle* readers were encouraged to send in photos of themselves, or with their pets, and sometimes they sent in short letters, such as telling of how they helped their daddy to tidy the garden. By the 1980s, the *Twinkle* club had evolved, and was now 'Twinkle's Magic Club'. The club membership had risen to 40p to join, and readers could (a sign of the times) send either 'a crossed postal order, or a cheque'. The page contained letters (Justine had written about her sister's guinea pig named Fudge) and a selection of readers' photos and drawings. Those who sent the drawings were awarded prizes of dolls.

Emma didn't seem to have a club as such, though the readers seemed loyal and supported the letters pages. Every writer whose letter was printed on the *Emma* letter page won 'a gold, red and black super-pendant with lettering to put your name on it, plus £2'. These pendants were known as 'Emma Awards', as they were decorated with that wording. Emma Awards also featured in some of the stories. Star Prize winners – who wrote the best letter in each issue – had the choice of a hairdryer, transistor radio, camera or pocket calculator. *Spellbound* had a club, called the Supercats Club. Members had a special cat pendant, rather than a

Free Gift booklet from Bunty.

badge. It cost 40p to join, and payment was by postal order. As well as the pendant, members received a colourful denim sew-on patch and a denim-look pouch containing the 'Zodiac Code'. Club members could enter various competitions or write letters, to win a *Spellbound* jeans' belt or a fashion tote bag. There were many, many other clubs in similar vein, especially during the 1950s, 60s and 70s when clubs seemed to play an important part in comics.

Enid Blyton seemed particularly fond of clubs; in *Enid Blyton's Magazine*, there is a form for enrolment of the Enid Blyton's Magazine Club. To join, you needed to send a 'Postal Order for 1s and a 2½ d stamp', and in return you would receive a shield-shaped badge. All club profits went to help the Centre for Spastic Children in Chelsea. Enid was especially keen on charity work; she also includes details of the Famous Five Club, which helped a Children's Home, the Busy Bees, which was affiliated to the P.D.S.A., and the Sunbeam Society which worked to provide funds for the Sunshine Homes for Blind Babies. The magazine contained competitions for the various clubs, which members could enter, to win books, sweaters and other goodies.

Competitions

Of course, you didn't always have to be a club member to enter the competitions in the comics. After all, that wouldn't be fair to the casual reader, and besides, there was always the risk that by limiting the entries to members the same people might keep winning. In *Judy* 24 August 1968, the competition showed a selection of Puzzle Pics – line drawings of objects and people with a question and multiple choice answers. Winners could choose their own prize from a comprehensive list which included: a charm bracelet, jumping jacks, top of the charts LP, roller skates, dressing-table set, nightdress holder, Tressy doll, book token or a pogo stick. The classic prize in *Bunty* was a *Bunty* scarf in colourful tartan, which was awarded to those whose letters were published.

Pester Power

A modern term, but the concept was used decades ago – advertise your product in a child's comic, and invariably she will start asking her parents for the items advertised. One of the pleasures of reading old comics is the array of adverts which appear dotted throughout. I remember, on reading comics as a child, being annoyed by the adverts – why did I want to know about foreign stamps or silly tricks to send away for? As far as I was concerned, the ads took up valuable reading space. Now, though, I find these vintage ads a joy. (See also Chapter 6.)

Particularly prevalent are the 'Stamps on approval' small ads, with wording such as 'Free! A fine pair of stamp tweezers and these five beautiful flower stamps in their full natural colours'. A few decades ago, stamp collecting was an exceedingly popular pastime amongst both girls and boys. Packets of stamps were cheap, and all you needed was an album and a few mounting hinges and you were away. It was an occupation which parents and teachers approved of too, because it taught geography and history. It was also quiet, and encouraged a child to sit down at a table with her stamps, moistening the hinges and sticking them into an album. Nowadays, to find a child actively taken an interest in stamp collecting is as rare as hen's teeth. The advertisers here wanted you to send off for their 'Approvals' – the child would be sent a few stamps, with prices, and the idea was that you kept what you wanted and sent the rest back with a postal order. Then the company would send you another lot. The stamps would keep coming, and the child was hooked into sending her pocket money each time, buying more stamps for her collection. After all, how could you resist that set of flowers from Rwanda or the 'Famous Australian Black Swan and approx. 500 stamps for only 1/-' once you actually had them in your hands at home? Some of the claims made, especially by the stamp sellers were ultra extravagant. One, advertising in *Mandy* in the 1970s, boasted 'A Million Stamps Free'. On closer inspection the advert actually said, 'your share of 100 different, plus Russians, plus space stamps' would be sent if you requested approvals.

Often manufacturers would take out a whole page ad, which they would 'disguise' as a picture strip story. *Bunty* in 1974, contained story-strip adverts from Matchbox promoting their Disco Girls sets of dolls. Britt, Dee, Domino and Tia had just been joined by Tony, all had hair which you could comb and style. Tony cost £2.11, while the others cost 'from £1.47'. The Boutique Record Sleeve clothing packs were priced from 54p. In *Sally*, dated 22 August 1970, Mattel had taken a full page advert to promote their latest Barbie model – New Living Barbie. New Living Barbie apparently had a head which turned and tilted, bending knees and ankles, legs which swung in and out, turning hands and much else besides. As well as the one-page advert, with drawings and a free 'Mattel Kiddle with every doll while stocks last' promise, two further pages were taken up with lists of addresses off stores and shops across Britain which sold the doll. Very blatant advertising here, but a perfect way to promote a doll.

Another popular group of adverts were those from the various joke shops, advertising their 'black face soap', floating sugar lumps, fake spots or nails-through-fingers illusions. You could buy gadgets to help you throw your voice, or to see round corners. Sometime manufacturers of toys or novelties would advertise their latest game; in 1939, Pepys were advertising their 'Mickey's Fun Fair Game', a set of playing cards, for 2/6d. By the late 1970s, Star Trumps cards were all the rage, and *Emma* carried adverts for Waddington's Junior Quartet 'New Pocket Size – Play Anywhere. Swap Them With Your Friends.'

A 1959 *Girls' Crystal* (which incorporated *The Schoolgirl*) contained adverts for Fry's Crunchie chocolate bars price 4d. Free Films courtesy of Gratispool (for camera sizes 620, 120 and 127 – no 35mm then, let alone digital!) – and genuine English Bedford cord jodhpurs, at only 39/6d, courtesy of Jacatex. You could get a riding cap from them, too, in a choice of colours, but they were another 10/-. Blue Cap Cheese were advertising Flixies which seemed to be a form of colour slide and came with boxes of the cheese. Advertised as a 'New Colourful Collecting Hobby', you could collect points for an album or a projector. By sending a shilling to Maxwell Studios, a girl could get ten free photos of ' Film Stars, TV Stars and Singing Stars', as well as a catalogue listing hundreds of stars. The ad was illustrated with a photo of Frankie Vaughan, who was a heart-throb at the time. And of course, there was a stamp-collecting advert – a 'complete stamp collecting outfit for only 1/-'.

Girl, in 1956, contained an advert for Rowntree's Fruit Gums. 'What kind of a Gumster are you?' it asked. It turned out that Gumsters were people who sucked fruits gums, and you could work your way up from a Junior Gumster (five to 15 minutes) right through to a Gumster-in-Chief who could make her fruit gum last longer than 60 minutes. Co-op Wheatsheaf were advertising girls' shoes – 'Schoolgirls' feet are happy feet' apparently, if they are wearing the shoes which began at 24/11 for a flat tan leather slip-on, up to 36/9 for a white leather lace-up with a brown heel and toe-cap. A few years later, adverts included those for 'Milky Way, the sweet you can eat between meals without spoiling your appetite' and 'Spangles give you extra flavour fast! Fast! Fast!' 3d a tube, they were double wrapped to keep all the flavour in. Best of all is an advert in a 1960 *Girl* comic which declared that inside every packet of Quaker Puffed Wheat was a free spinning sputnik! An advert like that sets the comic so firmly into its own time frame.

Often the adverts in the magazine had been placed by the publisher, announcing issues of other comics (also published by them), especially if they had free gifts inside. That gleaming plastic bangle or latest fashion hair clip always looked so tempting, and a girl knew that all she had to do was to spend her pocket money on that issue of the comic and her life would be complete. Only it wasn't, of course, because in the next issue more gifts were advertised. Today's girls are probably more worldly-wise and blasé regarding freebies. Practically every comic in the newsagents' nowadays has a pack of free gifts attached, so there is a tremendous choice. Besides, girls would need an awful lot of money to be able to afford more than one comic a week, because the prices seem to have escalated so much.

Advert for free gift.

CHAPTER NINE

What's Your Problem?

A look at problem pages and the way that the problems changed over the years – though many concerns still remain the same.

Formality

Perhaps more than anything else, it is the problem pages that have seen the most changes. Nowadays, it seems, anything goes. Young girls will openly discuss sex, men, contraception, and bikini-line waxing with abandon, and they won't hesitate to air their worries on the problem pages. Usually, the people who answer the questions are equally as forthright. Sometimes the girls' enquiries are funny, sometimes shocking, sometimes moving, and sometimes desperately sad. Looking through older magazines for girls, dating from a hundred years or so ago, I found that many of their queries centred on etiquette or formality. Which knife should you use? Should bread be buttered before it is served at the table? People were much more formal in those days, they used names in full, including their title. First names were only used between the closest of friends. Right up to the 1970s, children would rarely call an adult by their first name, and with family friends would quite likely prefix the name with 'Uncle' or Auntie'. It's only comparatively recently that we have regularly started to use first names, even with people we have never met.

Even up to the late 1930s, until the Second World War, although women had much more freedom than in previous centuries, young girls were still very much seen but not heard. Emphasis was still laid on etiquette and neatness of dress, and the air of formality was strong. Much of this altered during the Second World War; the late 1940s and the 1950s were more informal - by the 1950s, younger people didn't feel the need to don a hat every time they went out. Even so, compared to modern times, the problems in the magazines seem in the main quite tame; very personal and private problems would not be openly discussed in a magazine for many more years.

Back in Victorian times, the problem pages in publications (I hesitate to call them comics) such as *The Girl's Own Paper*, were very formal indeed. Often, the problems weren't even mentioned at all, just the answers, so it's fascinating to try to work out what the original query was. In 1895 Spider was admonished 'You should never go out alone, nor attend any place of entertainment with a man, excepting only your father, brother, or affianced husband', while Lilian Maude was told, 'You should send the boa to a furrier to be properly baked.' (I hope the boa in question was a furry stole and not a snake.) 'An Ayshan Girl and Marguerite' were informed, 'It would be a very impudent and shameful act on your part to ask any man to marry you, or to call at the house of a strange man. How could you so degrade yourself? You both appear to be crazy.' Many of the letters ask about music, painting or poetry, or are concerned with servants. This little gem was in reply to 'Pixie'. 'Much depends on how old little Miss Pixie is with reference to her verses. The first two

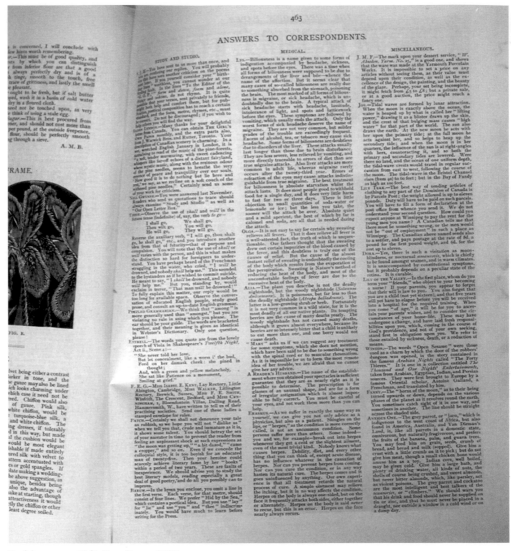

Problem page Girl's Own Paper, 1880s.

are the best, but Pixie, dear, what do you mean by 'the mass of surges'? Was the sea rolling into the valley? And were the soldiers performing their "dirges" while tramping "to and fro" in the water? It is to be hoped they wore high fishermen's boots. You might have relieved our minds by saying so.' Oooh, a bit of a put-down there for poor Pixie. Let's hope it didn't crush her poetic leanings too much!

Getting Bolder

History recounts that the 1960s was the decadent decade, the time when young girls went mad, threw away their inhibitions along with their long skirts and began smoking pot. Yes, of course 1960s' girls had more freedom than their predecessors. They had funky fashions and make-up too – regulation-length school skirts were hitched up round the waist to give them a kind of mini skirt look (though it wasn't really successful, as they soon slipped back down) – and white lipstick was surreptitiously applied in the hope that the teacher wouldn't spot it. I well remember being in class in the 1960s when our teacher stared hard at one of the girls before sarcastically remaking how lucky she was to have naturally blue eyelids. Blue or green eyeshadow was another sixties' fad. Compared to today's streetwise, designer obsessed youngsters, sixties' girls were babes in arms.

The comics of the era still reflect the delightful innocence of the girl readers – there may have been wayward, rebellious girls around, but the vast majority still lived by their parent's rules. Questions about boys, though, continually appeared – in a 1964 copy of *Mirabelle*, 'S of Birmingham' wanted to know when a girl has a choice of three boys, which should she go for? She was informed that she should go for the one she couldn't bear to have another girl go for, which, I suppose, was quite a clever reply. In the same issue, 'Dotty of Orpington' asked how a girl could tell whether a boy was really interested, or whether he was just making a fool of her. Adam (*Mirabelle* had a male to answer the letters' page), told her that if she had doubts about the boy, then she must 'play the game cool enough not to get burnt'.

Problem page Blue Jeans.

Problems published in *Boyfriend* were answered by 'The Talbot Twins', alias 'Johnny and Jennie'. In 1964 they were advising a hapless Dave from Macclesfield who was moaning that everything he did was wrong. Apparently if he kissed a girl, she slapped his face, and if he didn't kiss her, then she sulked. He was advised not to rush a girl into kissing, but if they look sulky and linger at the front door, then to go for it. They sensibly told 16-year-old Mary, from Tamworth, who wrote that her bags were packed and she was ready to move to digs in London where she hoped to find a job, that she was being silly. The twins explained that not only were there dangers lurking for unwary teenagers, but that also she might be lonely. They neatly summed up the situation by saying that the lonely girl in London was a prey for wolves and until she was older she would be wise to stick to the sheep at home. Edna of Isleworth had a dilemma, too, one very common in the 1960s – she hated her shorthand and typing course. After doing a term, and not getting on very well, she wanted to work in a factory or shop, but her mother said no, because an office would be much nicer for her. So Johnny – or maybe Jennie – told her to try another term, but after that, to tell her mother if she still felt strongly about it. They went on to stress that there was nothing wrong with working in a factory or a shop if that would make her happier.

Beauty problems were also tackled in *Boyfriend*. They were answered by a lady called Shirley Dean. Shirley dished out lots of advice, especially to all those sufferers of the dreaded teenage blight – spots. She explained how important it was to drink plenty of pure fruit juice, and to eat green vegetables and salads. Sufferers were told to not eat many carrots or potatoes, and to cut out sweets, alcohol and fizzy drinks. She also advised Terry, from Walthamstow, (I assume Terry was a girl, as in those days few men wore make-up!) who was agonising over whether she needed creamy foundation for dry skin or liquid for oily skin. Terry was told that, more than likely, she had combination skin, so the advice was oatmeal pack on the oily patches, astringent cleanser on nose and chin, and cold cream on dry parts. Then use two types of foundation, liquid and cream. It must have taken Terry ages to get ready after that routine. She probably regretted asking.

The teen magazine *Valentine* seemed to have a huge post-bag, judging by the number of letters and queries which appeared each week. It boasted a Pen Pal Club, too, and, in a 1962 issue, the ages of those seeking new pals ranged from 11 through to 19. Applicants gave their names and full addresses (something that would be most unwise in this day and age), as well as listing their hobbies. Hobbies included cycling, knitting, piano playing, bopping, collecting discs, motorbikes, modelling, dancing, swimming, riding, rock'n'roll, animals, films, reading, jiving, needlework, ballroom dancing and sport. Some also listed their favourite pop stars – most popular were Cliff Richard, Elvis Presley and Tommy Steele.

One and a half pages were devoted to answering queries about pop stars, actors and musicians, so we learnt all kinds of things, amongst them that there were seven members in Acker Bilk's Paramount Jazz Band, David MacBeth sang *Pigtails in Paris*, Tony Curtis loved painting and that Alma Cogan's full name was Alma Angela Cogan. Billy Fury as yet had no gold discs and that the tune Count Basie played in the Jerry Lewis film *Cinderfella* was *The Princess Waltz*. These pages also included a pop quiz, a photo offer, a list of Fan Clubs and a picture of Mark Wynter cuddling a koala bear!

But that wasn't all – because *Valentine* also had a 'Dear Stevie' problem page, or rather, two pages, which not only contained a selection of reader's problems, but each week, one was chosen to appear as a picture strip, illustrated by line drawings. One of the stories, from Josie Mason, was concerning her embarrassment regarding the shape of her nose.

She wanted to know if she should have it altered by plastic surgery – a very radical step in the early 1960s. The drawings showed Josie missing out on dances and dates. 'Must I resign myself to being an old maid?' asks almost-18-year-old Josie. Stevie advises her to consult her doctor, but also to first try a trip to a really good hairdressers, and to make herself join a club, accept invitations, decide to have a good time and to help other people have one too. That was sensible advice, and much better than telling the youngster to check in to the nearest plastic surgeon pronto.

Other questions on the page, not answered in strip format, include one from Suzy, who says that she had a date with a boy eight weeks before but she didn't turn up, and that she has stood him up on several other dates. Now he's ignoring her! Poor boy, I don't blame him, but the sensible Stevie tells her to write and say how sorry she is, and maybe he will forgive her. Ralph (a rare male reader) writes to say that it's his girlfriend's birthday soon, and he has known her for three months. He wonders if he should buy her a present. Stevie suggests cosmetics, jewellery or a pair of nylons (though stressed it was important to make sure they were the right size). Well, yes, of course – you try giving a slim girl an outsize pair of stockings (or tights as it would be now) and she will throw them right back at you.

Pat wrote to say she had known a boy for a year, and every time she saw him she said 'hello', and so did he. How could she make him notice her more? She was told to try smiling as well, and to pass a casual comment, while another Pat (it was a common name in the 1960s), who was in love with a friendly boy, had chased after him when she was younger. He had told her friend that he would never ask her out because of it, so what could she do? Stevie's advice to her was not to chase him any more, and perhaps he'd forget about it. Hmm.

Romeo had a problem page, too, which was called 'Dear Ann'. Ann gives not just advice, but a bit of a talking-to as well, when, in 1968, Hilary writes to say that she is in love with two boys, and when she goes out with one, the other is always on her mind. It transpires that Hilary is 13½. 'Now look here,' replies Ann, 'I've always said that love has no age limits but at thirteen (never mind the half) you're taking your feelings a bit too seriously. Shop around a bit – fall in love with six more. And have a lovely time until the real thing comes along.' That told her. Fifteen-year-old Linda wrote to say she had been going out with Dave for 18 months but he had never yet taken her home to meet his parents. She was afraid that if she asked, he would think she wanted to rush things. Ann replied, 'Let's face it, you DO want to rush things a bit. It's a little odd that Dave's never taken you home but he probably has his reasons'. She advises Linda to steer the conversation round to his home life and family, but 'not too obviously!' The most likely scenario in this day and age is that Dave is already married with two kids and a pregnant wife.

In another *Romeo* issue from 1968, a reader calling herself 'Lofty' was writing to say she had no self-confidence. She felt, at 5ft 7in she was too tall, was scared to go on a bus on her own, and dare not eat or drink in front of boys. Ann gently explained that she wasn't too tall, and the only way to get over her problem was to stop imagining she was at the centre of the universe. She continued by saying that Lofty must think about other people, and maybe have a chat with an understanding family doctor. This kind of sensible, kind, well-thought out advice must have proved invaluable, and would have comforted many girls with worries but who felt unable to confide in their parents. Early *Romeo* comics didn't have problem pages but instead they devoted a couple of pages to answering readers' letters on various pop stars and aspects of showbiz.

Problem page Romeo.

Jane is worried, in a 1962 *Cherie*, because her boyfriend Jack has asked her to get engaged for three months and if it doesn't work out they will break it off. Maureen wonders why all the screen heroes she falls for are dark and handsome but she's in love with a plump boy who isn't good looking, while Ruby wants to know why 'a girl of fourteen should be dragged everywhere with her parents like a kid of eight'. These problems all seem sweetly innocent when compared to those of a few decades later. Yet at the time, they were exciting reads for the early teens who read the comics. None of the problems fazed *Cherie*'s agony aunt, Sue Cartwright, who handed out oodles of good, sensible advice.

Cherie had quite an interactive readership; not only with packed problem pages, but a busy letters page and a Pen Pals section as well. Back to Sue Cartwright, still battling with reader's problems. When Shirley wrote in to say that she was very much in love with Henry, until she met his twin brothers Tom and Johnnie, and now she is in love with the twins

Problem page Cherie.

but not sure which she liked best, Sue chastised her. She said, 'I think you are misusing the word love. You like these boys no doubt, you might even be fond of them in a mild way – but if you were really in love with either then you would know with certainty.' Sue sympathised with Doris who unhappily wrote that her boyfriend wanted to marry her and then live in a room in his parents home, agreeing that it was far better to have a place of your own right from the start. She also assured Avril that she hadn't committed a dreadful sin just because she told her boyfriend she was 22, when actually she was 23. Phew, so that was all right then. In *Roxy*, the problem page was run by a rather stern looking lady called Joan Courage, though I am sure she was friendly really. Dorothy wrote in 1958 to say that eight months ago her fiancé had broken off their engagement and had been going out with another girl. Now he had returned and wanted to carry on as before, but Dorothy said she couldn't bear it if George left her again. She couldn't help wondering if the relationship would last any more a second time around. Joan's reply began rather ominously, 'Just why did George walk out on you, Dorothy? You'll have to ask yourself if the reason for doing so is likely to crop up again.' However, she then softens a little to say that it might be worth giving him a second try, and ends 'let me know how it works out, pet.' So perhaps Joan's bark was worse than her bite.

Jackie had the Cathy and Claire problem page. *Jackie* readers seemed a bit more forward than those from some of the other magazines of the time, though, then again, we were now into the seventies and eighties. Queries included, 'I'm fourteen and I've been going out with my boyfriend for six weeks. The trouble is he hasn't kissed me yet. Where do you think I'm going wrong?' Instead of the no-nonsense straight talk the writer might have received from Sue of *Cherie* or Johnny and Jennie from *Boyfriend*, Cathy and Claire replied, 'Next time you're out with your boyfriend, why not fling your arms around his neck and see what he does? You could have a pleasant surprise!' Umm. Or he might just turn tail and run.

A young schoolgirl wrote to say that she had been babysitting for her maths teacher, and he had stopped the car and made a pass at her when he gave her a lift home. She managed to jump from the car and run home, and since then she had been unable to look at him in class, and felt embarrassed. The reply was that it was a stupid and irresponsible way for him to act, and that no doubt he is regretting it. She was told to try to get the situation into perspective, but that if it he tried anything again, she must tell her parents. Nowadays, though, an incident such as that would probably have led to a court case and the teacher's dismissal. A 14-year-old wrote to say she had a crush on a 16-year-old boy, who knew she fancied him but didn't take any notice. She agonised that it could be because she only had a 32in bust. Cathy and Claire advised her to go all out to be as friendly as possible, but if he still didn't take any notice, then not to worry. It wasn't her bust size that was the trouble; it just meant he wasn't the right boy for her, so she must put her time to finding someone who was. Today, the girl would be frantically saving for a bust enlargement operation.

According to the Editor of *Jackie*, writing in a later compilation of issues, Cathy and Claire used to get up to 400 letters a week from readers aged from 10-16. Various leaflets were compiled to cover the most common problems, which could be quickly sent out with a covering letter – though sometimes mistakes were made. Once they received a letter from a reader complaining she had written about a problem, lopsided bust. In return she had received a knitting pattern for a little woolly hat!

Really advanced for the time was the girl – I assume it was a girl – who contacted the Doctor page (yes, *Jackie* had one of those as well) to say that she knew it sounded stupid, but it was important to her to know quickly whether it was safe to remove hair from the pubic area. She also asked whether people did remove it? The Doctor's reply was that, while it was safe to do so by shaving, there was no reason to do so, adding that most girls preferred to keep their hair on. Today's girl wouldn't have needed to ask, she would already have checked in to a beauty clinic for a Brazilian.

Dear Cathy & Claire...

If you're stuck with a problem, writing it all down often helps! If yours is getting you down, get it down — on paper, to us, Cathy and Claire, Jackie, 185 Fleet Street, London EC4A 2HS. We'll do our very best to sort it out. Don't forget to enclose a stamped addressed envelope, if you'd like a personal reply.

BRA BOTHER

DEAR CATHY & CLAIRE — I'm fourteen and I have a 34-inch chest, and I think it's about time I started wearing a bra.

The problem is my mum doesn't seem to notice — she's never mentioned it, or even talked to me about wearing a bra. All the other girls in my class have started wearing them, and I just don't know what to do. What do you suggest?

We suggest you have a word with your mum. It's likely that she just hasn't realised how grown up you're becoming. Approach her and explain it to her, the same way you told us, and we're sure she'll take your lead.

Or, if you prefer, write to us again, enclosing an s.a.e., and we'll send you our special leaflet, "Developing A Bust." It tells you all about choosing a bra and the importance of wearing one. Once you've read it, you could show it to your mum. We're sure she'll take the hint.

DOES HE LIKE ME?

DEAR CATHY & CLAIRE — I fancy my friend's brother like nothing on earth and I know all my other friends like him too.

When I'm round at his house, he's really friendly and talks to me a lot — but then Craig's like that with everyone. He's never had a girlfriend and I think he just sees us all as friends. I desperately want him to notice me as a girl and not just his sister's friend.

Can you tell me how you can tell whether a boy likes you or not?

If we could answer that question, we'd put all the problem pages out of business! It would be great if there was a sure-fire sign that he liked you — for instance, if he really did get stars in his eyes! — but unfortunately, life and love just aren't as simple as that.

In fact, it's often a very subtle thing. People are great at disguising their feelings, or covering them up so well that they give completely the opposite impression. Lots of girls have cut a boy dead when he's plucked up courage to speak to them — even though they're crazy about him!

Craig probably hasn't really begun to think of girls as possible girlfriends yet, and this could be why he's so popular; he's very natural with you all and isn't at all tongue-tied or shy.

The best thing to do here would be to take things slowly and to try to get to know him a bit better than you do just now. Don't be afraid to let him know you like him — but in a friendly, casual way. Don't overdo things, though. This way, when Craig does get around to noticing girls, you could well find yourself at the top of his list!

Douglas about your change of heart, though, and not keep him hanging on, believing you still think of him as your boyfriend. The best thing would be to write him a tactful letter, explaining that, because of the distance between you, you feel it would be fairer to both of you to finish. Mentioning your new boyfriend would only hurt him all the more, and we're sure you'd rather avoid this.

As for Mike, well, you need only tell him about Douglas if and when he asks!

Dear Fashion Ed,

I'm tired of looking fat and frumpy but until I lose some weight I suppose I'll just have to stay that way. I'm really envious of my slim friends being able to pick up inexpensive party dresses while I have to struggle into last year's "best" dress. Have you any ideas for a stylish look for a fed-up frump?

Surprisingly enough, Evans have got some great young-looking styles in right now. So, if you've never stepped inside an Evans store because you thought they only catered for middle-aged mums, think again!

For example, this leopard-print polyester dress would turn anyone's head at a special party or disco! It's available in sizes 16-30 from all branches of Evans and costs £12.99.

Note the accessories the model is wearing with it — boots to hide thick ankles, a sparkly shawl draped over one shoulder to hide any bulges, plus an up-to-the-minute bag and bangles that no girl could possibly look frumpy wearing!

SHE'S THREATENING ME!

DEAR CATHY & CLAIRE — Recently, my friend dared me to go shoplifting with her, and although I knew it was wrong, I went.

But now we've fallen out and she's threatening to tell my parents and schoolfriends unless I go shoplifting with her again.

I know I was stupid to do it in the first place and I don't want to take a risk and do it again. My parents would hit the roof if they found out and I'm really scared in case they do. Please help!

We can understand how scared you are, but calm down! It's hardly likely your friend — if you can call her that — will tell anyone what you've done, because to tell on you she'll have to give herself away.

The only way out is to stand up to her and put a stop to her threats now. Tell her you made one mistake and on no account do you intend to make another — no matter what she threatens to do.

Also, you should really tell your parents about the whole incident. They will be upset — that's only to be expected — but not half as much as if they'd heard about it from someone else. However, knowing how sorry you are, they'll probably realise you've been punished enough.

Finally, we all make mistakes — it's how we overcome them that counts!

29

Problem page Jackie.

Problem page Cherie.

Nikki's problem pages, from the mid-1980s, contained a letter from a young 'Wham! Fan' complaining that Fiona, her twin sister, insisted on swapping the hair ribbons which they wore for identity purposes, then caused trouble at school – and the Wham! Fan was blamed. The advice was to try to wear her hair in a different style to her sister, and to also confront her to say that it mustn't continue, because she couldn't fool people forever. Amongst the usual spotty skin, penpals and best friends problems, was one of a more serious nature. A young Irish girl had written in to say that she wanted to eat lots of food but was very thin, and once she decided that she didn't like something, she wouldn't eat it. Consequently, at 13 years old, she weighed only 4½ stone. The answer was that there was no normal weight for any set age because so much depended on height and build. However, she was told that her attitude towards food wasn't a good one and was advised to visit her doctor. As we progressed through the decades, sadly, eating problems were more frequently cropping up on the problem pages.

In 1970, *Sally* had a problem page, and the letters revolved about school and boyfriends – the usual topics which caused young girls the most problems. 'A Friend' writes to say that she is very worried because her friend has problems at home. The advisor, known as Sally, presumably as a magazine nom de plume advised her to be sympathetic, but there was no point in worrying as she couldn't do anything about it. It is a problem the friend and her parents must sort out together. One wonders if the 'friend' was actually the girl who wrote in; maybe it was a desperate cry for help. We shall never know. Sheelagh wrote to say that she grew tired of a boy pestering her, and had finally agreed to go out with him, but now she can't pluck up courage to say she is no longer interested. She was told that she must find the nerve from somewhere to tell him she no longer wants to go out with him. That problem can still arise today, though it has to be said that most girls now would probably be able to tell a boy the truth.

Although modern agony aunt columns are often more explicit, many of the questions which worried girls in previous decades are just as pertinent today, which is somehow comforting. Modern girls might seem outwardly confident and brash, but inside many of their worries are those which have troubled girls for hundreds of years.

Problem Page, Nikki.

CHAPTER TEN

Newspaper Strips

Most newspapers feature a comic strip. Some are adult orientated (such as 'Striker' and 'George and Lynne' from *The Sun*, or 'Faith, Hope and Sue' from the *Daily Express*), while others are more child-inclined. Some cartoon strips appear child orientated and will appeal to children even though being written for adults. Newspapers sometimes contained free comics, too. Another source of free comics was from manufactures trying to promote new lines or shops hoping to create a feel-good factor.

Comic Strips

Often, these comic strips were utilised in a children's section, occasionally being a pull-out special comic supplement, but more commonly a part-page feature with maybe a club, a badge and a 'secret' message. Just as with comics, many characters from newspapers were issued as tie-ins, in various forms. *Daily Express's* Rupert Bear or Calvin and Hobbes, *Daily Mail's* Teddy Tail, *Daily Mirror's* Pip, Squeak and Wilfred, Squibbet from the *London Star*, The Perishers – another *Daily Mirror* strip – and Peanuts, which was syndicated in several newspapers are all child-friendly. There are many more. Some characters, such as Rupert Bear, became so well known and so popular that the majority of people who bought the toys, books and other tie-ins, might never have read the actual comic strip in the newspaper.

Bobby Bear

Bobby Bear was the first teddy bear to feature in a British comic strip, appearing in the *Daily Herald* 1919. He was amongst the cast of characters in a strip called 'Playtime', but by the end of 1920, he was a star. Bobby was a rather thin bear with long legs, almost mouse-like in appearance, and was drawn for a while by William Haughton (who also drew the Mickey Mouse annuals), and illustrators such as Leslie Ellis. At one point, the Bobby Bear club boasted over four hundred thousand members. (See Chapter 8.) Bobby's friends included Percy Pig, Rabbit and Maisie Mouse, and the annual tie-ins are now becoming very collectable. These annuals first began in 1922 and continued well into the 1960s.

Bobby Bear Daily Herald badge.

Calvin and Hobbes

This much-loved, quite recent, cartoon, was devised by American artist Bill Watterson in the mid-1980s, and soon was syndicated worldwide. The humour particularly appealed to British fans, who found it easy to empathise with the stories of a small boy and his stuffed tiger. Both characters were, interestingly, named after famous philosophers. Calvin was once a sixteenth-century theologian who believed in predestination, while Hobbes, the tiger, was named after a seventeenth-century philosopher. However, in the strips, Calvin was a six-year-old boy who was constantly in trouble, much of which he blamed on Hobbes. To Calvin's parents and other onlookers, Hobbes was a toy, but to Calvin, he was an enormous, real, tiger, ferocious and cunning – if rather laid back and lazy – who usually accompanied him on his escapades, though sometimes Hobbes would go to sleep after making a few scathing remarks, instead. Cleverly, Bill Watterson drew the cartoon actually showing that Hobbes was a real tiger when no adults were about, but as soon as an adult was depicted in the same frame, he reverted to being a floppy toy.

Calvin and Hobbes became extremely famous, with a series of comic book compilations as well as the regular strips, which appeared in newspapers such as the *Daily Express*. Then, to the dismay of his fans, in 1995, Bill Watterson announced he had decided not to continue with the strip. So far, no artist has successfully managed to plug that gap of quirky, gentle childhood humour. Perhaps one day, he will begin drawing Calvin and Hobbes once more. Incidentally, he was so protective of his characters that, unlike most artists, he refused to sanction merchandise in the form of soft toys or other products.

Peanuts

Peanuts is a long-running comic strip by Charles M. Schultz, and made its debut in 1950. Originally, he wanted it to be called 'Li'l Folks', but the editor thought otherwise, and came up with Peanuts. Nowadays, fans think of Snoopy, Charlie Brown, Linus, Lucy, Schroeder, Marcie, Peppermint Patty and the rest as members of the Peanuts gang, but the main and favourite member is, of course, Snoopy, a loveable white beagle with black ears. Although Snoopy can't talk, he has a vivid imagination and can often be found typing out a

Peanuts toys, Golden Bear.

Snoopy as 'Joe Cool' McDonalds.

best-selling novel, hanging around in a pair of shades as his alter-ego Joe Cool, or lying in the sun on top of his kennel, dreaming of his days as a World War One flying ace. His best friend is Woodstock, a crazy yellow bird who has never managed to get the hang of flying, and his owner is Charlie Brown, a boy with a head like a billiard ball. Charlie Brown seems to come off worse in most adventures; even Snoopy gets the better of him. He tugs at our heartstrings – he's teased by his small sister Sally and bossed by his friend Lucy; Charlie Brown is the one who never wins the girl, the prize or even the right to bat in the baseball game. It's amazing to think that the Peanuts gang, with Snoopy, Charlie Brown and the others, have appeared in over 2,600 different worldwide newspapers since their debut, 60 years ago.

There are numerous collectable tie-ins, amongst them soft toys of Snoopy and all the main characters, which have been produced by various makers. There are also figurines, clockwork toys and, of course, hundreds of books of their cartoon adventures.

Perishers

The delightful cartoon strip called 'The Perishers' first appeared in the *Daily Mail* in 1958. It was written by Maurice Dodd, and drawn by Dennis Collins. The cartoon strip revolves around a gang of streetwise children and a dog, who live in the fictional town of Croynge (a cross between Croydon and Penge). The main character is Wellington, a thoughtful, resourceful, rather gloomy boy who seems to carry the weight of the world on his shoulders. His worries include wondering whether the weight of the atmosphere will eventually crush everyone to death. Wellington earns a living by building and selling soapbox carts, and he lives in a disused railway station with his dog, Boot. Boot is a large English sheepdog, though Boot seems to think he is actually an important aristocrat. Consequently, he doesn't like to do anything and is berated by Wellington for being lazy, although the two do bond together in times of adversity. Other characters include Marlon, Maisie and Baby Grumpling. Marlon is, to be frank, a bit dim, though he has ambitions to become a brain surgeon, or perhaps 'A-Bloke-What-Goes-Down-Sewers-In-Big-Rubber-Boots', while Maisie loves Marlon, though Marlon's only comment about that is 'Yeuk'. She thinks he is bright and clever and all the things he isn't, and enjoys bossing him around. Her little brother, Baby Grumpling, looks angelic but constantly causes mayhem in his search for food. Inventor of such delicacies as the worm sandwich, Baby Grumpling enjoys upsetting his cronies and also has a neat line in philosophy.

The cartoon strips continued until 2006, when a final 'into the sunset' version appeared as the Perishers said goodbye. Collectable memorabilia include books and annuals, a Robert Harrop figurine, playing cards and an excellent set of dolls. This latter item was made in the 1970s by Pedigree, and is fairly difficult to find today. The dolls measured around 15in tall, and were soft-bodied with vinyl heads and hands.

Pip, Squeak and Wilfred

An early picture strip, Pip, Squeak and Wilfred were a dog, a penguin and a long-eared baby rabbit, respectively. The strip cartoon first appeared in the *Daily Mirror* in 1919, and ran till 1956. It was extraordinarily popular, capturing the imagination of thousands of children, especially in its pre-Second World War heyday. The strip was drawn by Austin Bowen Payne, who always signed as A.B.Payne, and told of the adventures of three orphan animals, as well as their 'Uncle Dick' (Bertram Lamb, the writer who thought up the characters). Wilfred could hardly speak, because he was a baby, and just managed 'Nunc' – which was short for uncle – and 'Gug'. At first they were cared for by Uncle Dick and his maid Angeline in a house just outside London, but later they were given their own miniature house known as Mirror Grange. The house was designed by Maxwell Ayrton, F.R.I.B.A. and contained furniture, fittings and pictures contributed by distinguished artists. The exhibition of this 'dolls' house' raised funds for 'The Heritage Craft Schools for Crippled Children' which was situated in Sussex. In the 1920s a club was formed, known as the 'The Wilfredian League of Gugnuncs' (W.L.O.G.). It had its own special blue enamelled badge featuring two long rabbit ears. One of its rules was 'Never eat a rabbit'! Amazingly, the Gugnuncs attracted 100,000 members, and when they held their annual rallies, they filled the Royal Albert Hall, in the process raising thousands of pounds for the charities the club supported.

The cartoon strip also appeared as weekly episodes in the *Sunday Pictorial*, and in pull-out comics included in the *Daily Mirror* during the 1920s. These comics are rare and very much sought after today. The annuals were popular too, and appeared each year up until 1955, although by then the quaint, old-fashioned format had lost much of its appeal to modern, 1950s' children. As an example of the characters' popularity, the *Daily Mirror* reported that 100,000 copies of the 1923 *Pip and Squeak Annual* had been sold. Wilfred had a separate annual, ensuring extra sales as most young fans would want both, and there was also an *Uncle Dick's Competition Annual* which ran during the 1930s. There were plenty of collectable tie-ins issued at the time, from soft toys through to jigsaw puzzles – and even soap.

Rupert Bear

Rupert was created by artist Mary Tourtel, whose first cartoon strip appeared in the *Daily Express* on the 8 November 1920. In many ways he was similar to the little bear we know today, though a bit more 'bear-like', and with baggier trousers. He was shown setting out to the shops in the village of Nutwood, and the caption was in verse. Even today, verses still appear underneath the basic text.

We all recognise Rupert from his red jersey and yellow-checked scarf, yet when Mary's colour drawings first appeared, they showed him wearing a blue jersey and grey trousers. Mary dreamt up the strange, almost surreal world of Nutwood which featured people in medieval dress wandering amongst a mix of incongruities such as clothed animals who tended to keep unclothed animals as pets, 'normal' humans, and weird inventions with a scientific theme. She also thought up many of Rupert's chums, including Bill Badger, Edward Trunk and Podgy Pig. When Alfred Bestall took over the strip in 1935, he discarded Mary's use of magic to free Rupert from tricky situations, relying instead on proper twists in the plot. Alfred introduced a host of new characters, such as Pong-Ping, Tigerlily, Bingo Pup, the Professor and the Merboy. Alfred drew the stories up till 1965, his last adventure being 'Rupert and the Winkybickies',

Perishers, Pedigree.

though he continued to work on the annuals. (See Chapter 12.) Later John Harrold took over the drawing, and the current artist is Stuart Trotter.

Over the years, Rupert has appeared in many guises, from soft toys to ceramics, and from lampshades to slippers. Amongst the manufacturers of the plush Rupert bears have been Steiff, Merrythought, Burbank, Golden Bear, Chad Valley, Pedigree and Hasbro. Unlike most bear toys, which are fairly straightforward, the design of Rupert has always caused makers a headache. For instance, should the fur be white or brown? Most of the Rupert annual covers depict a brown bear, but when you turn the pages, you find the bear has white fur. Maybe he is a polar bear, not a brown bear at all. It must be especially confusing for youngsters – and no doubt, Rupert is baffled, too, for only he knows the truth! Another thing which causes manufacturing problems are Rupert's hands – or does he have paws? The strips seem to show that he has human hands, but when hands are given to a plush toy, the end result is very strange, as seen in the 1970s' Burbank Rupert Bear. This pull-string talking version had a brown furry face but pink dolly hands. The result was extremely disconcerting, However, this bear, who stands 21 inches high, is now sought after by today's collectors. Rupert Bear pieces made by Merrythought, Steiff and others for the collectors' market, do often try to depict the paws as hands. The toys intended

Rupert Bear, Hasbro.

Gugnunc badge.

Teddy Tail badge.

for children, though, tend to be more conventional in appearance and give Rupert paws, even though strictly speaking they are not following the drawings by Mary Tourtel and Alfred Bestall.

There are many other Rupert Bear collectable tie-ins, such as books, records, cassettes, jigsaw puzzles, die-cast model vehicles, badges and brooches. As well as the annuals, many of the original Mary Tourtel books now sell for hundreds of pounds. In the 1970s Pelham Puppets made a wonderful Rupert Bear string puppet, while more recently, companies

Free comics.

such as Wade, Beswick and Wedgwood have issued many Rupert Bear ceramic figurines, tea sets and even china clocks. Although Rupert Bear still appears each day in picture strip form in the *Daily Express*, he really has climbed the pinnacle of success and should be regarded as a literary character, as opposed to a cartoon character.

Squibbet

Squibbet was a favourite character of mine when I was little, and I used to have his adventures read to me when they appeared in the *London Evening Star* in the early 1950s. As his name suggests, he was part rabbit, part squirrel, and later appeared in a book called *Adventures of Squibbet* published in 1952 by Star Publications which told how Squibbet ran away from home as he was constantly teased, and was finally adopted by a little girl called Tuppenny. The stories were written by Nelson Davis and illustrated by Veronica Papworth.

Teddy Tail

Another of the popular anthropomorphic characters, Teddy Tail, in spite of his name, was a mouse. He was quite an early character, first appearing in the *Daily Mail* in April 1915, in which was the first daily strip cartoon. He was so much loved that he inspired the creation of many other strip cartoon characters of the time; editors realised that these cartoons were attracting people, thus increasing circulation of the newspapers. Following in Teddy Tail's footsteps came Rupert Bear from the *Daily Express*, Pip, Squeak and Wilfred from the *Daily Mirror* and the *Daily Herald*'s Bobby Bear. Teddy Tail of the *Daily Mail* was dreamt up by Charles James Folkard, who was a well known artist specialising in the illustration of nursery literature, and in the 1920s, his brother, Harry, took over the illustrations. Teddy Tail resembled a rather thin part mouse, part boy, who wore large Eton suits with white collars. His adventures were set in locations such as fairyland, often in the company of an insect called Dr Beetle. In the early 1930s, the strips became drawn by Herbert Sydney Foxwell, who had become famed for his work in *Comic Cuts* and, especially, the wonderful drawings of Tiger Tim and his friends in *Tiger Tim's Weekly and Rainbow*. His interpretation of Teddy Tail was different to Charles James Folkard's approach; he set the cartoon strip in a boarding school, run by Mrs Whiskers. Teddy Tail's friends were Kittie Puss, Piggy and a baby duck called Dougie. It seemed a lovely school to attend, with plenty of time to play, and Teddy Tail not only played impish tricks on his friends, but was able to drive a car and even fly a plane.

An inspired idea in 1933 increased Teddy Tail's popularity tremendously, when the *Daily Mail* decided to issue a giveaway comic for children inside the main paper. The comic was called the *Boys and Girls Daily Mail*, and it was to run for almost five years. It was issued at various intervals – sometimes weekly, but at other times two or three times a week. This free comic, coupled with the forming of the Teddy Tail League, boosted the newspaper sales tremendously. Thousands of young members were attracted, all keen to wear the enamelled badge and make the secret sign. (See Chapter 8.) On their birthdays the members received Teddy Tail cards, which were sent in matching Teddy Tail envelopes – something very special for a child to look forward to. There were plenty of merchandising spin-offs related to Teddy Tail, including jigsaw puzzles, annuals and various sew-on patches, all of which are collectable today.

Other free comics

If finding out about standard published comics is difficult, then finding out about free comics is virtually impossible. There must have been thousands upon thousands issued over the years, and form a collecting sphere in their own right. Sometimes the comics are substantial, full colour publications, which promote a new toy and are given away in a toyshop or with a purchase of the toy that the comic promotes. They may be comics given free from a restaurant, supermarket or chain store to promote customer relations, or perhaps they are mail-aways, buyer incentives or supplied at tourist attractions to keep children amused while the parents enjoy the venue. Comic supplements inside newspapers are still given from time to time. This practice was quite popular before the Second World War, when newspapers such as the *Daily Mail* gave away supplements, but isn't popular today. In the early 1990s, the *Daily Mirror* was giving the *Disney Mirror* free each Saturday. This conventional styled comic strip paper contained picture strips of Mickey and Minnie in 'Bat Bandit of Inferno Gulch', as well as ' Clarabelle's Hotel' and 'Pluto's Rival'. Another free newspaper comic, given away in 2008, was *The Comic Violet* in *The Guardian*, while in 2009, *The Guardian* gave away free reproduction copies of classic comics, amongst them *Tammy, Bunty, Beano, Dandy* and *Jackie*.

Typical of a toy-related comic was *Sweet Secrets*, based on the range of toys of the same name in 1987. Produced by The Colourful Comic Company for Rainbow Toys, this comic was a colourful glossy with an adventure starting the Sweet Secrets characters told in a picture strip. It contained details of the Sweet Secret club, and also an offer of free sweets in conjunction with various sweet shops. An example of a store-related comic was *Do It*, produced by Television South in association with the home maintenance chain stores B&Q. This lively magazine, dating from the 1990s, doesn't contain any picture strips but consists of 24 pages of quirky things to make ands do, all illustrated in cartoon style. Ideas include orange peel jewellery, a trick computer in a matchbox, secret image lampshades and mirror vases. If you decide to specialise in free comics, then it's worth keeping an eye out any time you go into a toy store or any shop that the parents of young children might frequent.

Squibbet book 1950s with Pip, Squeak & Wilfred Mirror Grange book, 1920s.

CHAPTER ELEVEN

Toy, Book, Annual and Game Tie-Ins

An annual at Christmas was a must; annuals featured favourite characters in new stories and usually contained puzzles and quizzes as well. Another popular tie-in were the 'Picture Libraries' and other booklets. Many comics had spin-offs, which told longer stories of the favourite characters in comic strip form. Board games, character toys, figurines, playing cards, books, shopping bags – all kinds of licensed products help generate more money for the comics' publishers.

Why Do Comics Need Tie-ins?

Tie-ins are a form of advertising; they bring a product into the public eye. Whether that product is a packet of soap powder, a tube of sweets, a tub of butter – or a comic – a tie-in generates more interest in the product. It also brings in more revenue, either directly through sale of goods, or indirectly, through licensing another company to use the items' promotional characters or logos. Usually the product will be advertised in the comic in the hope that the girl then brings it to the attention of her parents, for the majority of the items are

Korky the Cat, Robert Harrop.

more than pocket money toys. *Girl* in particular had many tie-ins, and some, such as the Girl doll or the Girl carpet sweeper, were substantial – probably more than a girl could hope to save even over a period of months.

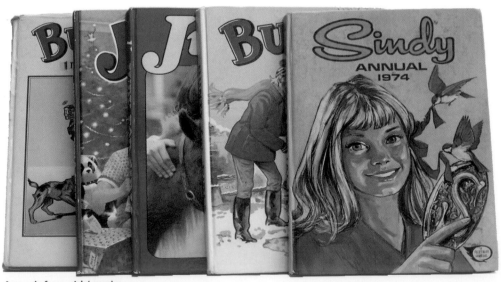

Annuals from girls' comics.

Annuals and Booklets

In earlier, post-war decades and in the 1950s and 1960s as well, Santa wasn't so generous as he appears to be nowadays. We were content with a few small toys, a 'main present' (such as a doll), a bag of chocolate money, a satsuma wrapped in tinfoil, a cardigan knitted by your auntie (if you were like me!) and, of course, an annual. If you were very lucky, you might receive two annuals – what a feast of reading they would be. Before the Second World War girls would probably receive one of the Schoolgirl titles, often packed with text stories and maybe a few picture strips and puzzles for good measure. After the war, things

Robin and Jack and Jill Annuals.

Summer Specials.

changed somewhat. For a start, the media – especially television – was very influential, and so annuals began to appear celebrating popular characters of the day.

Each year there was the agonising decision of which annual to ask for, because although you were rarely given more than one, if you were really fortunate, aunts and uncles might send postal orders, which you could use to buy another annual. So, did you play safe and choose *Bunty* or *Girl*, or did you decide to take a chance that, if you asked politely, you might be given the latest *Beano* annual, even though you knew Mum didn't really approve of you reading it? This plan could backfire, and you then ran the risk of being given an annual you didn't really want. Most comics had an annual tie-in, and some were better than others. Usually they were a mixture of stories about favourite characters from the comics, things to do, a full-page picture or two to admire, and a few factual articles.

Not all annuals were actually linked with comics; some were tie-ins with toys companies, television programmes, newspaper strips, pop stars or cartoon characters. *Girl* annual was a top favourite, as was *School Friend* and *Girls' Crystal*. And, slightly later, *Bunty*, *Judy* and others of that ilk. Alongside all these annuals were the traditional, proven favourites, the comic annuals in the true sense of the word, titles such as *Beano*, *Dandy*, *Beryl the Peril*, *Topper*, *Beezer* and *Sparky*. These annuals had their legion of fans, both male and female, and were regularly found beneath the Christmas tree. The media continued to influence the world of comics and annuals, not just the television titles, but annuals derived from films and even the toys that filled the toyshops to overflowing. Television annuals a girl might well have enjoyed included *The Avengers*, *Emergency Ward 10*, *Compact*, *Blue Peter* and *Charlie's Angels*. Amongst the 1980s' toy-related titles were *My Little Pony*, *Strawberry Shortcake*, *Sindy*, *Polly Pocket*, *Barbie*, *Glo-Bugs* and *Care Bears*. Toddlers were spoilt for choice with a wealth of annuals aimed at the pre-school market after the war and for the next few decades classic titles such as *Jack and Jill*, *Playhour*, *Play School*, *Twinkle*, *Robin*,

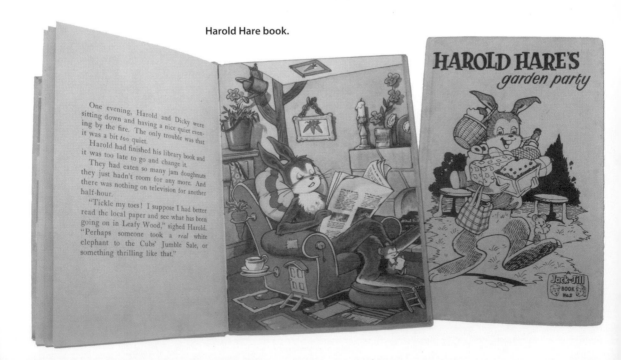

Harold Hare book.

Buttons and *Play-Group* kept the little ones amused. Sometimes, small books featuring loved characters appear. In the 1950s, Fleetway published a series from the *Jack and Jill* comics, amongst them *Harold Hare*. There were also several books featuring characters from *Girl – Belle, Wendy and Jinx* – while cookery books, ballet, pony, pop music and pet titles have also appeared as spin-offs from various comics. More recently, various compilations of articles and stories from girls' comics have been published. (See Book List.)

Very popular in the mid to late 1950s was the *News Chronicle I-Spy Annual*, which was based on the popular series of books and the accompanying column in the *News Chronicle*. These contained a mix of things to do, plays to perform and even a pop-up model, such as a castle, to build. *The Schoolgirl's Pets Annual* was another book that appeared in thousands of girl's Christmas stockings – or pillowcase – in the late 1950s, which is why they are so easy to find today. By the late 1960s there was a plethora of pop music titles aimed at young teens and pre-teens. These annuals were often a mix of pop star articles, pin-up photos, pop quizzes, fashion tips and beauty features, with maybe a token picture strip or two thrown in for good measure. Many of these pop music annuals are beginning to be collectable, especially those which contain Beatles pictures. Collecting pop annuals is a genre that is concentrated on by many; a collection of these books provides an intriguing insight to the musical world and the changes it has undergone. It's also interesting, and rather sad, to see how many of the stars of the annuals, once so famous, are now obscure, forgotten names.

Dandy and *Beano* annuals from the early 1940s can fetch hundreds of pounds, while some cult television series-related annuals are on the rise. Nowadays, many annuals are very collectable, with one particularly valuable one being the 1973 Rupert Bear annual depicting Rupert as a brown-faced bear, rather than the more usual white face. The story behind the two covers of this annual is that the illustrator, Alfred Bestall, had planned a beautiful painting around a brown bear as usual, but in 1973 it was decided to have Rupert's fur shown as white on the cover. Rupert was usually depicted as white inside the annual. When Alfred saw his painting altered into a white Rupert, he felt there was no contrast between Rupert and the pale sky behind him, and he was aware that, artistically, there should have been a shadow on Rupert's face. To appease the artist, just a handful of annuals from that year were printed with a brown Rupert. It must be every collector's dream to discover a 1973 annual with a brown-faced Rupert, as today they sell for thousands of pounds. Early Rupert annuals are valuable, too – if you have a very first, 1936 copy, or an early wartime edition – in mint condition – you could be sitting on a nest egg. Much later, the *Daily Express* issued a series of facsimile annuals of the early titles, a project later continued by Pedigree.

However, as a rule of thumb, it is comics, summer specials and other ephemera that are likely to be of more value. Annuals last longer, so there are a lot more of them around, though, as condition is all-important to a collector, mint copies of annuals will always demand a premium. Many of us concentrate on 'reading copies', which might be a bit scuffed or thumbed, but are more affordable and we don't feel guilty at opening them, looking at the illustrations and reading the text. Mint copies, once looked through, aren't, strictly speaking, mint any more.

It is easy to build up a collection of the more popular titles of annuals, just by searching through the piles to be found at any car boot fair, charity shop or flea market. Many will be worn and scuffed, but often, annuals were read once or twice, then not referred to again,

Picture library books.

so you could well strike lucky and pick up some pristine gems. My favourite annuals as a child were the Chicks' Own books – for ages I was puzzled by the story of a little girl who had been chosen as May Queen, and before she went to bed the night before the parade, told her mother 'Call me early'. I could never work out why she wanted her mother to call her 'Early' when that wasn't her real name! Eventually, I asked my mum, who laughed and explained the sentence. Years later, I found a copy of that annual in a second-hand bookshop. Eagerly I turned the pages, and there was the picture strip, just as I remembered. Needless to say, I bought the annual for the memories it contained. Another annual I remember was again a 1950s' *Chicks' Own*, which had two characters tricking their teacher over grammar by saying 'I sawed a piece of wood, see'. Other more general favourites included the *I-Spy Annual*, *Schoolgirls' Own Pets Annual*, *Princess Tina Ballet Book*, *Rupert Bear* and the *Princess Tina Pony Book*.

The 'picture library' booklets were a popular extra, and most comics produced them. With titles such as *Bunty*'s 'My Model Sister', 'No Place Like Home', 'The Bravest of Them All', *Mandy*'s 'Gilda's Golden Touch', 'Poor Little Rich Girl', *Debbie*'s 'Stella's Step Into Time', *Girl*'s 'Moments of Terror' and 'Welcome To the Old Mill', how could any girl resist them? They used to be advertised inside the comics, with a picture of the cover and a quick summing up leaving the reader desperate to know more. These booklets had colourful covers and cost around double the price of a comic, but they seemed more permanent. They could be stood neatly in a bookshelf, and so, unlike the comics, which tended to be discarded after a few weeks, the booklets endured. Today, many people prefer to collect these rather than the comics because they are much easier to store.

China
Ceramic tie-ins for comics are fairly easy to find, especially modern items such as mugs and plates featuring Minnie the Minx and similar characters. Many of the media stars who appeared in comics, as well as those featured in newspaper strips – Rupert Bear, Snoopy,

Sindy, My Little Pony, Barbie and Fifi and the Flowertots – can be found adorning pieces of tableware or as ceramic ornaments, with a little searching.

Perhaps the most interesting pieces, which crop up from time to time, are various items of nursery china which bear pictures of characters from the *Jack and Jill* comic and which were issued in the 1950s. These delightful pieces were made by Beswick china, and are marked, 'Fleetway Publications publishers of Jack and Jill and Playhour, Beswick England'. Amongst the items is a cup which

Nursery character china, Beswick.

bears a picture of Teddy and Cuddly, the two little bears on the front, while on the back Gulliver Guinea-pig can be seen, carrying a his belongings in a red-spotted bundle tied to a pole. Another attractive piece in the set is a high-sided nursery dish with a brightly coloured picture of Jack and Jill and their puppy, Patch, on the base.

Die-cast Models

Die-cast vehicles with Minnie the Minx by Lledo.

Die-cast vehicles featuring characters from girls' comics, by Oxford Die-cast and Lledo.

Buses, vans, lorries and other vehicles have long been used to promote items, usually the produce of the company or factory of which the vehicle belongs to. When miniature model vans were first made, they too would have replica logos so that they resembled the full size version. More recently, hundreds of die-cast models have been issued by various companies bearing many kinds of logos: often fanciful or based on a particular product. The designs of these models are usually dreamt up on the drawing board; they have never actually appeared on a full size vehicle, save in the designer's imagination.

Even so, these small die-cast models can be extremely attractive, and are an interesting addition to a collection of comics. Various companies, including Lledo and Oxford Diecast produce these vehicles, and they cover a surprising variety of comic titles that appeal to girls, including *Bunty*, *Girl*, *Robin*, *School Friend*, *Rainbow*, *Tiny Tots*, *T.V. Comic*, *Rainbow*, *Girls' Own*, *Girl Guide's Gazette* and *Bubbles*. There are also many cars and vans which feature various characters, amongst them Minnie the Minx and Beryl the Peril.

Fast Food Freebies

In 2000, McDonalds issued a set of nine characters from *The Beano*, as animated plastic toys. The figures consisted of the favourites; most would be easily recognisable to even a non-*Beano* reader. Of course, Minnie the Minx, was included. Minnie, 4½in tall was depicted wearing her usual red and black striped jersey and black skirt, and she put out her tongue when a button was pressed in her back. Amongst the other characters issued at the same time were Roger the Dodger, Headmaster, Dennis the Menace, Walter, Gnasher, Smiffy and Fatty. The only other girl in the set, apart from Minnie, was Bea, Dennis the Menace's baby sister. Bea is depicted as a seated toddler clutching a feeding bottle, and a button in her back puffs air through the teat of the bottle.

Burger King also released some characters from *The Beano*, amongst them a 3¾in high Minnie the Minx, mounted on a pair of snowshoes. Her arm was out to the side and her waist twisted. The others in this set were Dennis the Menace in a large sledge with his dog Gnasher, Bea with a snowman and Roger the Dodger on a smaller sledge. This Burger King promotion dates from 2003.

Figurines

The company Robert Harrop Designs have been creating collectable character figurines for over 20 years, and amongst them are many nostalgic licensed products. As well as such childhood favourites as Paddington Bear, Camberwick Green, Magic Roundabout and Clangers, Robert Harrop also produce figurines featuring characters from the *The Beano*, *The Dandy* and other D.C. Thomson comics. These include Korky the Kat, Biffo the Bear, Dennis the Menace and many others. Girl characters are not so plentiful, but even so Harrop has issued Minnie the Minx, Beryl the Peril, Bea, Keyhole Kate, Toots, Olive and even Katey, the niece of Desperate Dan. They are all modelled as accurate, highly detailed resin figurines. As it isn't particularly easy to find tie-ins featuring characters from girls' comics, figurines such as these make an attractive addition to a collection of comics, as well as being collectable in their own right.

Minnie the Minx, Burger King.

Some of the Harrop pieces are larger, set pieces, consisting of groups of several characters, while others show a single character posing, sometimes in a setting. There is a set of characters in colourful dodgem cars, and amongst these are Minnie the Minx, in a red and black striped dodgem, and the twins Toots and her brother Sydney in a blue striped car. Little Bea is very popular; models of her decorate picture frames and other items, while also obtainable is a series of message pieces which tie-in with special occasions. One of my favourite Harrop pieces depicts the Perishers, showing the children in a cart trying to get Boot the dog to pull it.

Minnie the Minx,
Robert Harrop.

Games and puzzles

There are plenty of tie-in jigsaw puzzles with characters shown in comics, so, for instance if you collect Rupert annuals or 1980s' Care Bears comics, you might like to collect the puzzles to go with them. A super jigsaw puzzle was sold through branches of Marks and Spencers in 2008, produced in conjunction with D.C. Thomson. The puzzle showed a collection of covers from girl's comics, amongst them *Jackie*, *Bunty*, *Diana*, *Mandy* and *Judy*, and consisted of 1,000 pieces. Other puzzles tied-in with girls' comics include a montage design jigsaw depicting cover images from *Jackie*, produced in 2009. This 1,000-piece puzzle was made by a company called Susan Prescott Games. Some greetings' card manufacturers have published small jigsaws with a comic-related theme, notably Halycon cards who, in 1976, issued several titles, amongst them *Girl*, *The Dandy* and *Rainbow*. These 'puzzle cards' made attractive gifts. Waddington's produced a set of six mini-puzzles in the late 1970s. The Waddington's puzzles were 40-piece giveaways, and subjects included Korky the Cat from *The Dandy*. Very hard to find and extremely collectable is a wooden puzzle made by Simpkin Marshall Ltd., of London, in the 1920s, which features the *Daily Mail* comic strip characters Pip, Squeak and Wilfred. If you are lucky enough to own one of these, they can sell for £100 or more if in perfect, mint condition. There are many other jigsaw tie-ins to find.

Card games and board games are another comic tie-in to look out for, and make a super addition to a comic collection. In the 1950s Castell Bros. under their 'Pepys' cards range produced a set of 44 playing cards, featuring many favourite characters from *Girl*. Amongst them were Wendy and Jinx, Belle, Lettice Leefe, Penny and Robbie. The cards were bright and colourful, featuring the characters on one side, while the reverse was red with a Girl logo. Each pack cost 3/11d. A company called Theydon Games using the 'Gayplay' name, made a shopping board game called Pik-Paks, in conjunction with *Girl*. The game included playing cards, shopping lists and miniature hand-painted people, while the box was decorated with Wendy and Jinx, as well as the Girl motif. The game cost 12/11d from Hamleys and other stores and was advertised in a 1957 issue of the *Girl* comic. More modern board games include those featuring characters from *The Beano*. One of the most popular is Dennis the Menace who has featured in several games, alongside Gnasher his dog. Top Trumps cards picturing Minnie the Minx, Toots and others are another collectables' games idea.

Beryl the Peril,
Robert Harrop.

Music and Media

An extremely difficult item to find is the sheet music of the *Lettice Leefe Hop* which was published in 1956. An advert from a *Girl* comic of the time says, 'the song was written by Murray Browne and is being featured by Ernest and April Catro. It has been recorded on HMV BD 1329, and the dance routine is available on song copies published by the BF Wood Music Co. Ltd, of Mills House, Denmark Street, W.C.2.' It cost 1/6d at the time.

Lettice was not the only character from a girls' comic to be feted in music – in 1924, a four-page booklet of sheet music entitled 'Bessie – The Pride Of the School' was given away with a March 1928 edition of *School Friend*. The song was a humorous ditty praising the favourite girls' comic character of the time, Bessie Bunter of Cliff House School, and was composed by Alison Travers, using her pseudonym of Toni Farrell. The words are by Tom Richards, which was probably a pseudonym as well. Around

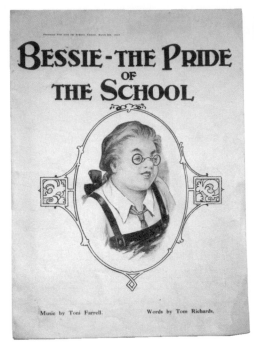

Bessie Bunter sheet music.

this time the *Daily Mirror*'s Pip, Squeak and Wilfred Gugnunc Sing-Song was popular. Money was raised for charity by the sales of printed song sheets. There was also a now, very rare, 78 rpm record produced by His Master's Voice of the Sing-Song.

More recently, several boxed sets of CDs have been issued, featuring popular music around during the time of *Jackie*. They have been released under the EMI label, and each

Puzzles depicting girl's comics.

set contains three discs containing tracks from the likes of David Cassidy, Donny Osmond, David Essex, The Bay City Rollers and other stars from the 1960s–80s. There are also earlier LPs, cassettes, videotapes, and DVDs featuring favourite characters from comics and comic strips, such as Rupert Bear from the *Daily Express*. His most notorious musical claim to fame was starring in the video 'Rupert and the Frog Song' which was composed by ex-Beatle Paul McCartney in 1984 and which won a BAFTA award. The song, *We All Stand Together* was based on the froggy design of the end papers in a Rupert Annual dating from 1958. An interesting Rupert Bear LP to look for is *Rupert Bear's First Album of Songs*, issued by the *Daily Express* in 1986 and featuring seventeen songs about Rupert and his friends. It was sung by 'The Nutwood Chums', and the colourful front cover was based on a design by John Harrold for the 50th Rupert Bear annual, while the reverse was a montage of Alfred Bestall's Rupert illustrations. All of these items would make interesting tie-ins for collectors of the relevant comics.

Pelham Puppets

Puppets seemed particularly popular during the 1950s and 60s, no doubt helped by the fact that so many children's television programmes featured them. Glove puppets, ventriloquist's dummies and, in particular, string puppets, appeared on many shows, and because children were not so sophisticated as their modern counterparts, they were perfectly happy to accept the somewhat wobbly, jerky action. Many of the puppets were featured in comics of the time, characters such as Andy Pandy, Bill and Ben, Muffin the Mule and the cult programme *Thunderbirds* – this latter show featured Lady Penelope who later starred in her own comic which today is very collectable. In those days it didn't seem to matter if strings could be seen or the puppet's mouths weren't synchronised.

The use of puppets in the theatre is probably one of the earliest forms of entertainment, it was known to the Ancient Greeks and many other cultures. Pelham Puppets made

Lettice Leefe.   Belle in ballgown.   The Schoolboy.

their first appearance in 1947, and remained in production till 1993. The company was founded by Robert 'Bob' Pelham, who initially sourced much of the necessary materials from government surplus stores, while many of the heads were made from the wooden balls used for coconut shies. The most interesting puppets for the collector of comics are those which were based on characters from the *Girl* and *Eagle*, and which appeared in the early 1950s. Amongst them were Lettice Leefe (the greenest girl in the school), and Belle of the Ballet, both from *Girl*, and the Schoolboy and Sir Harris Tweed from *Eagle*. The Lettice Leefe puppet depicts the bespectacled schoolgirl in her dark blue gymslip, white long-sleeved blouse and a red tie. Red and white spotted hair ribbons secure her dark brown plaits. Belle of the Ballet wears a light blue long dress, or tutu decorated with a pink flower. She has long blonde wavy hair, and she can also be found in a pink ball gown with a central patterned panel on the skirt. Lettice Leefe was obtainable as a glove puppet too. The *Eagle* characters are also very rare – The Schoolboy wears a navy blue blazer and short grey trousers, while Sir Harris Tweed is a mustachioed gentleman in a grey suit.

Stamps

Surprisingly, postage stamps can tie-in with comics. Occasionally, characters from comic strips are featured adorning postage stamps; in 1990 the laughing face of Denis the Menace appeared on a 20p stamp, while Rupert Bear was enjoying a balloon ride on a first class stamp in 1994. The best way to collect postage stamps as tie-ins is to go for those adorning first day covers (envelopes). Companies such as Buckingham Covers issue beautifully decorated (sometimes autographed) first day covers which would grace any collection of comics.

Toys and dolls

Dolls were popular girls' toys in the 1950s, appealing to girls up until the age of twelve or so, sometimes even older. Unlike today, there was no stigma attached to older girls playing with dolls – nowadays few girls over the age of five like dolls, or, if they do, it's the fashion teen type such as Barbie, Sindy or Bratz. Palitoy, a British toy company particularly famed for their dolls, launched the Girl doll in 1953 as a tie-in to the popular *Girl* comic published by Hulton Press. This doll was made from hard plastic and she stood 14in tall, probably representing a ten to twelve year old girl. Actually, she was rather an amalgam, as although her face was older and her body was slim, with a waist – she had obviously lost her puppy fat – she was completely flat chested.

This doll was of the walking type, and as she moved her head turned from side to side. She was jointed at neck, hips and shoulders, and her legs were slim and straight. Pretty, in a slightly old-fashioned way, her face was solemn, with delicate colouring, her mouth was closed with just the barest hint of a smile, and her eyes were an unusual shade of lavender. The plastic used for her construction was very shiny. Her slightly curved arms featured dainty hands with long, delicate fingers, and her hair was in an early 1950s' style of pin-type curls all around her face. Normally, though, most of the dolls found nowadays lack the majority of the curls because girls' enjoyed brushing and combing her hair. In those days dolls didn't have 'rooted hair' as they do today. This Girl doll was no exception, she had a wig glued to her hard plastic head, and if it got wet, then it tended to tangle and, eventually either moult or fall off. Palitoy claimed 'Her hair can be washed, combed and curled' going on to explain that the hair needed to be wetted with warm water and rubbed with shampoo 'until you have a good lather'. Afterwards the dolls' hair needed to be rinsed, towel dried, combed and wound onto curlers. When it was dry, it could be combed into the desired style – it's most unlikely many girls followed these instructions to the letter, which goes to explain why a Girl doll in perfect condition, wearing her original outfit, can sell for several hundreds of pounds.

The outfit was the most important part as it bore the logo of Girl's head as depicted on the comic masthead and on the club badge. The Girl badge was unusual, as instead of being the more traditional round metal badge this was a bronze-coloured sculptured head of a young girl. (See Chapter 8.) This logo was liberally featured in the doll – her short white taffeta dress was printed with the design in red, as were her matching knickers, while her hair ribbon bore the same design in either red or blue. Her red ribbon belt was fastened with a white plastic buckle fashioned in the shape of a girls' head. The Girl doll was marked on her back with the words 'Palitoy Made in England', arranged in a circle with a number 35 in the middle. Palitoy claimed that the dress could be washed and this was tried by many girls with dire results. The red tended to run! Even so, the instructions regarding the dress claimed 'Tub it gently in warm, soapy water and remember never twist the fabric'. Extra patterns could be obtained for clothes for the Girl doll, and they were advertised in *Girl*. Each pattern cost 10d including postage and packing, and amongst them were a sun dress and stole, square dancing outfit, overcoat, blouse and skirt, long, full-skirted party dress, cape and skirt, nightie, and a bloomer suit.

Other dolls to look out for include dolls of Minnie the Minnie the Minx, such as a soft fabric creation depicting Minnie in her usual red and black outfit, made by 'The Real Beano Gear', imported by Mr Lucky Bags. Dennis the Menace is available too. There are also various dolls from newspaper comic strips including the Peanuts characters and the Perishers. (See Chapter 10)

Girl also licensed Mettoy to make a Girl carpet sweeper in the 1950s. This cream and green sweeper was child-size and was made from metal. It really worked, it could pick up fluff, crumbs and dust, and it bore the Girl comic logo. The packaging was interesting; it was a long cardboard box decorated with illustrations of favourite *Girl* characters, amongst them Wendy and Jinx. Another *Girl* item available was by Winsor and Newton who produced an attractive red paint box, filled with small squares of watercolour paint. Bearing the logos of both *Girl* and *Eagle*, this smart metal tin must have been slipped inside many Christmas stockings in the 1950s. *Girl* also sold items such as a travel bag, made by Sports Utilities Ltd., available in beige, scarlet or green tweed effect fabric. The bag fastened with a locking zip, and cost 37/6d, back in 1957.

Woppit/Whoppit

Woppit was a favourite character in the *Robin* comic in the 1950s, continuing with the comic through into the 1960s, and Woppit has become something of a cult toy in the collecting world. Laurence Heyworth of Look & Learn, the company which now owns the rights to *Robin* explained, 'I have asked our honorary archivist, Steve Holland, about Mr Woppit. It seems pretty clear that the character belongs to Look and Learn as there is no evidence that its creator, Ursula Moray Williams, retained any rights, which would in any case be very unusual. It ran from the first issue of *Robin* under the title 'The Story of Woppit' until 1967. The famous Merrythought company briefly made a Woppit bear in 1955; it appeared in their 1956 catalogue and a year earlier Marks and Spencer produced a

Benham (A. Buckingham) Ltd., The Cover Shop, The Bayle, Folkestone, Kent ⬭Benham⬭ BLCS50

Postage stamps sometimes feature cartoon characters, as shown on this FDC from Buckingham covers.

Carpet cleaner, Mettoy.

Girl doll from Palitoy.

Girl products.

Mr Whoppit, Merrythought.

Woppit glove puppet. The Woppit bear then became famous because of Donald Campbell, who called his bear mascot Mr Whoppit (note the slight change of spelling). Merrythought made 5,000 limited editions of a Mr Whoppit bear in 1995.

Donald Campbell was killed on 4 January 1967 when his hydroplane *Bluebird* K7 flipped at Coniston Water in the Lake District. The craft completely disintegrated as Donald Campbell reached speeds in excess of 300mph. No one is absolutely sure of the cause, but it's probable that the jet engine suddenly cut out. The wreckage of *Bluebird* sunk, together with Donald Campbell's body, before the rescue boats could reach the site, but Mr Whoppit, the little teddy bear mascot, was found floating amongst the debris. It wasn't until 2001 that the wreckage of the craft, along with Donald Campbell's body, were recovered. Later, his daughter Gina, also used the bear as a mascot when she competed in offshore powerboat racing, setting a world water speed record of her own. The 1990s Merrythought version of Mr Whoppit showed the little bear dressed in his red jacket bearing an embroidered bluebird motif, blue shoes and with blue ear-linings. The bear was 8in tall and was made from light beige mohair. He was sold in a sturdy box bearing pictures and an account of the *Bluebird* tragedy.

Musical tie-ins.

CHAPTER TWELVE

Collecting Comics – What's Next?

Collecting and storing comics and annuals

Where do you start? With so many titles and genres to choose from, unless you are fortunate enough to own a barn or a warehouse, you will have to decide which to choose. Many people will collect the titles they knew as a child – often, it is the comics people remember from their very early years which make them feel most nostalgic, whether they might be *Chicks' Own*, *Jack and Jill* or *Twinkle*. Others enjoy the later ones, the *Girls*, *Buntys*, *Mandys* and *Jackies* – these were the comics which they would have discussed at school with their friends, and they might well have joined the clubs, sent in letters or entered competitions. So there are plenty of memories involved. You might decide to concentrate on media-based titles, or maybe pre-war comics. The scope is enormous. And then you will need to decide why you are collecting – is it for investment, or for reading purposes? If it is the former, you will obviously need to buy only the very best copies, but if you are buying for pleasure, to read them, then you probably won't mind them being a little frayed round the edges, or that the quizzes have been filled in.

Runs of comics will take up an enormous amount of space, as will sets of annuals – and even if you have the room, it isn't advisable to just stack the comics or squash the annuals tightly onto the bookshelf. Correct storage is essential if you want to preserve your collection, or at least keep it in a reasonable condition, and there are several things which could easily damage your items, so it is well to keep them in mind.

Damp, heat and light are all enemies of paper. Damp can cause mould or mould spots, and can buckle covers, smudge ink, stick pages together or make your treasured comics smell musty. Heat can make pages discolour or turn brittle, while bright light or sunshine will quickly fade colourful covers and turn the edges of pages brown. It isn't just sunlight that will fade inks, fluorescent lighting will too, and even tungsten will alter the colour if it is left on over a period of time. Ensure that your comics are well away from any heat source such as radiators or fires, as well as household pets. It's amazing how much damage a dog or cat can inflict on a pile of comics or even an annual if left to their own devices.

If all that isn't enough, there is the problem of insects. Many common insects like nothing more than to munch their way through a comic or tasty annual because the glue or starch is a particular treat. Even insects not normally noted for addiction to paper, such as greenfly or midges, can mar a section of a comic or annual if they happen to become trapped between two pages so you're left with the dreaded squashed fly decoration. This is why it isn't a good idea to place books or comics onto the carpet – tiny woolly bear larvae and other mites can be lurking in a rug (or even in the cleanest carpet), just waiting to nibble your precious hoard.

It's important to handle the comics correctly, paper tends to deteriorate over time, so the edges of pages can easily tear. If your comics are to last, then really you should wear

Assorted Comics.

white cotton gloves before you handle them, to protect the paper from the natural oils in your hands. However, for practical purposes, as long as you have washed your hands with soap and water to remove the natural oils, it should be fine. Hold the comics by the edges, trying not to put too much pressure on the stapled fold, as that is vulnerable to splits. It depends to a certain extent on the condition your comics are already in. As I pointed out, some people will only buy perfect copies, while others just seek to recreate their childhood, and so buy bundles of comics from boot fairs. The boot fair bundles are usually tatty, torn, with marks, and maybe scribble inside. As these are reading copies, which are unlikely to become valuable, the best thing is just to store them somewhere where they won't deteriorate further, and enjoy them.

Store comics in purpose-made comic storage bags – it's not a good idea to use ordinary polythene bags as they can react with the paper and the inks over time, Even worse are plastic freezer bags bearing printed designs which can transfer the design onto the comic. There are various types of storage bags sold; many people use Mylar bags, which are considered top of the range, though

Minnie the Minx in dodgem car, Robert Harrop.

if your comics aren't exceedingly valuable, the cheaper storage bags work fine. Mylar D is a chemically inert material, and bags made from this are used in many archival sites around the world. Never store comics in brown paper bags or boxes, because the dyes and the acid in the paper can stain the comic. Try to obtain an acid-free archival box in which to store your comics. It's a good idea to use white backing boards in with the comics to ensure they stay flat and don't get creased if the bag is moved. There are many suppliers of storage material for comics, especially on the Internet.

Annuals can be stored on bookshelves, though it's important not to squash them in as they will get distorted. One of the main causes of damage to annuals are split spines, especially at the top and bottom, caused by a finger being hooked into the spines to pull the books from the selves. To prevent this it is best to use both hands, or cup your hand right around the spine so that fingers and palm rest against the backboards and the thumb against the front boards, and the pull the book holding the middle of the spine. Better still, if there is enough room, slide a hand either side of the book and pull gently. It's best not to stack annuals, because the weight will warp those at the bottom of the heap. It might seem obvious, but it's worth pointing out that it isn't a good idea to leave an annual lying around when you aren't reading it, because people less enlightened than you are quite likely to use it as a handy surface on which to rest the paper while they write a note. Or even worse, put their teacup down on it.

**Facsimile comics from
The Guardian, 2009.**

Buying

So, you've decided that you would like to collect comics – where do you begin? Although much maligned, the ubiquitous boot sale is often a good place to start, especially if you are concentrating on reading copies. Flea markets, fêtes, charity shops and jumble sales are all worth trying. Ask around – it's surprising what friends and neighbours can have in their lofts, and if they know you are collecting, they might be only too pleased to know that the pile of comics which has been stored away since their children grew up has found a good home. Collectors' centres often have traders who sell comics and annuals, as do antique and collectables' fairs, while in some areas there are fairs just for solely to books and comics. Some second-hand bookshops have areas devoted to comics, and there are shops just selling comics and annuals. The Internet is another place to try; as well as the main auction sites, there are sellers and on-line stores who hold stocks of comics which you can buy immediately, using a credit card, without having to bid. Whichever you choose, ensure you are happy with the item and its condition before you buy, and, if buying over the Internet, remember to check the seller's feedback and that the site is secure before you make your payment. That way, you won't be disappointed.

Don't forget

You think that you know your collection, and the comics you already have – until you are confronted with a pile of them. It's amazing how the memory plays tricks; sometimes you can be convinced you have a certain comic or annual, then when you return home to check you realise that it only looked familiar because you saw a picture of it somewhere. In the case of annuals, often dust wrappers are removed and titles such as *Bunty* look vastly different underneath. It pays dividends if you have a small notebook listing all the comics and annuals you possess, together with their dates. You can then slip it into your pocket or handbag and it will always be ready if you happen to see some comics as you pass by a charity shop or boot sale. As your collection – and the length of the list – grows, you might find it easier to list the issues that you don't have and are searching for, instead.

Is it the real McCoy?

It's important to be wary when buying comics; though most of those you come across will be genuine, there are various reproductions around. For instance, in 2009, *The Guardian* newspaper gave away free issues of classic comics. These were facsimiles, and although on close inspection the differences are obvious, they might not immediately be spotted by a novice collector. The titles given away by *The Guardian* included *The Dandy, The Beano, Whizzer and Chips* and *Tammy*. The paper was of a different quality, and looked too new, and, on most, in small letters by the publisher's details the words 'facsimile issue' appeared – but even so, they could well turn up in a few years time amongst a batch of original issues.

Bill McLoughlin from D.C.Thomson, explaining how to differentiate their original comics from reproductions states, 'It is difficult and it isn't. The paper quality is different. Up until some point in the 1990s comics were printed letterpress or letterflex and were not full colour. Only when the comics went over to gravure printing did they get full colour and different paper for a different process. However the only real way to tell an original from a facsimile is that originals have imprint and copyright lines, generally on the back page and this contains the year of publication. Facsimiles will have the original date on the front cover, but should have a copyright line somewhere with the year of publication. If there is no imprint with the year of publication the chances are that it is a copy.'

British comic collecting gets overshadowed

Alan Notton of the British Comics Internet site says, 'There seems to be hundreds of sites dedicated to the American comic-book, but just a handful dedicated to their British counterparts. I, for one, do not want to see the British comic fall by the wayside and get totally lost in the mists of time. I want to remind people out there, young and old, that British comics were once a great and thriving industry, with great characters, great stories and great artwork. They really are, too good to be forgotten. British comics have long been the Cinderella of the comic world. Especially when compared to their counterparts across the pond. Love them or loathe them, American comic books can fetch big bucks. Issue 1 of *Action Comics* (where Superman made his first appearance) fetched £120,000 a few years ago. The Americans are very enthusiastic when it comes to collecting 'comic books', and I think it's about time the British caught up! In comparison, the first issue of *The Beano* was auctioned for £12,100 in March 2004 and *Dandy*'s first issue with the free gift went for £20,350 in September 2004. A *Dandy* without the free gift went for £7,261 in June 2004. The *1973 Rupert Annual*, with the very rare brown face, was auctioned for £16,000 in May 2000.'

British girls comics are collectable too

Up until fairly recently, British girls' comics were neglected by the collecting world. People who collected comics tended to concentrate on the boys' titles – probably because most of the collectors were male. Then it was realised that many of the comics issued for the fairer sex were, actually, rather good. In fact, many of them contained stunning artwork, and the stories weren't half bad, either! Also, the nostalgia trend has gathered momentum, and ladies of a certain age are anxious to recapture their youth by buying up *Girl*, *School Friend*, *Bunty*, *Misty*, *Judy* and many other comics. At the same time, others have decided to start collecting the pre-war girls' comics, the gung-ho jolly hockey sticks types so much loved in the 1920s and 30s. So now, many of these older titles are now becoming very difficult to source.

The result of all this is that prices of some girls' comics are soaring. As an example, recently a copy of a *Bunty Summer Special 1964* reached almost the £200 mark; not a bad investment for whoever first bought that way back in the swinging sixties. A first issue of a short-lived IPC girls' comic called *Lindy*, dating from 1975, sold for around £50, while a *1971 Bunty Summer Special* went for £35. Particularly popular with collectors are the cult girls' comics, such as the *Lady Penelope* titles dating from the mid-1960s. A first copy complete with the free gift of a Lady Penelope signet ring sells for £250 or so. *Lady Penelope* was a fairly short-lived comic. It began in 1966 with stories such as 'Marina', 'Girl from U.N.C.L.E.' and 'The Monkees', underwent a couple of name changes and became incorporated into *Princess Tina* two years later. Bound volumes of pre-war girl's comic classics have been rising in price recently, often reaching the £300 mark or more. Al Notton has noticed that *Misty*, *Jinty*, *Tammy* and early *Bunty*s seem to be the more modern comics which attract the higher prices, and which have most collectability.

Looking back and marching forward

It's tempting to look back to the good old days, when comics were a child's weekly treat, and when there were dozens of enticing titles from which to choose. The heady fifties, sixties and seventies – and, for those who remember them or are collecting them – the exciting pre-war comics, when classic characters such as Tiger Tim, Bessie Bunter and Pansy Potter first left the drawing boards. In the 1980s, comics changed, and magazine types became popular. These were consumer-led, featuring cosmetics, fashions, celebrities and all things girlie. Girls didn't want to read picture strips about life at boarding school anymore! There were still traditional-styled comics around, but the trend was towards magazine-styled colourful glossies and the newsprint types began to look dated. Many more free gifts were offered, too – in the decades up till the 1970s, free gifts were usually given with first three issues, and then as occasional extra treats. Nowadays, the girls' comics and magazines have at least one free gift each issue, often several.

The traditional comics haven't all gone from the newsagents' shops, but you will have to look harder to find a comic in the accepted sense of the word. Many have been replaced by magazines or activity-based publications, as opposed to the traditional idea of a comic filled with picture strips. Good old favourites are still around – you can still buy *The Beano* and *The Dandy*, for instance.

According to comic book artist David Roach, the decline began when the photo-strips became commonplace. Trialled with comics such as the romantics of the late 1950s and early 1960s, it wasn't long before they were commonplace in many mainstream publications – *Jackie*, later *Bunty* issues, *Debbie* and others. Once, there was so much work in the comics industry that British artists couldn't keep up, and much – in fact the majority – of the artwork in many comics was produced abroad by talented Italian and Spanish artists, such as Jordi Longaron in *Valentine*. (Hence the plethora of dark haired full-lipped beauties – you didn't see so many English roses in Barcelona!) As photo-strips increased, so the artists needed declined; their skills were no longer wanted and they were forced to seek new outlets. Everything moves on, in all walks of life; new inventions and techniques render older styles and attitudes obsolete.

There is another problem with photos when used to tell stories – they are too realistic. Perhaps this is rather an obvious observation, but because they show 'real life', there is no room for fantasy. A drawing is a softer art form, and can show interesting backgrounds, dreams, different locations or fabulous outfits. Drawn picture strips allow imagination to flow, the reader sees an idealised image of the heroine or hero, and can much more easily identify with them. A photographic strip shows the heroine and hero as they are, including spots, iffy hairstyles and odd outfits, which can be immensely off putting. Also, drawings allow the writers to depict schoolgirls, girls in exotic locations, historical adventures and 'brave animal' stories – all these are much more difficult to show in the harsh reality of a photo strip story. So the modern photo strips, though hailed as an innovation, depicted modern life – and there was only a limited number of times you could repeat the same 'boy meets girl, they quarrel, they make up' story themes.

It's more difficult for today's children to buy what we think of as 'traditional' comics; as we have seen, most are centred around a television programme or toy character. Inside is a mix of puzzles and features, with maybe a token picture strip or two – but everything is simplified. It is almost as though there is a policy of making things as easy

Modern girls' magazines.

as possible. Publishers seem loathe to believe that children might actually enjoy reading a longer story or comic strip. Having said that, there are still many lively and creative comics around. Titles such as *Sparkle World*, *Girl Talk*, *Go Girl*, *Disney Girl* and *Fifi and the Flowertots* are just a few of the bright comics which can still be found in newsagents and supermarkets.

Compared to earlier decades, comic prices are much dearer. No longer are they spur of the moment purchases, bought with loose change; they are priced in pounds. Says Sharon White, mother of two young children, 'I'm afraid Holly and Lucy are into *Barbie* and *Disney Princess* magazines but they're so expensive', while Kathy Martin points out that, with regard to her daughter, 'Amy's only regular magazine is *Pony Magazine* which she adores. She doesn't really like any of the others although she likes the fact that there is one called *Amy*!' Many children nowadays will choose to take a magazine reflecting their interests, rather than buy a comic, and with magazines often not costing much more than a comic, it's a wise move. Most magazines are far more substantial than a comic, and though the majority of the special interests magazines are aimed at adults, they will appeal to any intelligent child. Wildlife magazines, such as those published by the BBC, are deservedly popular, while specialised subjects such as ballet dancing, horse riding, sports and crafts such as scrap-booking are well-catered for. A child interested in these subjects will have no difficulty in finding enjoyment in a magazine on the subject, even if it is adult-orientated.

Thousands of children are members of societies and clubs which have regular newsletters and magazines, especially geared towards the topic. Sometimes these are children's organisations, but often they are adults', which make a point of welcoming children into the groups and publishing special 'junior versions' of the magazines to encourage youthful members. Organisations such as Girl Guides, Brownies, ornithological and wildlife societies and many, many more, publish plenty of junior literature.

Another sphere many children are drawn to is the part-work genre. Again, many of these tend to be more substantial than a comic (See Chapter 7) and build up into a collection, often with a binder and various related gifts. Some, such as the *Magic of Ballet*, were packed with useful and fascinating information on all aspects of the dance world, while the gifts of ballet charms, make-up and adornments were of a high standard. The comic market as such seems to have changed drastically: will it die a natural death, or is there still hope? Children still want to read, girls especially have a voracious appetite for favourite authors such as Jacqueline Wilson. However, nowadays there are far more distractions than there were in the heyday of the comic; girls go out much more with friends, shopping, to clubs and to parties. They have iPods, mobile phones, games consoles and computers, all of which take up leisure time, while schoolwork and related projects seem to spread into spare time, too. The influence of the media means we are all au fait with other cultures, their music and their art styles and as we live in a multicultural society we absorb new ideas and exciting images. So, especially to young eyes, the comics we used to read and enjoy look quaint and old fashioned.

Modern Girls' Comics and Magazines

There are still plenty of titles available for today's girls, and though, as previously mentioned, the format has changed – picture strips are on the way out – there are some lively titles around. Interestingly, the 'pink power' has influenced the magazines, especially the covers – a look at a shelf of girls' titles in a newsagents' shop nowadays reveals a sea of candyfloss. I first mentioned this phenomenon in my last book, *Collecting Girl's Toys*, when I commented on how manufacturers were using the colour pink on much of the packaging for girls' toys, having decided that girls were influenced by the colour. Today, pink is very popular for the covers of girl's comics, followed by lilac. Below are a few of the current crop of publications intended for girls. (See Chapter 5 for current media based titles.) Will they become sought after by future collectors? You never can tell.

Animals and You

Perfect for the pet-loving girl – and aren't they all? This title, by D.C. Thomson, breaks away from the usual pop/fashion magazine, and consequently is something a bit different. Full of cute animals – an October 2009 copy features a pin-up spread of a young panda – it costs £2.10 every three weeks. Amongst the interesting features in *Animals and You* are instructions on how to draw an owl and how to draw a flamingo, and there is a double-page photo story telling of a dog who stole his owner's school tie, and her efforts to retrieve it. Other items include how to make a butterfly dream catcher, quizzes, embarrassing pet moments, caring for chinchillas and a puzzle page. As with most magazines, it comes with a free gift, which, in this issue, is a quality spiral, bound notebook with a puppy cover, and a pen.

Girl Talk

The three-weekly BBC Magazines publication *Girl Talk* costs £1.99 and is a lively publication with plenty to attract the top primary/early secondary girl. It is especially good on fashion. Depicting the latest trends, mainly with affordable chain store buys, it also contains behind the scenes gossip and quotes from girl personalities. An October 2009 copy includes an interesting peek at who makes the dresses for the programme *Strictly Come Dancing*, and what happens to them after the show, while there is also a feature on how to give yourself a free 30-minute make-over. Interestingly, unlike many modern comics, *Girl Talk* also has a photo picture strip story, 'Best Friends', which looks at a group of schoolgirls who unwittingly break the school rules by jazzing up their school uniform. Competitions, letters page, and pet photos make this a friendly and entertaining publication. With this issue comes a free gift of an attractive notebook, pencil and hair bow.

Go Girl

This 2009 issue of the comic/magazine, *Go Girl*, which is published every three weeks by Egmont, cost £2.75. It's an activity based mix of fashion, quizzes, readers' letters, pop pictures and fun facts on favourite stars. It contains an illustrated review of the latest Pixar movie, *Up*, a couple of pin-up pictures and a cut-out mask to make of celebrity Ashley Cole. Some of the pages are designed to be cut and folded into a mini magazine to accompany a sleepover, which is the theme of the issue. Free gifts are a brush, hair clips and a sleep mask.

Goodie Bag Mag

As the title suggests, *Goodie Bag Mag* comes with plenty of free gifts. It's a publication from D. C. Thompson, and is issued monthly costing £2.99. As it promises on the cover, this one contains 'All the celebs! All the goss!' and that's precisely what is inside. It's lightweight, fluffy, no stories – apart from a few captioned pictures showing an incident from Hannah Montana. But even so, with the (it seems compulsory nowadays!) crop of 'embarrassing moments', as well as quizzes, competitions, fun features and how-to-look-like-your-favourite-star type articles, there is still plenty of entertainment value. The free gifts in issue 65 included two sets of beads, a cute poster of two puppies, a pot of body glitter gel, a bottle of nail polish, two emery boards and a set of nail transfers. Maybe the actual

reading matter is scarce but the lively magazine and free gifts will appeal to many girls. It's interesting to speculate if magazines such as this, especially if left intact with their gifts in the original sealed polybag, might one day become collectable.

Shout

Shout is definitely a magazine, not a comic. It's a super, substantial good-value read of 100 pages, and is aimed at schoolgirls. There are masses of fashion ideas and beauty tips, as well as pages of 'Embarrassing Moments', quizzes and real-life features. Problem pages, confessions of a smoker, best buys in handbags and jewellery ideas make this a magazine which will provide more than a few hours entertainment value. The problem page includes gems such as this from an anonymous reader, 'I was on the way back from a school trip on the coach when a boy behind me slapped me on the bum. She goes on to ask 'what does this mean?' The reply, from agony aunt Laura, explains that boys can be weird, and that they also enjoy pinging bra straps. *Shout* is a D. C. Thomson magazine, which has been running since 1993, and includes free, high quality gifts, such as a large phial of mascara. It's published fortnightly and costs £2.30.

Up to date - Manga

What comes now? Well, how about turning to Japan? Over the last couple of decades, the Japanese art form, Manga, has been gathering momentum, influencing not just art and the media, but toys and dolls, even teddy bears. And, especially, comics. Many young girls in their early teens are turning to the manga comics which, under the genre shojo manga, are providing the entertainment an earlier generation found in *Jackie*, *Bunty* or *Girl*. With titles such as *Fruits Basket*, young girls assimilate these comics readily, even dressing up as the characters in role games they refer to as 'Cosplay'. Various Internet groups provide ideas, and girls can make or buy costumes and wigs, to enable them to dress as their favourite manga heroines.

Shojo manga translates as 'comics for girls', but unlike our typical British comic strip stories based on boarding school, ballet, gymnastic or pony riding themes, these Japanese magazines are far more thought provoking. Often using imagery or emotion-play, manga magazines are not only stunning to look at but provide a very complex and stylised read. Themes include science fiction, humour, romance and even gothic-influenced horror. Young girls probably became first aware of the manga style in Britain in the early 2000s with the advent of the Sailor Moon range of dolls, which were linked to Japanese cartoons and publications. These dolls, with their strange, almost blank expressions and large, staring eyes, seemed alien, but their quirkiness was admired and they were soon snapped up. When the Japanese cartoons were shown on television and the manga magazines began to appear in UK bookstores, as opposed to just the specialist shops, girls were intrigued by the large eyed girls

featured, and word of mouth soon spread the news. Manga comics were excitingly different, and were a stimulating read.

In Japan, shojo manga is everywhere, and is read by the youngest children as well as mature women. One recent survey estimated that manga was read by 75% of Japanese teenage girls. Now British teens – and younger girls – are discovering manga and its glorious artwork. It's interesting to speculate what *Bunty*'s 'Four Marys' would make of the phenomenon. Mary Cotter, Mary Radleigh, Mary Field and Mary Simpson would be transformed into lithe, large-eyed girls wearing tight clothing a million miles away from the slightly frumpish styles worn at St Elmo's!

Fruits Basket, probably the most popular of the shojo manga publications in Britain, tells a complex fantasy-based tale of an orphan girl who discovers that 13 members of the Sohma family are possessed by creatures from the Chinese zodiac. If they embrace someone of the opposite sex, or if they are stressed, they will transform. As Tohru Honda, the orphan, becomes more involved with the family, she resolves to somehow break the curse. The characters and the storyline were devised by Natsuki Takaya. Tohru falls in love with Kyo, who is cursed by the cat. As can be seen the story line is complex and involved, and coupled with the stunning, lively graphics it is easy to see why this comic book form appeals to British girls, just as it does to their Japanese counterparts.

Why do we still love comics?

It's a nostalgia thing, a yearning for times past, for things lost which can never be recaptured. We all remember curling up on a rainy day in a warm room, reading our *Beano*, or sitting on our desk at school, legs swinging, as we read the next instalment of Lorna Drake in *Bunty*. We giggled with our friends over the problem pages in *Jackie*, and sighed over the romantic kisses in *Cherie* or *Roxy*. We scared ourselves silly reading *Misty* under the bedclothes at night with a torch, and we sat underneath the letterbox, eagerly waiting for the paperboy to post our copy of *Tammy* through the slot. That is probably why so many of us are now searching the car boot sales, flea markets and the internet, hoping to find copies of our favourite comics. We might not ever be young again – but we can certainly recapture that magical glow. All it takes is a crumpled few pages featuring our favourite characters and the childhood memories rush back. Happy days!

Minnie the Minx cloth doll, by 'Real Beano Gear'.

APPENDIX

Part-Works Lists
Adventures of Vicky **(Fabbri)**

Issue 1   On Safari
Issue 2   At the Stables
Issue 3   In Tudor England
Issue 4   At the Ballet
Issue 5   On a Coral Reef
Issue 6   In Spain
Issue 7   In the Wild West
Issue 8   Gymnast
Issue 9   In the Rain Forest
Issue 10   In India
Issue 11   Is a Journalist
Issue 12   In Ancient Rome
Issue 13   In a National Park
Issue 14   In a Space Centre
Issue 15   Is an Actress
Issue 16   In Switzerland
Issue 17   Fire Fighter
Issue 18   Is a Pop Star
Issue 19   Is a Vet
Issue 20   Meets King Arthur
Issue 21   Is a Pilot
Issue 22   In Russia
Issue 23   Is a Chef
Issue 24   Is a Stunt Girl
Issue 25   Meet the Doctors
Issue 26   In Japan

Vicky, Pop Star.

Angelina's Fairy Tales **(G.E.Fabbri)**

Issue 1	Cinderella	Issue 9	Beauty and the Beast
Issue 2	Snow White	Issue 10	Goldilocks and the Three Bears
Issue 3	Sleeping Beauty	Issue 11	Rumpelstiltskin
Issue 4	Little Red Riding Hood	Issue 12	The Nutcracker
Issue 5	The Princess and the Pea	Issue 13	Hansel and Gretl
Issue 6	Thumbelina	Issue 14	Snow Queen
Issue 7	Rapunzel	Issue 15	Jack and the Beanstalk
Issue 8	Little Mermaid	Issue 16	the Frog Prince

Issue 17	Aladdin	***Discover the World With Barbie***
Issue 18	The Enchanted Princess	**(Eaglemoss)**
Issue 19	Swan Lake	Issue 1	Austria
Issue 20	The Twelve Dancing Princesses	Issue 2	Russia
Issue 21	Coppelia	Issue 3	Italy
Issue 22	Snow White and Rose Red	Issue 4	California
Issue 23	The Red Shoes	Issue 5	Czech Republic
Issue 24	The Goose Girl	Issue 6	New Orleans
Issue 25	The Magic Flute	Issue 7	Denmark
Issue 26	The Sorcerer's Apprentice	Issue 8	Holland
Issue 27	Giselle	Issue 9	Germany
Issue 28	Peter Pan	Issue 10	China
Issue 29	The Little Princess	Issue 11	Turkey
Issue 30	East of the Sun, West of the	Issue 12	Romania
	Moon	Issue 13	Greece
Issue 31	The Lemon Princess	Issue 14	Ireland
Issue 32	Hearts of Glass	Issue 15	India
Issue 33	Robin Hood and Maid Marion	Issue 16	Canada
Issue 34	The Firebird	Issue 17	Chicago
Issue 35	Feather Girl and Morning Star	Issue 18	Morocco
Issue 36	Town Mouse, Country Mouse	Issue 19	Belgium
Issue 37	A Midsummer Night's Dream	Issue 20	Chile
Issue 38	The Toy Princess	Issue 21	New York
Issue 39	The Elves and the Shoemaker	Issue 22	Argentina
Issue 40	The Wizard of Oz	Issue 23	Egypt
Issue 41	The Princess on the Glass Hill	Issue 24	Philippines
Issue 42	The Kingdom Under the Sea	Issue 25	Nepal
Issue 43	The Magic Porridge Pot	Issue 26	Poland
Issue 44	The Ballerina and the Tin Soldier	Issue 27	England
Issue 45	The Runaway Princess	Issue 28	Mexico
Issue 46	Diamonds and Spiders	Issue 29	Sri Lanka
Issue 47	Princess Splendour	Issue 30	Bulgaria
Issue 48	Alice in Wonderland	Issue 31	Thailand
Issue 49	The Clever Princess	Issue 32	Columbia
Issue 50	Apple Pie Anna	Issue 33	Scotland
Issue 51	The Sisters and the Swan	Issue 34	South Korea
Issue 52	The Contest of Fairies	Issue 35	Sweden
Issue 53	The Little Pear Girl	Issue 36	Japan
Issue 54	Little Dusty Face	Issue 37	Mongolia
Issue 55	The Mystery Dancer	Issue 38	Nigeria
Issue 56	The Enchanted Knight	Issue 39	Iceland
Issue 57	The Wood Fairy	Issue 40	Fiji
Issue 58	The Rainbow Goddess	Issue 41	Paris
Issue 59	The Crystal Heart	Issue 42	South Africa
Issue 60	The Beautiful Storyteller	Issue 43	Hawaii

Issue 44   Finland
Issue 45   Australia
Issue 46   Kenya
Issue 47   Samoa
Issue 48   Cuba
Issue 49   Jordan
Issue 50   Brazil
Issue 51   French Polynesia
Issue 52   Venezuela
Issue 53   Syria
Issue 54   Uganda
Issue 55   Myanmar
Issue 56   Algeria
Issue 57   Panama
Issue 58   Vietnam
Issue 59   Jamaica
Issue 60   Senegal

Outfits from Discover the World With Barbie.

Discovery

Issue 1   Elizabeth I/The Armada
Issue 2   Guy Fawkes/Gunpowder Plot
Issue 3   Columbus/New World
Issue 4   Shakespeare/Theatre
Issue 5   Joan of Arc/Siege of Orleans
Issue 6   Leonardo/Man of Genius
Issue 7   Henry V & Agincourt
Issue 8   Galileo & The Heavens
Issue 9   Cortes & The Aztecs
Issue 10   Richard III & Wars of the Roses
Issue 11   Michelangelo & the Sistine Ceiling
Issue 12   Henry VIII & the Church
Issue 13   Julius Caesar, Life & Times
Issue 14   William & The Norman Conquest
Issue 15   Cleopatra, Queen of Egypt
Issue 16   Richard the Lionheart
Issue 17   Marco Polo in the Orient
Issue 18   King Alfred & the Vikings
Issue 19   Alexander the Great
Issue 20   King John & Magna Carta
Issue 21   Hannibal, Crossing the Alps
Issue 22   Charlemagne's Empire
Issue 23   Tutankhamen & his Tomb
Issue 24   Minamoto Yoritomo & the Samurai

Issue 25   George Washington
Issue 26   James Watt, the Industrial Revolution
Issue 27   Mozart, Genius of Music
Issue 28   Captain Cook & his Voyages
Issue 29   Louis XIV & Versailles
Issue 30   Cromwell & the Civil War
Issue 31   Nelson Hero of Trafalgar
Issue 32   Bonnie Prince Charlie
Issue 33   Samuel Pepys & The Great Fire
Issue 34   Peter the Great/Russia
Issue 35   Isaac Newton/Scientific Genius
Issue 36   Marie Antoinette
Issue 37   Abraham Lincoln/Civil War
Issue 38   Vincent Van Gogh/Art Revolution
Issue 39   Queen Victoria
Issue 40   Louis Pasteur/White Knight of Science
Issue 41   William Cody/Wild West
Issue 42   Florence Nightingale
Issue 43   Napoleon Bonaparte/Waterloo
Issue 44   Charles Dickens/Social Reform
Issue 45   Ludwig van Beethoven
Issue 46   David Livingstone/Darkest Africa
Issue 47   Karl Marx/Dawn of Communism

Issue 48 Charles Darwin/Descent of Man
Issue 49 Robert Falcon Scott/Antarctic
Issue 50 Emmeline Pankhurst
Issue 51 The Wright Brothers
Issue 52 David Lloyd George/WW1
Issue 53 Charlie Chaplin/Movies
Issue 54 Lenin/Russian Revolution
Issue 55 Henry Ford/Craze for Cars
Issue 56 Albert Einstein/Atomic Age
Issue 57 Winston Churchill/WW2
Issue 58 Mahatma Ghandi/Indian Independence
Issue 59 Neil Armstrong/Space Age
Issue 60 Martin Luther King

Disney Princesses, Wicked Queen, Snow White.

Disney Princesses (De Agostini)

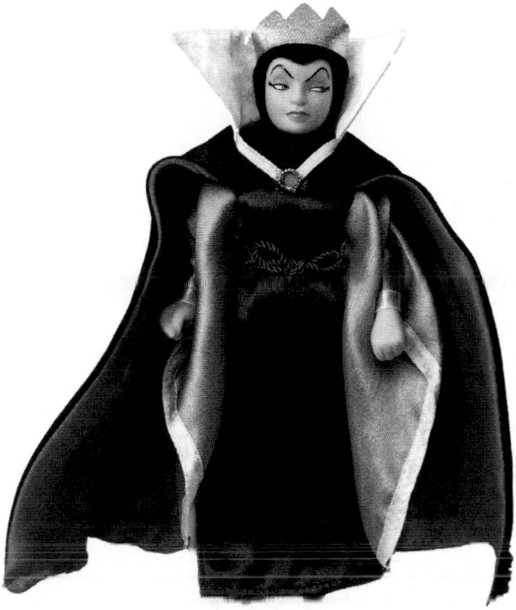

Issue 1 Snow White SW
Issue 2 Ariel (Mermaid) LM
Issue 3 Cinderella C
Issue 4 Belle BB
Issue 5 Pocahontas P
Issue 6 Jasmine (Harem Outfit) A
Issue 7 Mulan M
Issue 8 Sleeping Beauty SB
Issue 9 Ariel (Bride) LM
Issue 10 Aladdin (Street Rat) A
Issue 11 Cinderella C
Issue 12 Snow White's Prince SW
Issue 13 Belle (Village Dress) BB
Issue 14 Prince Eric LM
Issue 15 Mulan (Warrior outfit) M
Issue 16 Cinderella's Prince C
Issue 17 Sleeping Beauty (Woodland Outfit) SB
Issue 18 Beauty's Prince (Beast) BB
Issue 19 Snow White (Rags) SW
Issue 20 Sleeping Beauty's Prince Phillip SB
Issue 21 Jasmine (Ball Gown) A
Issue 22 The Queen (Wicked Stepmother) SW
Issue 23 Cinderella's Fairy Godmother C
Issue 24 John Smith P
Issue 25 Good Fairy Flora SB
Issue 26 Aladdin (Eastern Groom's Outfit) A
Issue 27 Cinderella (Bride) C
Issue 28 Maleficent SB
Issue 29 Shang M
Issue 30 Belle (Festive Outfit) BB
Issue 31 Triton LM
Issue 32 Fauna SB
Issue 33 Kokum P
Issue 34 Jasmine (Disguise) A
Issue 35 Cinderella's Stepmother C
Issue 36 Merryweather SB
Issue 37 Jafar A
Issue 38 Pocahontas (London) P
Issue 39 Fa zhou M
Issue 40 Melody LM
Issue 41 Fa Li M
Issue 42 Prince Philip SB
Issue 43 Prince Eric (wedding Outfit) LM
Issue 44 Nokoma P
Issue 45 Grandmother Fa M
Issue 46 Drusilla C
Issue 47 Anastasia C
Issue 48 Happy & Dopey SW
Issue 49 Bashful & Doc SW
Issue 50 Sneezy, Grumpy & Sleepy SW

Key:

A – Aladdin
A – Ariel
BB – Beauty and the Beast
C – Cinderella
LM – Little Mermaid
M – Mulan
P – Pocahontas
SB – Sleeping Beauty
SW – Snow White

Dolls of the World (**Eaglemoss**)

Issue 01	Japan
Issue 02	France
Issue 03	Brazil
Issue 04	India
Issue 05	Russia
Issue 06	Palestine
Issue 07	Peru
Issue 08	Scotland
Issue 09	Senegal
Issue 10	Norway
Issue 11	Lebanon
Issue 12	Nigeria
Issue 13	Germany
Issue 14	Thailand
Issue 15	Cuba
Issue 16	China
Issue 17	Martinique
Issue 18	Denmark
Issue 19	Bolivia
Issue 20	Tunisia
Issue 21	Mexico
Issue 22	Indonesia
Issue 23	Madagascar
Issue 24	Czechoslovakia
Issue 25	Alaska
Issue 26	Guatemala
Issue 27	Philippines
Issue 28	Sweden
Issue 29	Tibet
Issue 30	Turkey
Issue 31	Switzerland
Issue 32	Bulgaria
Issue 33	New Zealand
Issue 34	Afghanistan
Issue 35	Morocco
Issue 36	Albania
Issue 37	Mongolia
Issue 38	Portugal
Issue 39	Columbia
Issue 40	Holland
Issue 41	Cyprus
Issue 42	Algeria
Issue 43	Kenya
Issue 44	Romania
Issue 45	Eskimo

Issue 46	Iran
Issue 47	Poland
Issue 48	Panama
Issue 49	Lapland
Issue 50	Burma
Issue 51	Greece
Issue 52	South Africa
Issue 53	Ukraine
Issue 54	Honduras
Issue 55	Yemen
Issue 56	Ireland
Issue 57	Kazakhstan
Issue 58	Egypt
Issue 59	Lithuania
Issue 60	Ecuador
Issue 61	Slovenia

Issue 62	Mali	Issue 72	Korea
Issue 63	Pakistan	Issue 73	Cameroon
Issue 64	Argentina	Issue 74	Libya
Issue 65	Ethiopia	Issue 75	Venezuela
Issue 66	Finland	Issue 76	Belarus
Issue 67	Syria	Issue 77	Ivory Coast
Issue 68	Croatia	Issue 78	Paraguay
Issue 69	Vietnam	Issue 79	Iraq
Issue 70	Hungary	Issue 80	Chile
Issue 71	Saudi Arabia		

Dora Dress Up and Go (G.E. Fabbri)

Issue 1	Ty Dora doll	Issue 21	Skier
Issue 2	Ice-skater	Issue 22	Chef
Issue 3	Cowgirl	Issue 23	Red Riding Hood
Issue 4	Surfer	Issue 24	Mouse
Issue 5	Schoolgirl	Issue 25	Flamenco Dancer
Issue 6	Pirate	Issue 26	Christmas
Issue 7	Fairy	Issue 27	Gymnast
Issue 8	Gardener	Issue 28	Princess
Issue 9	Cat/Fancy Dress	Issue 29	Bath Time
Issue 10	Pyjamas	Issue 30	Clown
Issue 11	Winter Magic	Issue 31	Ballerina
Issue 12	Hula Dancer	Issue 32	Picnic
Issue 13	Tennis Player	Issue 33	Birthday Party
Issue 14	Artist	Issue 34	Farmer
Issue 15	Butterfly	Issue 35	Musician
Issue 16	Doctor	Issue 36	Rainy Day
Issue 17	Flower Girl	Issue 37	Easter Bunny
Issue 18	Magician	Issue 38	Sailor
Issue 19	Lifeguard	Issue 39	Witch
Issue 20	Fiesta	Issue 40	Little Bo Peep

Felicity Wishes (G.E. Fabbri)

Issue 1	I wish I was a cake-maker	Issue 12	I wish I was an journalist
Issue 2	I wish I was a nurse	Issue 13	I wish I was a chef
Issue 3	I wish I was a ballerina	Issue 14	I wish I was a lifeguard
Issue 4	I wish I was a pop star	Issue 15	I wish I was a artist
Issue 5	I wish I was a flowergirl	Issue 16	I wish I was a party planner
Issue 6	I wish I was a hairdreser	Issue 17	I wish I was a Waitress
Issue 7	I wish I was a explorer	Issue 18	I wish I was a gardener
Issue 8	I wish I was a fairy fashion designer	Issue 19	I wish I was a make-up artist
Issue 9	I wish I was a teachers help	Issue 20	I wish I was a ice-skater
Issue 10	I wish I was an actress	Issue 21	I wish I was an inventor
Issue 11	I wish I was an beautician	Issue 22	I wish I was a decorator
		Issue 23	I wish I was a flight attendant

Issue 24   I wish I was a model
Issue 25   I wish I was a shopkeeper
Issue 26   I wish I was a magician
Issue 27   I wish I was a cheerleader
Issue 28   I wish I was an Eco worker
Issue 29   I wish I was a photographer
Issue 30   I wish I was a TV presenter
Issue 31   I wish I was a detective
Issue 32   I wish I was a tour guide
Issue 33   I wish I was a archaeologist
Issue 34   I wish I was a jewellery maker
Issue 35   I wish I was a perfume designer
Issue 36   I wish I was a postworker
Issue 37   I wish I was a weather girl
Issue 38   I wish I was a sweet maker
Issue 39   I wish I was a skier
Issue 40   I wish I was a circus clown
Issue 41   I wish I was a bee keeper

Issue 42   I wish I was a architect
Issue 43   I wish I was a film maker
Issue 44   I wish I was a musician
Issue 45   I wish I was a shoe designer
Issue 46   I wish I was a park warden
Issue 47   I wish I was a hotel manager
Issue 48   I wish I was a butterfly house attendant
Issue 49   I wish I was a furniture maker
Issue 50   I wish I was a stylist
Issue 51   I wish I was a sports coach
Issue 52   I wish I was a travel writer
Issue 53   I wish I was a hat maker
Issue 54   I wish I was a theme park attendant
Issue 55   I wish I was a window dresser
Issue 55   I wish I was a friendship fairy

Porcelain Dolls (De Agostini)

Issue 1   Anna, a picture of prettiness
Issue 2   Louise, a tomboy at heart
Issue 3   Elizabeth, a radiant beauty
Issue 4   Emma, precious little angel
Issue 5   Sally, an adventurous spirit
Issue 6   Tricycle, a Victorian keepsake
Issue 7   Bonnie, a bathing belle
Issue 8   Deckchair, a relaxing treat
Issue 9   Sarah, the perfect pupil
Issue 10   Miss Julie, a Victorian Teacher
Issue 11   Scarlett, Belle of the Ball
Issue 12   Emily, a delightful dancer
Issue 13   Jean, a photographer doll
Issue 14   Grace, a blushing bride
Issue 15   James, the proud butler
Issue 16   Polly, a perfect bridesmaid
Issue 17   Paul, the bonneted pageboy
Issue 18   Betsy, the sailor girl
Issue 19   Bobby, the sailor boy
Issue 20   Florence, the Victorian nurse
Issue 21   Robert, a family doctor
Issue 22   Unknown
Issue 23   Lily, the flower girl
Issue 24   Alexandra, a Victorian mother
Issue 25   Albert, a Victorian father

Issue 26   Elspeth, a Stylish nanny
Issue 27   Jemima, a Victorian daughter
Issue 28   Jack, the Victorian boy
Issue 29   Dorothy, the milkmaid
Issue 30   Unknown
Issue 31   Barbara, the shepherdess
Issue 32   Billy, the busy bellboy
Issue 33   Felicity, the artist
Issue 34   Lily, the flower child
Issue 35   Matthew, the beggar boy
Issue 36   Cedric, the young Lord
Issue 37   Heather, the country lassie
Issue 38   Unknown
Issue 39   Tom, the American farmhand
Issue 40   Geoffrey, the medieval boy
Issue 41   Twinkle, the snow girl
Issue 42   Gabrielle, the Christmas angel
Issue 43   Basil, the winter boy
Issue 44   Lucinda, the ballroom dancer
Issue 45   Josephine, the flapper girl
Issue 46   Nadia, the acrobat
Issue 47   Harriet, the girl clown
Issue 48   Henry, the boy clown
Issue 49   Roland, the ringmaster
Issues 50–53   Unknown

Teddy Bear Collection (**Eaglemoss**)

Issue 1	Henry the Hiker
Issue 2	Alphonse the Artist
Issue 3	Peter the Pilot
Issue 4	Gordon the Golfer
Issue 5	Edmund the Explorer
Issue 6	Fergus the Fisherman
Issue 7	Barney the Bellboy
Issue 8	Donald the Doctor
Issue 9	Scott the Skier
Issue 10	Louis the Lumberjack
Issue 11	Matt the Mechanic
Issue 12	Sam the Schoolboy
Issue 13	Francis the Florist
Issue 14	Pedro the Pirate
Issue 15	Clement the Chef
Issue 16	Freddie the Fireman
Issue 17	Colin the Captain
Issue 18	Bob the Baseball Player
Issue 19	Geoff the Gardener
Issue 20	Patrick the Postman
Issue 21	Tim the Tennis Player
Issue 22	Santa Bear
Issue 23	Clint the Cowboy
Issue 24	Carl the Conductor
Issue 25	Phillip the Photographer
Issue 26	Harvey the Huntsman
Issue 27	Bert the Builder
Issue 28	Graham the Graduate
Issue 29	Sebastian the Surgeon
Issue 30	Simon the Sleepyhead
Issue 31	Clive the Cashier
Issue 32	Guy the Guardsman
Issue 33	Bill the Burglar
Issue 34	Lionel the Lion Tamer
Issue 35	Stanley the Stockbroker
Issue 36	Dick the Detective
Issue 37	Walter the Wine Waiter
Issue 38	Hank the Hotdog Seller
Issue 39	Kim the Karate Expert
Issue 40	Milo the Milkman
Issue 41	Sidney the Scientist
Issue 42	Bruno the Blacksmith
Issue 43	Ned the Night Watchman
Issue 44	Toby the Tailor
Issue 45	Basil the Butler

Issue 46	Ambrose the Ambassador
Issue 47	Derek the Decorator
Issue 48	Sandy the Sailor
Issue 49	Pete the Park Keeper
Issue 50	Winston the Weightlifter
Issue 51	Caesar Bear
Issue 52	Steve the Stationmaster
Issue 53	Giorgio the Gondolier
Issue 54	Sancho the Salsa Dancer
Issue 55	Iain the Icecream Seller
Issue 56	Miguel the Mexican
Issue 57	Hugo the Harlequin
Issue 58	Maurice the Musketeer
Issue 59	Gary the Goalkeeper
Issue 60	Napoleon the Bear
Issue 61	Terry the Tourist
Issue 62	Gino the Gangster
Issue 63	Andrew the Angler
Issue 64	Aladdin Bear
Issue 65	Roy the Racing Driver
Issue 66	Paul the Policeman
Issue 67	Mervyn the Monk
Issue 68	Rex the Roman
Issue 69	Prince Pippin
Issue 70	Manual the Matador
Issue 71	Robin Hood
Issue 72	Vik the Viking
Issue 73	Zorro Bear

Issue 74   Nik the Newsboy

Issue 75   Charlie the Clown

Issue 76   Carson the Cop

Issue 77   Michael the Minstrel

Issue 78   Ming the Mandarin

Issue 79   Nigel the Knight

Issue 80   Reg the Referee

Wonderful World of Teddy Bears (De Agostini)

A list of bears which came with every fourth issue (other issues contained fabrics, patterns and accessories).

Sleepy Sam

School Girl Sally

Holiday Harry

Belinda Bride

Gentleman Johnny

Yoko Japanese Opera Singer

P.C. Bruin

Nurse Nora

Claude Chef

Lady Lavia

Toddler Tim

Princess Polly

Cowboy Clint

Little Running Bear

Sporty Sue

Morgan the Pirate

Wilbur Pilot

Horsey Henrietta

Hamish McBear

Colin the Cricketer

Dealers/Auctions

http://www.ebay.co.uk

http://www.silveracre.com/

http://www.thirtiethcentury.free-online.co.uk

Useful Websites

http://www.26pigs.com

http://comicsuk.co.uk

http://www.dandare.info

http://www.friardale.co.uk

http://www.ggbp.co.uk

Book List

Brewer, Susan *Collectable Girl's Toys*, Pen & Sword 2010

Cadogan, Mary *Chin Up, Chest Out Jemima!*, Girls Gone By 2004

Cadogan, Mary *Mary Carries On; Reflections on Some Favourite Girls' Stories*, Girls Gone By 2009

Cadogan, Mary & Craig, Patricia *You're a Brick, Angela! The Girls' Story from 1839–1975*, Girls Gone By rev. ed. 1986

Clark, Alan *The Children's Annual; A History and Collector's Guide*, Boxtree 1998

Gifford, Denis *Discovering Comics*, Shire Publications 1991

Gifford, Denis *The International Book of Comics*, W.H.Smith 1988

Gifford, Denis *Happy Days! 100 Years of Comics*, Bloomsbury 1988

Gravett, Paul & Stanbury, Peter *Great British Comics*, Aurum 2006

Green, Paul & Taylor, Laura *Green's Guide to collecting TV, Music & Comic Book Annuals*, GT Publications 2000

Kibble-White, Graham *The Ultimate Book of British Comics*, Alison and Busby 2005

Compilations
Best of Boyfriend, Prion 2008
Best of Girl, IPC Media 2006
Best of Girl Annual 1952–1990, Webb & Bower 1990
Best of Jackie, Sevenoaks 2005
Best of June and School Friend, Prion 2007
Bunty for Girls; Golden Age Classic Stories, D.C. Thomson 2009
Jackie: Growing Up as a Jackie Girl, D.C Thomson 2009

Acknowledgements
Bill McLoughlin (D. C. Thomson), Melanie Legatt (Egmont), Emma Thackera (Eaglemoss) Sarah King (IPC) Laurence Heyworth (Look and Learn), Steve Holland (Live and Learn), Emma Pumphrey (De Agostini) Jacey Bunker (Mattel), Erika Davis (Pedigree), David Roach, Alan Notton (British Comics), Robert Harrop Ltd, Steven Taylor, Gaz Summer, Dr. Mel Gibson, Dr. Peter McCall, Mary Cadogan, Sylvia Reed, Clarissa Cridland, Andrew Whelan (Tokyopop Ltd), Cathy Banda (Hachette), Eddie Baxter, Colin Casey, Jules Parsons (Buckingham Covers), Martin Ayres, Jan French, Anne McAndrew, Sharon White, Kathy Martin, Tricia Smith

Picture Credits
Buckingham Covers www.buckinghamcovers.com 190
Eddie Baxter 55, 100 (top), 115, 187
Photos by Susan Brewer of items copyright of: De Agostini Courtesy De Agostini UK Ltd www.deagostini.co.uk 135, 143 (top r, centre, lower), 144
Photos by Susan Brewer of items copyright of: Eaglemoss Eaglemoss www.eaglemoss.co.uk 135, 138, 142
Photos by Susan Brewer of items copyright of: Egmont © Egmont UK Ltd and used with permission. 90, 98, 202 (r)
Fruits Basket Licensor: Hakusensha Inc. (TMA) Creators: Natsuki Takaya 204
Robert Harrop 103, 111(lower l), 178 (top r), 185
Photos by Susan Brewer of items copyright of: IPC© IPC+ Syndication 26, 54, 58, 63, 130
Jan French 191
Photos by Susan Brewer of items copyright of: Look & Learn c Look and Learn. 31, 33, 34 (top), 38, 39, 40, 42, 117 (top), 179 (top), 180
Bill McLaughlin 115 (lower)
Photos by Susan Brewer of items copyright of: Pedigree Courtesy of Pedigree Dolls & Toys 107, 135, 143 (top l)
Steve Taylor www.dandare.info 148, 152, 155
Photos by Susan Brewer of items copyright of: D.C. Thomson 14, 19, 21,23, 28, 34 (lower), 35, 45, 46, 50, 51, 53, 66, 67, 70, 71, 74, 75, 78,79, 82, 83, 86, 91, 94, 95, 99, 100, 101, 106, 107, 111 (top), 113, 117 (lower), 118, 119, 120, 121, 122, 123 (top), 127, 125, 131, 133 (lower), 146, 147, 161, 164, 165, 167, 168, 169, 178, 179 (lower), 182, 201, 202, 203
William Warne 11, 125
Mark Wynter 8, 9

All other images property of the author.

All characters depicted remain copyright of their respective owners.

Every effort has been made to ascertain the owner of the copyright of the publications pictured in this book.

Index